"I PROMISE YOU, THE HIVE WILL BE HELD ACCOUNTABLE FOR EVERY DEATH THEY'VE CAUSED . . ."

Captain Benjamin Sisko said, "but this is not the time to start a fight."

"So we just do nothing?" Major Kira cried.

"No." Sisko gave her a very firm stare. "We help the survivors. Then we think about revenge. Do you understand me, Major?" Before she could reply, Security Chief Odo called out to him.

"Captain!" the changeling looked up from his panel. "I'm reading signs of a power overload from the Daranian vessel. Its engines are going critical."

Dr. Bashir paled. "They must have had a malfunction."

"No malfunction," Odo corrected him. "The crew has done this deliberately. They are moving in towards the intruder on a collision course. They're on a suicide run."

Look for STAR TREK Fiction from Pocket Books

Star Trek: The Original Series

Star Trek: The Next Generation

Star Trek: Deep Space Nine

Star Trek: Voyager

STAR TREK
DEEP SPACE NINE®

OBJECTIVE: BAJOR

John Peel

POCKET BOOKS

New York   London   Toronto   Sydney   Tokyo   Singapore

An *Original* Publication of POCKET BOOKS

POCKET BOOKS, a division of Simon & Schuster Inc.
1230 Avenue of the Americas, New York, NY 10020

A VIACOM COMPANY

This book is published by Pocket Books, a division of Simon & Schuster Inc., under exclusive license from Paramount Pictures.

ISBN: 0-671-56811-6

First Pocket Books printing June 1996

10 9 8 7 6 5 4 3 2 1

POCKET and colophon are registered trademarks of Simon & Schuster Inc.

Printed in the U.S.A.

OBJECTIVE: BAJOR

CHAPTER
1

"TARGET COMING in range now, Captain."

Captain Benjamin Sisko nodded. "Thank you, Major." He leaned forward in the command chair of the *U.S.S. Defiant* and stared intently at the viewscreen. "All weapons to full power. Raise shields."

"All weapons powered." Kira Nerys glanced up from her panel to Sisko's left. There was a gleam of excitement in her eyes, and the more-than-fleeting suggestion of a smile on her lips. "Ready on your command."

Sisko could understand her feelings perfectly. It had been more than a month since any of them had been off *Deep Space Nine* at all, and it felt really good to be back in space and back in action. Though commanding DS9 was hardly a simple desk job, it was good to spread one's wings and head out among the stars again. "Hold steady."

"Shields at full, Captain," Chief O'Brien reported from his panel.

"Thank you, Chief." Sisko could feel the thrill of the hunt now. He watched the forward image intently, waiting for the first glimpse of the . . .

"There she is, Captain," Jadzia Dax said. She was seated at navigation, between Sisko and the screen. Her superior eyesight had caught the briefest flicker of movement that he now belatedly noticed.

"It's a Calderisi raider, all right," added Odo from his station. "Classic configuration. And they've powered up their weapons, too." The shapeshifter was the only one who didn't look eager for this confrontation. That was mostly because he still hadn't mastered the art of shaping his somewhat rudimentary features into semblances of human emotions.

"They can outrun most ships in this quadrant," Sisko murmured. "But they can't beat this one. Open a hailing frequency," he called out.

"Open," Dax responded.

"This is Captain Benjamin Sisko, of the Federation starship *Defiant,* to Calderisi raider," he said, slowly and clearly. "You are ordered to stand down your weapons and prepare to be boarded. We have reason to believe that you are running illicit weapons to the Maquis." He gestured to Dax for her to terminate the transmission. "Now," he said, "let's see what their reply is, shall we?" He hunched forward in his command chair, feeling the tension building within him.

"They've changed course," Odo announced grimly. "They are now heading directly for us." He shook his head. "Foolish. And typically humanoid. They are also opening fire."

The screen dimmed automatically as twin phaser bolts lanced out from the dart-shaped ship that skimmed toward them. The *Defiant* trembled slightly as the bolts impacted on the ship's deflectors.

"I think we can take that as a *no,*" Kira commented.

"No damage to shields," O'Brien called.

Sisko raised an eyebrow. He hadn't really expected the Calderisi to surrender. They were a volatile species at the best of times, and he had been certain that they were indeed the gunrunners he was after. Still, he hadn't expected them to do anything as foolish as trying to attack the *Defiant*. "Even so, I think we had better defend ourselves, Chief." He spun to face Major Kira. "Fire a warning shot across their bow."

"Across?" Kira sounded disappointed.

"Across," he repeated, with a slight smile. "For the first one, at any rate. And . . . fire!"

Kira obeyed. The *Defiant* shuddered slightly as the phasers lanced out across the void at the twisting raider.

"Open a channel," Sisko ordered Dax, "and stay as close to them as you can manage." When Dax nodded, he called aloud, "Sisko to Calderisi raider. I repeat: Stand down, or we shall be forced to disable you. I cannot be certain that this will not result in some loss of life to you."

Another twin blast of phasers shot from the raider, again dissipating harmlessly against the shields. Grim, Sisko turned to his Bajoran first officer. "All right, Major—target their engine nacelles and take them out."

"Aye, sir," Kira replied with a great deal of satisfaction. Her hands flew over the phaser controls.

"Captain," O'Brien called out suddenly. "I'm registering a drop in shield strength." He sounded harried and puzzled. "They're down to ninety-five percent and dropping."

"What?" Sisko spun to face him. "What's causing it, Chief?"

O'Brien glared down at the panels. "Outside interference," he said. "There's some kind of jamming signal coming from the raider. It's causing interference in the generator wave somehow. I've never seen anything like it. Shields are now down to eighty percent."

Sisko turned back to Kira. "Now would be a good time to fire," he said gently.

"I'd agree with you, Captain," Kira agreed, frustration evident in her voice, "but whatever's affecting the shields is affecting the targeting sensors, too. I just can't get a lock on a confirmed target. Plus," she added angrily, "power levels on the phasers are dropping. We soon won't be able to fire them at all."

"Best guess, then," he ordered, scowling. "Any damage you can do to stop this attack." He spun back to O'Brien. "Any idea yet what's causing this, Chief?"

"None," the engineer answered, irritated with the reply. "As Major Kira says, all our sensors are being affected, too, so I can't get a straight reading on this thing. Off the top of my head, I'd say it was some sort of modified delta-emitter array, but how they could power one from a craft that small beats me. I could do with a bit of time to study it. Say, a couple of weeks." He gave a mild grin.

"Not funny, Chief," Sisko objected. "Status?"

Embarrassed, O'Brien checked his panel. "Shields down to sixty percent and falling."

"They're coming about," Odo announced. "I'd guess they aim to attack us now. It's difficult to read my instruments, but it looks like they're preparing to fire again."

As Sisko watched the viewscreen, he saw the dart-shaped raider heading for them. Twin phaser beams lanced out, slashing into the *Defiant*. The ship shuddered as the inertial dampers struggled to keep her steady. The lights in the cabin dimmed, flickered, and then settled down to about half their former level.

"That's it," O'Brien announced. "The shields are down completely. The power interference is spiraling around inside the systems now."

"We've lost the phasers," Kira reported grimly. "I'm firing a photon torpedo." She glanced up and managed a tight smile. "Best guess, so you'd better hope I'm feeling lucky today."

Sisko nodded. There were very few options left to them. Whatever weapon the Calderisi were using, it was wreaking havoc with his ship. Another run like the last one would destroy them. He watched as the ship on the screen began to turn. Then the picture started to break up as the power levels continued to fall. "Damn," he muttered. If he was going to die, he would prefer to stare his fate in the face as he did so.

There was the flash of a photon-torpedo ejection, and the ship shook with the strain—a strain that they wouldn't normally have even felt thanks to the dampers. Now it seemed as if the *Defiant* was falling apart about their ears.

Then there was a bright flash on what was left of the picture screen—the torpedo detonation.

But had Kira hit the target?

For several seconds, everyone on the bridge stared at the screen, holding their breath. Nothing came into sight. Finally, Odo called out, "I'm registering debris ahead. The raider was completely destroyed."

"Well done," Sisko said, sighing with relief. "Very nice shooting."

"Thank you," Kira said with a smile.

From where he'd been sitting watching the others, Julian Bashir spoke up. "Remind me not to play darts with you today, Major. Even blindfolded, I think you'd beat me."

The only one of the crew not smiling was O'Brien. With a scowl, he said, "I just wish we hadn't been forced to destroy their ship." He shook his head. "I'd have loved to get a good long look at that weapon of theirs."

"We all would, Chief," Sisko agreed. "But under the circumstances, I think we did well just to survive. How are the systems now that the raider is gone?"

"Recovering slightly," O'Brien answered. "But not by much. We're going to be limping back to DS9, Captain."

Sisko nodded. "I'm in no hurry right now. How long will it take to get the *Defiant* back up to par when we do reach home?"

O'Brien shook his head. "It depends on how many systems were damaged and by how much," he replied. "I can't get consistent readings here. It could be days, or even weeks—if we've got the spares, and if there aren't too many repairs on the station to keep my crew busy."

"I understand." Sisko turned back to Dax. "Set course for home. Best speed." He managed a small smile. "If you could manage a rough estimate of how long it'll take us, I'd appreciate it."

"As soon as I can, Benjamin." Dax bent to her task. Sisko saw that her hands, instead of flying across her board as they normally did, lingered and repeated tasks several times.

Finally, she looked up. "Course laid in and executed." She shook her head. "It's really slow, I'm afraid. It's going to take us at least six hours to get back."

"Understood. Can you patch through a channel back to DS9? We'd better let them know we'll be late for dinner."

"I'll try my best." She bent back to her board again. A moment or two later, she said, "I've got a weak audio link, Benjamin. It's all I can raise."

"I'm glad for even that," Sisko told her. "Sisko to Ops: Can you read me?"

"Ops here," came a faint, crackling voice. "Your signal is very faint, Captain. Are you all right?"

"Not exactly, Mr. Soyka," Sisko replied. "We've destroyed the Calderisi raider but sustained damage. We should be home in about six hours."

"Understood," Lieutenant Soyka's weak voice came back. "Do you need assistance? I could have a runabout out to you pretty quickly."

"Thank you, no," Sisko said ruefully. "We'll just head back under our own steam, licking our wounds. Sisko out." He cut the link. Gazing at the screen, he sighed. The picture was still rather fuzzy—symptomatic of the ship's damage. Still, at least they had survived, and stopped the weaponry shipment. Whatever new weapon the Calderisi had, it would be up to Starfleet now to try and track it down and neutralize it. He'd have O'Brien transmit a full report when they reached home.

Then the chief was going to be very busy getting the *Defiant* back into order. Sisko could only hope that until it was fixed, there wouldn't be a need for it.

And he knew how weak his chances were that this would be so. On DS9, crises were the order of the day. . . .

CHAPTER
2

"YOU HAVE BETRAYED us all, and everything that we believe in!"

Even though he had been more than half expecting this accusation, Tork winced at the words that Harl spat out. There was a pain in his thorax as he faced his oldest and once-dearest friend. "Harl, it is not like that. Believe me, I have no intention—"

"It does not *matter* what you mean *now*," Harl retorted, his anger and disappointment clear on his face. "They have sucked you in. In a short while, you will be just like them. And I thought you *believed* in what we talked about." He gave a snort of disgust. "I should have known better."

"Harl—enough." As always, Sahna's voice was quiet and yet piercing. Despite his mood, Harl subsided. When Sahna wanted something, she inevitably got her way, and without undue effort. "You are not being fair to Tork, and in your hearts you must know this. You have not given him a chance to explain." Her lips twitched mischievously. "And isn't that your main complaint against the Hivemasters? That they will not listen?" She gestured toward Tork. "Now, here

7

is an apprentice Hivemaster, and you will not allow him to speak. Is that fair?"

"He's not an apprentice Hivemaster," Harl replied sulkily, but somewhat chastened. "He's our ex-friend who's gone over to the side of the enemy."

"Please," begged Tork. "Listen to me. Harl, I have *not* betrayed you. You know very well that my Determination was what led me to become a Hivemaster. I did not seek the position; it was thrust upon me."

"Of course it was," sneered Harl, his nostrils dilating rapidly, showing his disgust. "But *why?* Was it because such elevated positions are hereditary in your Lineage?" He snorted again. "Or because the other Hivemasters are trying to buy your silence by offering you the post? And expecting you to silence the rest of the student critics as payment? Have they asked that of you yet? Or are they waiting until you discover that you can no longer live without all the privileges of the exalted position of Hivemaster?"

Tork knew that it was mostly Harl's anger speaking, but he couldn't help being hurt and irritated by his old friend. "Harl," he said, trying to stay reasonable. "You know me. You know my commitment to the truth. Surely you must see that I am not going to abandon all that I believe in simply because I have been appointed a Hivemaster?"

"All I see," Harl snapped back, "is that badge on your carapace." He gestured at the symbol of the Hive that Tork now wore. "The badge that we all agreed stands for repression of thought and maintenance of the status quo. How *could* you?"

Tork's patience was wearing thin now. "Because I believe that there are some Hivemasters who are not against us," he replied. "Because I think that it is not the *office* that is wrong, but some who hold the position. Because I think that working from within I can effect changes. Because if the public sees even just one Hivemaster who will listen instead of simply giving orders, then change is possible. Because I think that in this thing, I am right and you are being a thick-skulled idiot!"

Harl stabbed out one long, bony finger, quivering with

anger. "Perhaps—just *perhaps*—you believe that now," he snarled. "But it will not last. Remember your precious texts: *Power is its own reward—and curse.*" He grimaced. "Or have you already forgotten all of your studies?"

"I have forgotten nothing," Tork answered, striving to keep his temper. "But you, it appears, have forgotten one thing: our friendship."

"Friendship?" Harl deliberately turned his carapace on Tork. "You have already murdered our friendship. The Tork I once thought I knew and respected is dead. All that is left is a *Hivemaster.*" He spat the last word, and then stormed from the meeting room. The door hissed shut behind him.

Sahna placed a hand on Tork's shoulder. "Well," she said gently, "that went better than I expected it to."

His hearts lifted slightly at her touch, as they always did. But it could not erase the pain he felt. "He would not listen," Tork said bitterly. "He did not try and understand."

Laughing, Sahna shook her head. "Harl? Tork, *now* who is having unreasonable expectations? You know what he is like. Anger consumes him too often." She shook her shapely head. "But it will not last. *The flame that burns brightest, dies fastest,*" she quoted. "His anger will be gone shortly, and he will begin to think again."

"I hope so." Tork gave a long sigh. "I know it was foolish of me to expect otherwise, but I had hoped—"

"Yes," Sahna said gently. "And that is where you are so different from Harl. You *hope.* You work hard, and strive for reason and change. Harl simply wants to sweep away the old and bring in the new. And this is not possible. Your way is the better way."

It warmed his thorax to hear her speak so well of him. "Then you approve of my acceptance?" he asked eagerly.

Sahna smiled at him. "I have always approved of you, Tork," she replied. "You are a calm, reasoning, and caring individual." She touched his carapace again, and Tork felt a thrill of mingled love and lust pass through him. "And you are my hope."

It took a great deal of self-control for Tork to quash the burning feelings within him. Though he had undergone his

Determination, and was now officially an adult, Sahna had
not. If he made his feelings for her known, it would not only
be immoral but illegal. Perhaps as a Hivemaster, Tork
would be immune to such charges as immorality, but he
simply could not chance it. It wasn't just the fear of being
caught—he knew that Sahna would say nothing even if he
were to make unwelcomed and illicit advances to her—but
that he could not use his office as a shield for his crimes.
After all, wasn't that one of the things that had always most
disgusted him about the Hivemasters? One rule for the
Hive, and one for the Masters?

He *had* to be better than that. Not only for the sake of his
own soul, but also as an example to everyone. Especially
Sahna.

She looked at him with her wise eyes, and he was pierced
by an arrow of certainty. She knew what he had been
thinking.

"I am sorry, Tork," she told him, removing her hand. "I
should not have done that. It was wrong of me to test you in
that way."

"You—" he started to say, to tell her she had done
nothing wrong. She didn't allow him to finish.

"I was deliberately tempting you," she said, smiling
slightly. "I should have known that you would not suc-
cumb."

"I . . . wanted to," he replied. As an adult, he was mor-
ally bound never to approach a single female child. Despite
the fact that she was from the same Hatching Year as
himself, Sahna had not undergone Determination herself,
and was thus still technically a child.

"But you did not," she said fondly. "Whatever Harl
thinks, you have proven that your sense of honor remains
untouched. And as a *child,*" she added ironically, "I am
allowed to say what you cannot at present. I love you, Tork,
and want to be One with you." She held up a hand. "Do not
say anything—yet."

Tork understood once again how much wisdom she
possessed. Sahna always knew exactly how far to go. She
had effectively promised herself to him, without compro-

mising his morals. With her love and his new position, he had almost everything he had ever desired from life. "Do you have any idea when your Determination will be?" he asked her. Of course, it was supposed to be a surprise—his certainly had been—but there were always ways that the news could get around.

"Within the next few cycles," she replied. "And I also suspect what the outcome will be." Seeing his amazement, she laughed. "Do not be so naive, Tork. Some Determinations are quite obvious. Most, in fact."

"Mine was not," he answered.

"Perhaps." Sahna's lips twitched again. "But it is not exactly unexpected. I believe you will make an exemplary Hivemaster. Perhaps the first such in several centuries."

Her support and love made his thorax warm again. Tork fought down his emotions, striving to be what she expected of him. "And what do you believe your Determination will make you?" he asked.

"An astronomer."

If she had told him that she was expecting to become a sex provider, she couldn't have shocked him more. "An . . . astronomer?" he gasped weakly. "You can't be serious?"

"Why not?" Sahna cocked her head to one side and regarded him evenly. "It's an unpleasant job, agreed, but a necessary one. Especially now."

"But . . . you . . ." Tork struggled weakly with his prejudices. "Sahna, how *could* you?"

"It is because I *can* that I expect to become one," Sahna answered. "If this disgusts and repels you, I am truly sorry." She smiled ruefully. "That is one reason, beyond the impropriety, that I did not wish you to declare your love for me. If you no longer wish to associate with me, I will understand. It might be poor for your public image."

"My image be damned," he snapped back, still struggling to accept the idea. "And my feelings for you have not changed."

"Of course they have," Sahna said simply. "I understand."

"Well, I do not," Tork told her, bluntly and with candor.

"I do not understand how you could wish to be an . . . *astronomer.*" He almost choked on the word. "But . . ." He took a deep breath. "If that is what you wish to be, then I will do all I can to support your decision. I may not understand it, but I do not care about that. I will *try* to understand." He drew on every ounce of courage he had and tried to reinforce his hearts. "Show me."

Sahna stared at him in something like alarm. "Tork, there is no need—"

"There *is* a need," he said, almost roughly. "If this is to be your chosen pathway, then I will be forced to share it with you. I must understand it. Show me."

She bowed her head slightly. "It is not wise," she replied.

"Love is not always wise," he told her.

"So be it." Sahna raised her head, and he could see the love in her eyes. Ah, if not for the boundary that separated them, what passions they could share this night! "Very well," she agreed. "Come with me."

She led him through the web of the student quarter. Tork followed, trying to steel himself for the ordeal that was ahead. He was scared; there was no point in denying that, either to himself or to Sahna. But he *had* to do this, for both of their sakes. They left the more traveled byways, and Tork knew they were coming close to the wall of the Hive.

Their destination was an almost empty room. The walls, as always, were metal, but these had no decorations or furniture. The only thing in the room with them was a small control panel. As she locked the door behind them to prevent accidental intrusion of the unprepared, Sahna turned to Tork.

"I love you," she told him. "You do not need to do this for me. I will understand and respect you without this."

"I know that you will," he agreed. "But I do this for *us.* And I will not respect myself if I do not share it with you."

Sahna sighed and bowed her head in acceptance. "Very well," she agreed. She crossed to the control panel, her hands hovering uncertainly above it. "Try hard to endure this, my love."

He didn't dare speak. Instead, he simply gave a single, curt nod. Her fingers danced over the controls.

The wall in front of them both began to iris open. Panels slid back into their recesses with a hiss. As they moved, the lights within the room died down.

And the stars became visible.

Thousands, perhaps millions, of stars, littered across the whole vast space in front of Tork. Stars that burned with beautiful, entrancing intensity. Stars that went on without end, to the openness of space.

Tork felt the vast emptiness beyond the fragile, transparent shielding reaching out from the stars and into the core of his being. The openness pierced his soul.

The immensity of it all overwhelmed him. Striving to escape the vast nothingness, he shrieked, then curled reflexively into a fetal ball, his carapace sealing off the universe without and sealing him safely within his own being.

And still he kept on screaming at the nothingness beyond the vast metal womb of the Hive.

CHAPTER
3

"GODS, HOW I hate this job."

Garaia looked up from her science station at the captain of the Cardassian science ship *Vendikar*. He was, as usual, pacing like a caged animal up and down the walkway beside her. This was not the first time that she had heard his complaint, and she strongly doubted it would be the last. Tak was a handsome young officer—with a sleek neck, and very nice eye ridges—but he was, after all, both career military and something of a loser. A shame, really. He might otherwise have been at the very least an interesting diversion on this routine mission.

"This is an important task we perform," Garaia said diplomatically.

"Mapping the positions of a bunch of stupid *rocks?*" he spat, gesturing to the asteroid belt on the ship's viewscreen. "It's dull, it's pointless, and it's eternal."

Though she, too, felt bored by the routine, Garaia felt compelled to defend their mission. "We have to be able to chart safe paths through the belt," she pointed out.

The rest of the bridge crew wisely remained outside this

discussion, finding their instrumentation suddenly fascinating. They were, no doubt, listening to the exchange very carefully. Though Tak was flapping his mouth foolishly, Garaia had no intention of saying anything that might cost her if it was reported back to the wrong people—as it inevitably would be. How Tak had lasted this long with such a negative attitude was inexplicable to her.

"Why?" he demanded, histrionically. "We're on the edge of Cardassian space here. Virtually on the rim of the galaxy. There's nowhere out there to go to." He gestured at the screen. "Just more empty space. And if we *had* to come out here for any logical reason, we could just go around this stupid belt. No, this is just punishment work for us." He laughed bitterly. Garaia knew he'd probably had a drink or two before coming on duty; it was getting to be a habit with him of late. The longer this mission lasted, the worse he became. Another sign of a loser. "Well, I know what *I'm* being punished for. What's your crime, Science Officer?"

Garaia managed a slight smile. "Curiosity," she replied, lying slightly. "I find this fascinating, so I am assigned to the job." Since the captain seemed to be quite talkative, she decided to probe further than she usually bothered. "And what was *your* crime?"

"Foolishness," Tak replied. The crime didn't surprise her, but his admission did. He gave another of his barking laughs. "I thought I was outside the usual backstabbing." He gestured at his chest. "You wouldn't think to look at me that I was once Gul Gavron's most trusted assistant, would you?"

No, Garaia thought. "Yes," she lied. "You are obviously very capable, Captain."

"Well, I was," he went on. It was hard to tell whether he'd heard her reply or not. "I was his favorite, and thought I was untouchable. But I forgot the most important rule in the Cardassian military: No matter how much your commanding officer likes you, he likes his rank much better." Tak made another spitting sound. "When he was accused of a poor decision, I was the one he blamed for making it—even though I had advised strongly against it. Somehow, that

15

record was expunged." He glowered at Garaia. "And I was reassigned."

The story didn't surprise her. She knew what it was like in the Cardassian military. Actually, he was lucky he hadn't simply been executed. That was the sort of barbaric punishment they usually went in for. If he was still alive and working—no matter how pointless the task—he must have had *some* political connections remaining. She shrugged elaborately. "And if you perform this task well," she said, "you will undoubtedly be given a better one."

"Hah!" Tak snarled. "Mapping *more* rocks, no doubt." He slammed his right fist into his left palm. "I want to be out there, hunting the damned Maquis, not baby-sitting a bunch of female scientists." He glared at her. "No offense, Science Officer, but I hate being here."

And we hate having you here, she thought. She was saved from having to invent some polite response by the navigation officer.

"Captain," he called. "I'm picking up something odd directly ahead of us."

Tak spun around. "Identify!" he ordered.

"I'm . . . sorry, sir," the navigator answered, his face twisted with puzzlement. "It does not conform to anything I have ever seen before."

Tak whirled back to Garaia. "Science Officer—why didn't you spot this?"

Because you were talking to me, you idiot, she thought. Ignoring his stupid question, Garaia studied her instruments. Her eye ridges raised in astonishment. "Whatever that craft is," she said slowly, "it is unlike anything we have ever encountered before. Or heard of, either."

Returning to the command seat, Tak glared at her. "I'd appreciate a few details," he told her sarcastically. "What are you talking about?"

"Forward scanners," Garaia ordered. "Sector three nine four green." The navigator obeyed her command, and the intruder sprang to life on their screens.

Garaia had always been very curious, and had spent

hours studying data from many alien species. What she saw displayed now on the *Vendikar*'s screens reminded her mostly of a Terran fish called a manta ray. The craft had a large central body, with wide-spreading wings. Behind it trailed a long, tail-like antenna.

Tak frowned. "It has an unusual configuration," he agreed, "but it is not unprecedented, surely?"

"The shape, no," Garaia commented. "But the size . . ." She let her eyes stray back to her instrumentation. "Captain, that vessel is approximately eight thousand miles long, and the wingspan is about twelve thousand miles. We are still almost an hour from its present position at current speeds."

Tak paled, his eyes riveted to the screen. "Eight . . . thousand . . . miles?" he repeated in awe. He shook his head in disbelief. "What kind of a craft is it?" he asked.

Garaia shrugged. She was almost as awestruck as he, but she refused to allow her scientific training to suffer as a result. "Captain, the central core of the vessel is eight thousand miles long, and approximately one hundred miles in diameter. That gives an interior surface area of over two million, six hundred fifty thousand square miles. That is the size of a moderate continent."

Bored and slightly drunk though he might be, Tak wasn't stupid. "You mean that ship is some kind of colony vessel?" he asked, leaning forward and staring hard at the image in front of him.

"It would be a logical assumption," agreed Garaia. "And one probably containing several billion inhabitants."

Tak gave a sharp intake of breath. "Then we had better deal with it now," he decided. He spun about to face the communications officer. "Relay a message back to Central Command on Cardassia with all of the information we currently have," he instructed. "Inform them that we are moving in to contact the alien intruder." Without waiting for acknowledgment, he turned back to the navigator. "Plot an interception course," he ordered. "Maximum velocity." Then he turned back to Garaia. "Get me as much information on the thing as you can before we reach it. I want to know *exactly* what we are dealing with here. Specifically look for indications of weapons capabilities."

Men, thought Garaia in disgust. *It's about time he finally got around to attacking it!* "Acknowledged." Trying to hide her feelings, she turned back to her instruments, and began coaxing as much information out of them as she possibly could.

Whatever that vessel was, it had clearly come from outside the galaxy. A quick backtrack of its probable trajectory showed that much. Assuming it had taken an energy-conserving course, the computers estimated that it must have come from one of the Magellanic Clouds.

And if it had crossed the galactic void at the low velocity it was now employing, then the journey must have taken the inhabitants almost half a million years. . . .

The figures were almost mind-numbing. Whoever the inhabitants of the craft were, they could not have had contact with any other species in that time. But that was about to change. Within the next hour, the *Vendikar* would be approaching it.

Garaia worked hard, poring over her instruments, trying every last trick she could think of to gain even a meager amount of extra data from them. Finally, she stood upright and approached Tak. "I've gathered as much as I can at this range," she announced in a quiet voice. If the captain wanted the rest of the crew to share her findings, he'd tell them. "To learn more, we'd need to go inside the craft."

"So?" he asked her, pointedly.

"It's an extremely old craft," Garaia answered, striving to keep her irritation with his brusque manner in check. "Somewhere in the region of half a million years old. Its origin would appear to have been in one of the Magellanic Clouds. It has spent most of its life crossing the void to arrive here. Those big wings are dust-gathering devices; their size is dictated by the need to gather the finely scattered dust in extragalactic space. This is undoubtedly turned into energy and raw materials inside the vessel." She shook her head. "It would need to be a very efficient system.

The craft is proceeding at sub-light speed. Given the construction of the vessel, I would not expect it to be able to exceed that velocity. To accelerate faster would undoubtedly tear the wings apart. We are therefore looking at a very slow, ponderous ship. We could literally fly rings around it."

Tak tapped his fingers impatiently on the arm of his seat. "And the weaponry I specifically asked you to investigate?" he asked.

Garaia paled with anger, but kept her voice even. "I am unable to detect any weapons. Our sensor devices cannot penetrate the alien ship's hull. I cannot even get a reading as to what the hull is composed of. For all I know, the aliens could be completely defenseless—or able to blast us out of space without even thinking about it."

"That isn't a great deal of help to me," Tak snapped.

Garaia shrugged. "It's the best I can do—for the moment." She gestured at the manta-ray image. "The sensors do indicate that there are openings at the prow of the vessel, and several along the body of the ship. These are presumably airlocks and entry ports. Once we are closer, I might be able to get a scanning beam inside one of these and obtain some of the answers that you require. Until then, there is nothing that I can do."

"Very well," growled the captain. He leaned forward in his seat, staring intently at the screen. "If that is all, then you may return to your post until you can get me further facts." When she didn't move, his eyes flickered over her. "Well?"

"There is one thing that does puzzle me," she added. "That vessel must have smaller ships within it, surely. Explorers, shuttles, and perhaps even war vessels."

"So?"

"Well," she replied, her unease growing. "After half a billion years in the void, wouldn't you have launched some small ships to explore the first solar systems that you have ever seen?" She pointed to the screen. "Yet they have not. Why not?"

Tak considered her question and then nodded. "A good point," he conceded. His eyes narrowed in concentration.

"Their ship has been on a very long voyage," he suggested slowly. "Perhaps not a successful one."

He was clearly having the same thought that had crossed her own mind. "You think, then, that there may no longer *be* any inhabitants within the vessel?"

"It is one possibility," he agreed. He abruptly gave her a smile. "I recall reading a story once in which the inhabitants of a generation starship reverted to savagery. When their ship reached its destination, they had become uncivilized louts who couldn't even operate an airlock door. That is another possibility in this case. After all, a great deal can be forgotten in half a million years."

"Indeed," she agreed. "Or, of course, learned. Perhaps they have entered a new stage in their evolution and no longer need machinery to do their bidding?" She gave the captain a smile of her own. "I have also read such speculative fiction."

Tak nodded. "Well, all we can do is to wait," he said. "In a short while, we will have all of the answers we need." He turned to face the communications officer again. "Open a channel using as wide a band of frequencies as you can to the ship ahead of us," he ordered. "Send our identifying code and demand a response. Inform me immediately of any reply." He turned back to Garaia. "And now we wait," he said. There was a gleam in his eyes.

As she returned to her station, Garaia smiled to herself. This was certainly far more interesting than scanning rocks. And Tak seemed to have dragged the shreds of his personality together. Whatever happened now, he would be pleased. Their routine punishment mission had suddenly become something very important. If he handled it well, it would put him back in favor with the military.

And if he handled it badly, then he would die. Either result would probably suit him much better than commanding survey charting.

As they continued their approach, Garaia scanned and rescanned the ship, trying to eke out just a little more information. She didn't have very much luck, however. The vessel guarded its secrets well. As she couldn't penetrate its skin, she had no way of knowing whether they were approaching a floating cemetery or a mobile fortress. The uncertainty was wearing on her nerves, and she suspected that none of the crew was immune. Every now and then, Tak would start rapping his fingers nervously on his command-chair arm. Then he would catch himself and force himself to stop. Only to begin again a few moments later.

Then, finally, there was a change. "Captain!" she called, urgently. "The sensors register the opening of the main portal in the craft."

Tak glanced at the screen. "I see nothing."

Fool! she thought. The prow of the craft was a hundred miles across. One small portal a mere two hundred feet across wouldn't be visible at this distance. "I'm registering smaller craft emerging," she announced. "Twelve of them, in a very loose formation." She tried bouncing a sensor beam past the craft and through the airlock, but it dissipated rapidly. Then the portal irised closed again. *Damn!* Still, now she had something other than the main ship to play with. She turned the sensors onto the smaller craft. "Each is approximately eighty feet long," she called out. "They're a lot more fragile than the main ship, and— Captain, each vessel is armed. I'm reading energy weapons powering up."

"Sound alert," Tak ordered, his eyes dancing with joy. He was in his element now. "Raise shields. Power the weapons systems."

The weaponry officer moved swiftly to obey. Garaia frowned. She understood the need for this move, and she had no qualms about combat, but she hated to see the loss of research material.

"Any response on our hail yet?" Tak demanded.

"No reply at all, Captain," the communications officer called back. "I'm running it again, with greater variation in frequencies and—Captain, incoming signal, audio only."

"That's better," Tak said with satisfaction. "Put it on the speakers."

There was a second or two of noise while the translation

computer hooked into the signal and scanned it. Then the noise cleared into words.

"Approaching craft, identify yourself and your purpose."

Tak scowled. "This is the Cardassian vessel *Vendikar,*" he answered. "Identify yourself."

"We are the Hive." The voice was neutral, without any apparent emotion.

"You are entering Cardassian space," Tak said bluntly. "You will not do this without permission. Bring your ship to a halt and prepare to meet us."

There was a slight pause. "Unacceptable," the voice finally replied. "We will continue our journey. You will not attempt to interfere."

Sitting up straighter in his chair, Tak snapped, "You will not be allowed to enter Cardassian space. Halt your vessel now, or else we shall be compelled to use force."

"This contact is terminated," the voice commented coldly. The carrier went dead.

Garaia scowled. "How do you propose to stop that craft?" she demanded. "We could detonate every weapon aboard our ship and still not even dent its hull."

"They do not know that we are alone," Tak told her. "They will not risk beginning a conflict without further information. All we have to do is to hold them off until reinforcements arrive."

Garaia was about to dispute that assertion, but was saved the trouble.

"Incoming vessel," the navigator announced. "They have powered up their weapons for the attack."

"Ready response," Tak ordered, eagerly. He looked like a wild beast who had just been set free from his cage and smelled a victim ahead. "Steady all weapons."

Garaia watched as two of the small craft came spinning toward them. She kept a sensor lock on them, waiting to see what kind of weapons they would be using. They were both much smaller than the *Vendikar,* and probably less well armed and armored. This attack was both unprovoked and foolish. There was no way at all that it could succeed.

She died with that last thought on her mind. The two

ships whipped past the *Vendikar* on opposite sides. There was no sign of any energy discharge, no sign of any weapons system being used.

As their pass was completed, however, all that was left of the science vessel were tiny shards of metal and plastics, and smaller pieces of flesh that spread out in ever-widening circles, all that marked where the *Vendikar* had been annihilated.

CHAPTER
4

"THE OPERATION WAS a complete success!"

Hivemaster Dron glanced up sharply from his position at the conference table. He shuffled his report comp rather ostentatiously until Hivemaster Pakat subsided.

Pakat cast his eyes down to the floor. "I am sorry for my overt enthusiasm," he said quietly.

"It is good." Dron allowed a small smile to creep across his face. "And it is, in part, at least understandable. Your fledgling force has done very well. But we shall hear your report at the correct time. If you please." He gestured to one of the two empty seats at the table. Pakat, still humbled, sat beside his thirteen other colleagues.

Now that he had complete attention—as he always demanded—Dron could begin the meeting that he had called. He nodded to the person on his right. "You may commence recording." Every deliberation had to be kept for posterity. After all, they were at the most crucial point in the history of the Hive, and Dron had every intention of being recalled by future generations as a great visionary and savior of his people. "I see that we have one member missing." He pretended to think for a moment. "Ah, yes, our junior colleague, Tork."

"He sends his apologies, Grand Master," explained Boran, two seats to Dron's left. "He is currently with a medic."

"Nothing serious, I trust?" Dron had plans for the young rebel, and he didn't want them ruined by an untimely sickness, or—worse—death.

Boran cleared his throat. "I understand he was looking at the, uh, stars and was taken ill."

There was a murmur of surprise and irritation around the table, which Dron cut off with a wave of his hand. "I am sure Tork must have had a good reason for his actions. When he recovers, he will undoubtedly explain." Privately, Dron already had a good idea what had happened, but there was no need to go on the record with that. "So—to the point of this meeting." He looked slowly at the expectant faces around the conference table. "As I am sure you are all quite aware, we have now entered our target galaxy. The Crossing is complete, and we can now commence the next phase in the Great Design." He waited a moment for this to sink in, to see that there were no untoward displays of emotion. Though several attendees looked almost ready to burst with pride and joy, they wisely suppressed any outbursts. Nodding his satisfaction, Dron turned to Premon. "Hivemaster Premon, how has the Hive borne up under the journey?"

Premon was something of a fatuous fool, but he ran a tight department. His engineers were in charge of the structure and operation of the Hive. "As you know," he began, "for the past several months my engineers and I have been going through the Hive with the greatest of attention to even the smallest details. We have checked out all of the primary, secondary, and tertiary systems." He permitted himself a slight smile. "And in many cases, even the functioning of children's toys." He patted his report comp. "The statistics and results are all compiled here, and will be duly fed into the official archives. To avoid boring you with the facts and figures, though, I can summarize our findings quite simply. The Hive is in far better shape than even the First Hive Founders could have predicted. Our people have taken good care of our world, and we have survived the Crossing remarkably well. There are, of course, some repairs that need to be undertaken—but remarkably few, and none at all in any critical systems."

Dron cut him off before he could keep his almost endless flow of prattle going. "It seems that every member of the Hive owes you and your staff a tremendous vote of thanks, Premon. You have managed no small miracle." Dron addressed the meeting at large. "I move that we register a strong message of approval for the marvelous work that the engineers have done—both in our generation and in all previous ones. Agreed?" There was, of course, a chorus of approval. "Excellent." Dron turned back to face Premon again. "So, we are in good shape for the next phase of the Great Design?"

"We are in excellent shape," Premon replied, preening himself happily.

It was remarkable how little it took to please some people. Dron sighed mentally; a few words of praise, and Premon was ecstatic. Ah, well, perhaps it would keep him silent for the rest of the meeting for once. "Commendable." Dron turned to Boran, the head of Industry. "Your report, Hivemaster Boran?"

"My departments are all ready," he replied. "As soon as the raw materials become available, then we can commence the next phase."

"Good." Dron faced Makarn. "And what of your department, Hivemaster Makarn?"

Makarn cleared his throat, somewhat embarrassed. He hated to be dragged away from his work for these meetings, and was obviously looking forward to the end of it so he could scuttle back. "Science is mobilized," he answered. "We are, ah, working triple shifts at present to, ah, analyze all details." He gestured to his comp. "All the details are here, and will be, ah, fed into the report. Summarizing, though, we have already discovered one, ah, target world that appears perfect for our requirements." Tapping the controls before him, he called up a holographic projection of the area of space they had entered. Several dozen stars showed up, and Makarn zoomed in on one. This resolved into another picture showing the yellowish star and six orbiting planets. "The fourth world of this system has all that we require for the next phase."

"And how long will it take us to reach it?" Dron asked patiently.

"The course corrections have already been fed into the guidance systems," Makarn answered. "The computers indicate that we shall reach the target world in three days." He coughed. "Ah, of course our smaller vessels will be able to make a better determination within two."

"Thank you." Dron had already known these facts—and approved the course change—before the meeting had begun. The gathering wasn't to inform him but the other Hivemasters and posterity. "Pakat, it is your turn now."

Pakat nodded, barely able to contain his excitement. "As we entered this star system, we were challenged and then attacked by a warship from a local race. They called themselves 'Cardassians.' Despite this unprovoked attack, our warriors were able to defend themselves and annihilated the aggressor. If this is symptomatic of the reception we will get, then clearly the local species are warlike, aggressive—and no match at all for our technology."

Dron was more than happy to let him brag about his department's success. It established in the record that they were not the aggressors. Not that it mattered, but Dron did like the slight moral edge it would give him. He had already altered the records of the transmission from the Cardassian ship to agree with Pakat's propaganda. "And our pilots suffered no ill effects?"

"None at all," Pakat said happily. "They functioned perfectly."

"Forgive me." This was Hivemaster Hosir. He was the oldest among them, almost twice Dron's age, and the only member of the Masters whose motives and responses Dron couldn't predict with any certainty. "I do not quite understand this. Are you telling us that several of your young pilots flew an attack mission outside of the Hive and came back utterly unaffected by their experience? While one of our own exalted members"—he gestured at Tork's empty seat—"couldn't even look at the stars without becoming very ill?"

"Yes," replied Pakat eagerly. "You see, the pilots in my craft never actually looked into space. With the help of my colleague Boran, we simply manufactured fighter craft without any external portals. All of the piloting was done by the crew using computer simulations. And it worked perfectly. To all intents and purposes, the pilots were simply undergoing another training exercise within the Hive."

Hosir nodded. "I see. Pardon my question."

"There is no need to excuse asking a perfectly sensible question," Dron said. If he hadn't asked it, Dron would have been forced to do so. He had wanted their rather tidy solution to the problem on record. "I feel certain that we are all pleased with the resolution that Pakat and Boran have found to overcome exposure to open space." There was, of course, a murmur of assent at this. "Be it so noted," he commanded. "Now, if there are no further matters, this meeting is adjourned." Naturally, no one raised any objection to this.

As the Hivemasters filed out to return to their duty, Hosir made his weary way across to Dron. "My compliments on resolving the agoraphobia issue." Not expecting a reply, he then limped from the conference room. In a matter of minutes, only Pakat and Raldar remained behind. Raldar had contributed nothing overtly to the meeting, but he was not expected to. He was Dron's strong right hand, and in charge of security for the Hive.

"Off the record, now," Dron said quietly, "I am very pleased with your results, Pakat. The weaponry and pilots performed flawlessly. Training will be accelerated, of course, since we now have a target world. Everyone must be prepared."

"Of course," agreed Pakat. With a happy smile and a low, deferential bow, he left the room.

"A very capable officer," Raldar commented.

"Very," agreed Dron. "His work is progressing the Great Design. Now, to other matters. What is this about Tork being hospitalized? Has it to do with a female?"

The security officer smiled. "Naturally. Youngsters are often driven to foolish acts when trying to impress a potential mate. But I am assured that he will be released shortly, without permanent damage. He looked out at the stars."

Dron frowned. "And why did he attempt such a foolish thing? Merely to impress a female? It does not sound like Tork. He is normally rather levelheaded—if obstinate and filled with misplaced enthusiasm."

"Ah." Raldar smiled again. "The particular female he sought to impress is most likely to be Determined an astronomer."

"Oh, I see." Dron chuckled. That was interesting. "He is serious about this female, then?"

"Yes. She has not yet passed Determination, so he can't do anything overt, of course."

Dron nodded. "And Tork is far too high-minded to consider an illicit relationship, even though he knows he could get away with it."

Raldar inclined his head. "He likes to think of himself as incorruptible."

"I'm sure he does." The Grand Master considered for a moment. "Then I think it's time we corrupted him, don't you? I believe that this female's Determination is definitely due. And I have a strong suspicion that she'll be designated an astronomer. See to it that she is then assigned to Team Two." He smiled. "I'm certain that Tork will hear about this very quickly and want to change her assignment."

Nodding his understanding, Raldar said, "And he will request that her Determination be changed. . . ."

"Precisely. I, of course, will insure that it is, so that he and his female can be One." Dron chuckled again. "And that first, small corruption will begin his descent, Raldar. And the second step . . . What about that loudmouthed, rebellious friend of his?"

"Harl?" Raldar spread his hands. "He's as noxious as

ever, claiming that the Hivemasters must be overthrown—
preferably with a lot of our internal organs decorating the
walls and floors." The security officer frowned. "He could
be dangerous. We should execute him."

Dron shook his head. "He could be *useful*. Besides,
executing a child would not be good for morale. Until he has
passed his Determination, we can do nothing to him. I
would therefore suggest he also be given a speedy Determination. And after that . . ." He looked up at Raldar. "Could
one of your agents convince him to perform some small but
nasty act of sabotage? Preferably one with a small loss of
life? Say, a child or two?"

"Convince him?" Raldar gave a sharp bark. "I doubt he'll
need much persuading. He's ready to do almost anything at
the moment. He is doubly frustrated since Tork was made a
Hivemaster."

"As I suspected he would be." Dron considered the
matter for a moment. "See that this happens, and then
arrest him. We shall be forced to stage a trial at the next
Hive Meeting. I think it would be interesting to have Tork's
name chosen by accident to conduct the investigation, don't
you?"

"You mean him to have to beg for the life of his friend?"
asked Raldar thoughtfully.

"Either that, or force him to condemn his friend to
death." Dron shrugged. "Either way, we shall have our
solution. If he condemns his friend, then Tork will feel
guilty and he'll be easier to manipulate. If he spares Harl,
his morals will be compromised, and we shall have him. In a
short while, he will be with us in all things." He stood up,
and collected his comp. "And at this momentous point in
the Great Design, it is vital that we be unanimous in our
resolve. The future of our species is at stake. We must seize
the opportunity we are offered. We must fully exploit the
target world to insure the survival of the Hive.

CHAPTER
5

SISKO SIDESTEPPED THE truck filled with spare parts, managing to slide onto the bridge of the *Defiant*. He stopped, aghast at the mess that met his eyes. Most of the panels had been removed, and it looked as though a midget with an axe and a bad temper had attacked every system in the room. Wiring, connectors, chip sheets, crystals, and circuit boards lay in total disarray.

He could only hope that it looked like something very different to Chief O'Brien.

There was nobody visible at first as he edged his way across the deck, carefully avoiding stepping on anything. It might only be junk, or it might be vital to the repair of his ship. There was no way to tell. As he approached the navigation console, he finally saw a pair of legs sticking out from under the mess.

"Chief?" he asked, trying not to startle the engineer.

"Mmff," came a reply, and then the legs slid out. It was quite obvious that this wasn't the chief from the contours that emerged even before the good-looking blond woman's face appeared. Technician Fontana removed the laser driver from her mouth. "Sorry, Captain," she said with a grin. "It's just me."

Sisko smiled back at her, and gestured around the bridge. "Tell me that this isn't as bad as it looks."

"You want me to lie to you?" she asked bluntly. She brushed hair from her face, making another smudge that joined the dozen or so already there. "It's not too good, sir." She pointed over to the science console. "I think the chief's over there," she said. "Unless the damn thing's swallowed him up. And that wouldn't surprise me."

"Keep it down out there," a cross voice called from the indicated station. "I'm trying to concentrate." There was a flash and a curse, and then O'Brien's head emerged from behind a stack of wafer chips. "Bloody Nora," he snapped, shaking his right hand. "That *hurt.*" He vanished again under the console.

Sisko raised an eyebrow and glanced down at Fontana. "Has he been like this long?" he asked, sympathetically.

"All my shift," she replied, grinning slightly. "He's a walking curse, if you ask me, Captain."

"Then you won't mind if I take him out of here?"

"Mind? I'll remember you in my will." She grinned wider. "Assuming the chief doesn't murder me before I can write it."

Nodding, Sisko crossed the deck with exaggerated care. "Chief," he said in his sternest voice. "Come on out of there."

O'Brien scowled back at him from the open panel. "Look, Captain, I'm kind of busy," he complained. "Can't whatever it is wait?"

"No." Sisko glowered at him. "According to Dr. Bashir, you've worked four straight shifts without more than a cup or two of coffee. I'm ordering you to take a break with me. Come on."

O'Brien snorted. "Typical of him to cause trouble. And exaggerate. It was *four* cups of coffee." He spread his hands in appeal. "Look, sir, I've really got a lot of work to do here, and I—"

"—and you're getting on your staff's nerves," Sisko finished for him. "Chief, I really do appreciate the overtime you're putting in, but you're so tired you're making mistakes. Take a break, get a meal, and then sleep." He held up a hand to stifle the chief's protest. "That's an order. Do you want me to have Odo lock you up in the brig to enforce it?"

With a sigh, O'Brien laid down his tools and clambered slowly to his feet. "No," he said. "He'd enjoy that far too much." He wiped off his hands on the seat of his pants. "And now that you mention it, I am kind of hungry." He looked over at Lieutenant Fontana. "Will you be okay on your own for a while?"

"Okay?" Fontana gave him a wide smile. "I'll be deliriously happy, Chief. My ears are still tingling from your last bout of swearing."

"I was that bad, eh?" O'Brien managed a rueful grin. "Well, don't repair too much while I'm gone. I don't want the captain to think I'm dispensable."

"No promises." Fontana winked at the chief, then vanished back under the console.

"They're a good crew, Chief," Sisko said, as he led the way gingerly back to the elevator shaft. "They'll be fine while you get some rest."

"I know that," O'Brien said proudly. "It's just that there's so much to be done," he added, his shoulders sagging.

"And so much you've already accomplished," Sisko pointed out. "How much of the *Defiant* is back on-line?" The elevator doors hissed shut as they stepped in.

"Well, we've restored life support and power to most decks." O'Brien scowled. "Navigation should be finished in a few hours. Fontana's doing wonders there. But weapons are still off-line, and the shields are balking a bit. They took the biggest hit from that Calderisi weapon." He shook his head. "I still can't figure out quite what it was, but it did a remarkable job of burning out the command systems, even through the shields."

"Well, Starfleet's sent the *Hood* out to the Calderisi homeworld to ask some rather pointed questions," Sisko told him. "We may have some answers for you soon. No pressure, Chief, but how long before the *Defiant* is back up to strength again?"

The chief shrugged. "Hard to say. We can have her flying again by the end of the day, as long as you don't want phasers or more than minimal shields. Beyond that . . . Well, I'm hoping another two days, but there's always something to bollix matters up, isn't there?"

Sisko nodded. "I've always felt that entropy was the fundamental ruling force in the universe," Sisko admitted. "Still, it's been remarkably quiet these past three days. Maybe it'll stay peaceful till you're finished?"

"I wouldn't want to take odds on that," O'Brien muttered. "I doubt even Quark would."

"Probably not," agreed Sisko. "Now, where would you like to eat? My treat." He grinned. "There's a new Bajoran restaurant opened on the Promenade that does heavenly bat-bird stew . . ."

Despair gnawed within Sahna as she exited the Determination Center. She gripped her comp fiercely, its message burned into her brain. Theoretically, the Determination was supposed to be the happiest day of her life; she now had a career and was an adult. She could become One, could have a voice in the day-to-day running of the Hive, and could petition the Hivemasters in cases of grievance.

Except, of course, in the one case that was *causing* her grief.

Sahna stumbled away from the Center, not paying attention to the others about her who were heading in or out themselves. She stumbled against several of them, too numb to really care, and they were rejoicing too much to notice her.

One of the ones she bumped into grabbed her suddenly. Sahna started to mumble an apology, and then she managed to focus on the face of the one who held her. "Oh. Harl."

"I am overjoyed to see you, too," Harl replied, his lip twisted sardonically. "I take it that you have had your Determination, and that you are so delirious with happiness that you are not paying attention to the paths you take?"

"I have had my Determination, yes," she agreed. "But I have never been so unhappy."

"What is wrong?" he asked. "Did they make you a sewage worker? A sex provider?" He managed a wide smile. "I could live with that Determination, though I doubt Tork could."

"No," Sahna answered, too upset to be either amused or offended. "I am to be an astronomer."

Harl grimaced. "Oh. That is bad news. But it *is* what you expected, isn't it?"

"Actually, it's also what I wanted," she agreed. "I prayed to the First Hive for this Determination. I have always longed to be an astronomer. I love to observe the stars."

"Sooner you than me," Harl answered. "The only thing I'd see if there was a window open to the void would be my last meal hurtling forth from my mouth." He placed an arm gently on the edge of her shell. Technically, since she was now an adult and he was not, he was transgressing. But at this moment, neither of them cared too much, and she was grateful for his touch. "So, what is so wrong about getting what you wished for?"

"Because I have been appointed to Team Two."

"Oh." Harl was sometimes foolish, but he was not stupid; he knew what the problem was. "And Tork is on Team One," he observed. "That is a problem." Then he twitched his nose derisively. "Still, now he is a Hivemaster. I am sure that he will have you reassigned."

Sahna looked at him in shock. "He would not do that!"

Harl grunted. "Why not?"

"Because . . ." Sahna couldn't believe that Harl was asking such a thing. "You know very well that the Determination is never wrong. The comp assesses our skills, our personalities, and our abilities and places us where we shall be most fulfilled and most productive."

"I know nothing of the sort," he told her bluntly. "*You* know nothing of the sort. You're just repeating what we've been taught. For all we know, the Determination could be wrong any number of times, only nobody complains about it because it is supposed to be infallible."

Sahna stared at him in utter bewilderment. She had known for years now that Harl was a rebel, questioning most things, but she had never dreamed that he would go this far. "The Determination is the basis for our society," she said, struggling to keep her head and temper in check. "It *cannot* be wrong."

"No wonder you'll make a good astronomer," Harl said sarcastically. "Your brains are already out there among the stars instead of down on the deck where they belong. Look," he tried to explain, "if I told you that the stars were simply illusions, that there *was* nothing outside the Hive, and they were just illuminations placed there to test my belief, what would you say?"

"That you were simply repeating the Six Hundred and Fourth Hive's heresies," she snapped back. "Nobody seriously believes that nowadays."

"But they did then," he pointed out. "And with just as little proof for their beliefs as you have for the infallibility of the Determination. You are a scientist, Sahna, and you have a good brain. So *use* that brain. Ask questions. Don't simply accept what you have been told: demand proof of it."

Sahna shook her head. "I would make a poor revolutionary," she replied. "I shall have to leave that to you. Meanwhile, I have to break the sad news to Tork." She stared at her friend. "I know you think he will abuse his power to have me reassigned, but I do not believe he will. He is too moral for that."

Harl snorted again. "Too moral to change a stupid system in order to be One with the female he loves? I would call that too *stupid*."

Not offended, Sahna managed a weak smile. "And if he *did* have my Determination changed, you would call that corrupt."

"Yes," Harl agreed. "It's nice being a rebel; you can always find justifications for anything you wish to believe in. Even if those reasons contradict something else you believe in. No one expects me to be consistent—merely obnoxious." He stroked the edge of her shell. "And, despite my temper, I do care for both you and Tork. I think he is a fool, but he probably is an honest one. Just this once, I would be happy if he did abuse his power to keep you with him. You belong together." His comp beeped. "And I belong in the Center," he added. "I have been summoned for my Determination also."

That did cause Sahna to smile briefly. "Which you do not believe in. So why are you here?"

"Because until I have passed it, I am forbidden to communicate with mature females like yourself. And I do not wish that to continue."

Sahna looked at him fondly. "I wish you success," she informed him. "What do you believe you will become?"

Smiling, he started away. "I don't know. Do you think there are any positions for revolutionaries? Anyway, with luck, maybe *I'll* get to be a sex provider." He shook his tail at her, and vanished into the crowd again.

Feeling slightly better for having talked with him, Sahna returned to thinking about her woes. Harl was wrong to doubt the Determination. He had to be. It was just that Harl liked to question everything. He didn't really have any doubts as to the process. He couldn't have. It was the basis of their civilization.

Summoning all of her resolve, Sahna tapped the code for Tork's comp into her own. She had to meet with him as soon as possible to inform him of her changed status. She had no idea what he would say, but she knew that he would be deeply saddened.

"Hivemaster Tork is not available," the comp informed her.

He had never refused a call from her before! Sahna stared at the comp in confusion. "But why not?" she asked. "Is he ill?"

"No," the comp replied. "He is in session with the other Hivemasters. It is forbidden to interrupt them."

"Oh." Sahna knew what was happening now. It was what

37

she had tried to tell Tork the other day, before he had insisted on staring into space and became ill. She had been doing her observations and knew that the Hive was close to its target. Somewhere ahead of them in space was the world that would provide them with everything they needed to implement the Great Design—and the moment when she would lose Tork forever.

CHAPTER
6

GUL DUKAT SAT easily in his command seat, watching the
quiet efficiency of the operatives inside Cardassian Central
Command. There were some thirty-five officers working in
the room, but the noise level was low. Dukat disliked
unnecessary sounds. His staff knew that and paid close heed
to what they were doing—and how softly they could carry
out their tasks.

From this room on Cardassia Prime, the military vessels
of the Empire could be monitored and controlled. Dukat
enjoyed his time here, at the very heart of Cardassian
strength and will. He kept close watch on what was happening through controlled space, and even the occasional
problems were more stimulating than irritating.

The technician at the communications desk before him
half turned in his chair. "Incoming message from the
Karitan, sir," he reported. His voice was pitched perfectly
to just carry to Dukat's ears.

"On my screen," Dukat ordered, tapping the control to
bring it to life. The face of the captain of the ship sprang
into view. "Report," Dukat commanded.

"We have caught up with the alien intruder," the captain answered. He looked tense and unhappy. "We can confirm the transmission from the *Vendikar:* the craft is several thousand miles long."

"Intriguing." Dukat rubbed the back of his left hand absentmindedly. "And is it still in Cardassian space?"

"Yes, Gul," the captain answered. "But it will cross into the Darane system in just under two hours. There is still time for us to intercept it."

Dukat sighed. "Be sensible, Captain. What would you do with a vessel that size if you did intercept it?" He was pleased to see a chastised expression on the young officer's face. "There is still no indication of how the aliens managed to destroy the *Vendikar?*"

"My science crew has been examining what wreckage we recovered," the captain replied. "All they are able to say is that the ship was literally shredded somehow in flight. Shields did not prevent the attack."

It wasn't exactly a lot of information, but Dukat hadn't really expected better. "Very well, Captain," he answered. "Your orders are simple: Follow the intruder, but take no action against it unless you come under attack. Maintain sensor sweeps and observe. Report to me anything that happens."

The captain scowled. "Understood," he said reluctantly.

Dukat glared into his screen. "You do not like your orders?" he asked, with deceptive mildness. Some of these younger captains were quite presumptuous. Standards in the military these days were seriously slipping.

"It's not that, Gul," the captain said hastily. "It's simply that . . . Well, we are going to allow them to go unpunished for destroying one of our ships?"

Dukat shook his head slightly. "What did they teach you before allowing you command of a ship?" he chided. "They will not go unpunished. However, if you tried to attack them, I have a strong suspicion that the *Karitan* would end up in small pieces like the *Vendikar.*" He allowed himself a small smile. "I'm sure that doesn't appeal to you. It doesn't appeal to me—I'd then have to dispatch another ship to take your place, and that would be a waste of time. As you reported, the intruder is about to enter the Darane system. This will make it a Bajoran problem. Let *them* attack the vessel and have their ships destroyed. You will monitor the event and record it. This way, we can discover what weapons the aliens possess without your having to lose your life and my having to sacrifice a science vessel. *Now* do you understand?"

The captain smiled. "Yes, Gul," he replied, admiration in his voice. "It is a sound plan."

"Of course it is," Dukat informed him. "So, obey my instructions to the letter. Out." He snapped off the contact, and settled back in his seat. Hardly a promising officer, but you had to make do with whatever tools were at hand. . . . He considered his next move. The intruder was about to become a Bajoran problem, which amused him. Let those weaklings try and figure it out! Of course, their first response was likely to be a request for aid from Captain Sisko on *Deep Space Nine*. They always went mewling to him for help at the slightest provocation.

That would be interesting. The Federation was a lot more likely than the Bajorans to get answers about this vessel. And if the *Karitan* paid proper attention, then Dukat would get the information, too.

A ship eight thousand miles long . . . Normally, technology didn't greatly impress Dukat, unless it was in the field of weaponry, but this was no mean achievement. The secrets that the intruder revealed might prove to be quite helpful.

Should he give Sisko a call and alert him to the incoming problem? It would be a friendly gesture, after all. And Dukat enjoyed being friendly with the human . . . from time to time. As humans went, Sisko was almost likable. On the other hand, there was no need to overdo friendship. Why not simply let the Bajorans send for Sisko and leave him in the dark? It might be more fun to watch him fumble his way about without help.

Yes, that was it. Wait and see what happens, Dukat

decided. He had a feeling that the intruder was up to something interesting in the Darane system. It would be educational to see just what that might be.

Dron surveyed the conference room and noted with satisfaction that every Hivemaster was present, including Tork. The youngster looked a trifle pale, but otherwise unaffected by his recent experience. He might be an idealistic fool, but he was obviously also resilient.

There was an air of excitement in the room, as everyone already knew what was happening. Dron indicated that the recording was to begin and then rapped on the edge of the table.

"Hivemasters," he said in a strong, clear tone, "the hour of fate is upon us. The next stage in the Great Design is about to commence. Makarn?"

The Science Master shuffled to his feet. "Ah, the target planet has been selected," he announced. "It is the fourth planet from the sun that we are now approaching. It is a world of some small industry, which will be of assistance to us, and it contains much vegetation. Preliminary surveys indicate a fair amount of mineral and metallic wealth on the planet, though there has been extensive mining already performed there. We assume this was done by an off-planet species, since there is little evidence of much refined metal on the surface of the world."

Dron glanced at him sharply. "There will be sufficient remaining for our needs, though?"

"Ah, yes, without doubt," Makarn responded. "There will be no delay in the Great Design."

"Excellent." Relieved, Dron turned to Pakat. "And how is our readiness?"

"We have three wings of attack vessels standing ready," Pakat reported. "The pilots have all achieved high scores in simulated runs, and I anticipate no problems. Our surveys show fewer than one hundred vessels currently in flight in the system, and their weaponry is inferior to ours."

Tork shuffled in his seat and leaned forward. "You are

preparing to attack the inhabitants?" he asked, concern in his voice.

"We are preparing to *defend* ourselves," Pakat answered, snuffling loudly to show his displeasure. "Had you attended the last meeting, you would know that the local race—calling themselves 'Cardassians'—attacked our ships without provocation when last we met them. I am sure that none among us wishes to wait until they attack again before we prepare to defend ourselves?" He stared pointedly at Tork, who sat back in his seat and closed his mouth.

"If that is quite clear?" asked Dron. There were no further comments. He hadn't expected there would be. Even Tork couldn't complain about defending themselves. "Boran?"

The Industry Master stood up. "My teams are all prepared," he reported proudly. "We stand ready to harvest the coming fruits of our labor. Production is completely ready to commence as soon as the raw materials are obtained."

"Excellent," Dron complimented him. "Then it is clear that we are ready—that the Great Design can go ahead. After half a million years, the plans of the First Hive come to fruition, and we achieve our destiny." He gestured at the holographic representation of the planet that spun in the air above the table's surface. "All departments will come to full strength," he commanded. Turning to his Security Master, he said, "Raldar, the time has come to speak with these 'Cardassians,' in this system. Have a link established immediately."

"Of course," Raldar agreed. He set about tapping instructions into his comp. What only Dron and he knew was that there would be several layers of recording taken when they established contact. Dron couldn't take the chance that something might go amiss and spoil the records he intended to be kept for future Hives. However, if the aliens said or did anything untoward, it could be redesigned in the records Dron decided.

A moment later, the spinning globe above the table was replaced by a hologram of an alien race—the first that the other Hivemasters had ever seen. There was a murmur of shock and disgust from those assembled about the table. Even the liberal Tork and the elderly Hosir couldn't restrain themselves.

Well, the alien was ugly. It was also quite obviously not a Cardassian, but there was no need to mention that. This might be some subject species, for example. The being was roughly the size of a member of the Hive, and it stood upright, but that was about all the resemblance there was. It—possibly a *he*—was shell-less, and its skin was a pallid pink, instead of a rich gray. There was hair visible on the crown of its ugly head, and the being wore what appeared to be cloth draped over the larger part of its body. Dron wasn't too surprised—a creature that grotesque would *have* to cover itself.

The being spoke for a moment, and then the translation computers could begin to decode its vocalizations. "—First Minister Worin, of Darane Four," the creature was saying. "Please identify yourselves."

Dron took a breath, and then said, "I am Hivemaster Dron of the Hive. You will leave your world immediately. We will allow you two days to evacuate your population."

"What?"

Was this alien stupid as well as deformed? Dron repeated his message patiently. "Do you comprehend?" he added.

"You're . . . insane," Worin finally spluttered.

"No," Dron answered. "We are not insane. You have two days. If you require assistance in evacuating your people, we will be willing to assist." He moved to cut the communication.

"Wait!" Worin exclaimed, holding up a hand. "You . . . you're *serious* about this?"

"Of course we are serious," Dron replied. "This is not a matter we would joke about."

"But you *can't* be!" The alien looked almost panic-stricken. "What you ask is . . . unthinkable!"

Dron sighed. "It is not unthinkable," he explained. "And we are not *asking*. We will allow you two days, and then we shall commence harvesting this world. If your people are not removed by then, they will simply have to suffer the consequences. We have no desire to injure anyone, but we will not alter our schedule."

"No!" Worin seemed to have a grip on whatever low intelligence he possessed. The message had obviously sunk at least partway into his brain. "This is our world, and you cannot have it without a fight!"

Dron had been afraid of this: the alien was clearly insane. "You are not utilizing the world," he explained. "We have need of it, and therefore we shall make use of it. Please stand aside and allow us to do this."

"Darane Four is our *home!*" cried Worin. "We won't let you have it."

"Home?" Dron shook his head in astonishment. "You are clearly not an intelligent species if you believe that a ball of mud and rock is a *home*. It is simply a resource, neither more nor less. You are not using it, so we shall."

"He can't be serious," muttered Premon to the table at large. "He thinks that this world is his home? What kind of deviants are these people?"

"The kind we will have trouble with," predicted Pakat. "They're obviously intelligent enough to build crude weapons, but too stupid to build a home of their own."

Worin had been conferring with someone out of Dron's line of sight, in feverish haste. He now turned back to face the Hivemaster. "You will cease your flight," he ordered. "If you move any further into our system, we shall take it as a declaration of hostile intent and will be forced to defend ourselves."

This was going far better than Dron had imagined possible. It was quite obvious to all the others about the table that they were being threatened first. There would be no need to edit this recording at all. "We are not an aggressive species," Dron replied carefully. "We do not wish you any harm. But we need the planet that you call . . ." He shuddered. ". . . *home*. If you try and interfere with the Great Design, we shall be forced to retaliate. Any injuries or deaths your people sustain will therefore be your own fault."

"You're not having our planet!" Worin howled, and cut the communications link.

Dron allowed the picture to fade, and waited a few heartsbeats before he spoke again. "It appears that we are dealing with a dangerously deranged species," he said sadly. "Pakat, it would appear that your brave pilots will be forced to defend the Hive."

"And they all stand ready," Pakat answered proudly. "The alien aggressors will not harm the Hive. That I vow."

"Good." Dron smiled. "We all knew that we could count on you." He spread his hands in resignation. "Well, we tried to do this without pain and bloodshed. Unfortunately, these aliens seem to completely lack logical faculties. We will be forced to fight them for what we need. Are there any further questions or comments?"

As he had expected, Tork stood up. "Is this really necessary?" he asked. Dron could see the pain on his face, his nose wrinkling almost uncontrollably. "Must we . . . kill to obtain what we need?"

"We all heard their spokesman," Dron told him. "They threatened us; any killing will begin with them and be on their own consciences."

"No, I mean is there no other world we can use instead?" Tork explained. "One without such insane inhabitants? I am reluctant to condone the removal of a species that is obviously so feebleminded."

"As are we all," Dron agreed, hypocritically. Sometimes decisions simply needed to be made, and then enforced. "And there are indeed further worlds that offer what we need."

"Then why do we not use one of them?" asked Tork, almost desperately.

"Makarn?" prompted Dron.

"Ah, because they lie beyond this one," the Science Master explained. "And we shall indeed use them. Once the process of deconstructing Darane Four is finished, then we shall need at least two further worlds. Ah, and there is no telling whether their inhabitants will be any less maniacal than the ones here. We must face the possibility that we could be in an area of space whose inhabitants are all terminally deranged."

"Thank you." Dron signaled for Tork to reseat himself. "None of us wish harm even to such a subintelligent species. But we have no choice. If they attack us, we will defend ourselves. Darane Four will be the source of material for the next stage in the Great Design. Now, if there are no further comments, can I ask for a sign of assent?"

Pakat and Raldar signified their approval instantly. One by one, the rest of the Hivemasters complied. As expected, Tork's vote was the last. But even he had agreed.

"So be it," Dron announced. "The Great Design goes forward today!"

Gul Dukat watched the transmission from the *Karitan* with great interest. The messages between the intruder and Darane IV had been intercepted. The aliens were not backing down, and those idiotic Bajoran colonists on Darane IV were equally stubborn. The intruder's craft was advancing into the Darane system, and the small fleet of ships the colonists possessed were massing to meet it.

This should prove to be a most interesting day. . . .

CHAPTER
7

WORIN TURNED TO his aide in near panic. Rubbing the bridge of his nose between thumb and forefinger as he always did when worried, he snapped, "Those maniacs are going to destroy our world!" He forced himself to think for a moment. "Get Major Marel, and order an immediate launch of every fighting vessel we have. Tell him our very existence depends on his skills."

"Yes, sir," the aide said with alacrity, vanishing toward the communications room.

Hurrying that way himself, Worin tried hard not to collapse in shock. It was unthinkable that anyone would be doing just what the alien intruders threatened, but they were quite clearly as serious as they were demented. Given the size of the incoming ship, he was virtually certain that they'd never hold this attack off alone. He needed help, and he needed it fast. Entering the communications room, he rushed to the nearest console.

"Clear whatever you're doing immediately," he snapped. "And open a channel to Bajor, highest priority."

"Yes, sir." The woman obeyed promptly, simply cutting

the channel she'd been using and opening a new one. "Whom shall I ask for?"

"First Minister Shakaar, and no one else," Worin answered, feverishly. He tapped his fingers on the top of the console impatiently as the woman patched through the call. A moment later, Shakaar's harried-looking face appeared on the screen.

"Yes?" he asked, an edge in his voice. "I'm very busy, so—"

"Darane Four is under attack by an unknown alien species!" blurted out Worin, unable to contain his panic any longer. "They've threatened to destroy our world and kill us all!"

Shakaar's face went almost blank, but Worin could see in his eyes that he was thinking fast. "All right," Shakaar snapped. "Hold them as long as you can. What kind of defense do you have?"

"Not much," Worin answered. "Just a few dozen interceptors. We never dreamed that anything like this could ever happen!"

"I'll mobilize whatever forces I can to help," Shakaar promised. "And I'll contact Captain Sisko for help from the Federation. Keep this channel open, and send us all the information you can." He looked away from the screen. "You," he called. "Over here. Record everything that comes through at this board." He turned back to Worin. "Do your best. Help is on its way." He moved out of sight, and a young woman took his place.

Worin wrung his hands together. *Help is on its way.* . . . But from Bajor, two systems away. It would be hours before anyone could arrive, assuming they were already in space. As for help from the Federation—how long would that take? By treaty with the Cardassians, they weren't allowed any permanent show of force in this sector. Any starships they'd send would have to take days to get here. . . .

It looked very, very bad for Darane. . . .

"All units," Marel transmitted, "signal in and identify yourselves." He stood on the bridge of the *Morvan Falls,* the largest ship in the Daranian fleet. Largest! It was a smallish battle cruiser, with a crew of fifty-eight. It didn't have the firepower to take out a starship, let alone whatever their unknown enemy might fling at them. And, judging from what his sensors were showing, the aliens must have a tremendous force. Their main vessel was thousands of miles long—how many attack ships might it hold?

Still, it was all irrelevant. There was no question of his duty and his responsibility. He had to do his best to defend Darane IV, and at the very least buy the planet all the time he could until reinforcements arrived.

"All ships reported in," his first officer announced. She grimaced slightly. "Eighty-six ships, most of them low-level interceptors. We've got just three further cruisers, sir."

"Then that will have to be sufficient," he replied firmly. "Anything yet on the aliens?"

"Not yet." She gestured at the screen, where the huge ship was already visible, even though it was still half the system away. "They've not launched anything at all." She chewed her lip uncertainly. "Do you think the whole craft is a fighter?"

"We'd better pray it isn't," he answered. "If it were, I can't think of anything this side of a Borg ship that might be able to stop them." He considered for a moment. "All right. Signal all ships to begin closing in. Let's take the battle as close to the enemy as we can."

She nodded. "All ships," she called out. "Prepare for action. Target, ahead, bearing one nine oh mark four. Distance—"

Tuning her out, Marel studied the image on the screen ahead of him. *What kind of weapons do they have?* he wondered. *And why are they so arrogant, so confident?*

Pakat moved closer to Dron. All of the Hivemasters were still in the conference room, and would be until the battle was over, but they had broken into smaller clumps to talk quietly. Only Dron sat alone, watching his comp to keep up to date with everything that was happening.

"They have launched attack vessels," Pakat reported. "They have begun the fight."

"Excellent." Dron gave his friend a smile of satisfaction and confidence. "Nothing your pilots cannot handle, I take it?"

"Of course not." Pakat sounded slightly shocked at the mere thought. "At your word, I will launch the first flight."

Dron considered for a moment, then decided. "Allow them to get closer," he said. "I want it perfectly clear that they have commenced this action. They are scared," he added. "They will fire the first shots. *Then* annihilate them."

"Understood." Pakat moved off to his communications station. His eagerness for the impending battle showed in his jaunty steps. Dron smiled again.

The Great Design was almost upon them, and he had the honor and glory of leading the Hive to their destiny! He glanced around the room, taking in the faces of the other Hivemasters. They all looked tense, but none of them looked worried—except for Tork. He was as nervous as a *shallath* tossed in water.

And he was talking animatedly with that old fool, Hosir. Dron frowned. What did the two of them have in common? Then he shrugged the matter off. It wasn't really important. Neither of them had voiced any dissent to his policies. Neither of them would dare to object to the implementation of the Great Design.

"Target closing fast," the first officer reported.

Marel nodded. "Still no sign of their ships?" He was juggling plans in his head. With his small fleet, there was no feasible way of attacking the main vessel.

"Not yet," she answered.

"And how about sensor readings on the intruder itself?"

"They reveal nothing at all," the first officer reported. "The sensors simply seem to slide off that metal—if it is metal. I can't read anything at all inside the craft . . . city . . . whatever it is. There are several places in the skin of the ship that look like portals and—" She broke off, and bent over her screen. "Sir, one of the portals has opened. The aliens have launched . . . one hundred ships."

"On screen," Marel ordered. The picture flickered and then showed a close-up of one section of the intruder. A portal had irised open, and dozens of small, dartlike ships were flooding out. Interestingly, they traveled in pairs. Marel's mind clicked on this. Was this an attack formation, or did they have some kind of need to be together?

"Signal all ships," he ordered. "Engage the enemy at will."

"Yes, sir." She bent to the panel to issue the order.

Marel studied the ships as they spiralled out from the alien craft. They were smaller even than most of his ships. They didn't look to be that formidable.

Why, then, did he have a very bad feeling about this?

"Weapons?" he called out.

"Primed and ready," the gunner answered. "Shields at maximum."

"Take us in," he ordered the helmswoman. "Sublight drive at half, full sensor sweeps." He turned back to his first officer. "Any readings on those craft?"

She studied her board. "Similar metallic construction to the intruder," she replied thoughtfully. "Not as dense, but still almost impossible to break through. I read the power source from its reactor, but no sign of weapons buildup. They do possess shields." She scowled. "Pretty good ones, too."

"No weapons?" Marel shook his head. "That doesn't make sense," he complained. "They're intercepting us. They must have *some* sort of weapons."

"I'm not reading any energy buildups," she insisted. "Nothing to show that any weapons systems we know are being brought on-line."

What was going on here? Marel nervously chewed at his thumbnail. "What about projectile weapons?" Maybe they weren't very sophisticated?

"Nothing that I can detect," she replied, sounding as

puzzled as he did. "There's nothing at all that I can pinpoint as a weapon on any of those ships."

"Suicide bombers?" he mused. Maybe their plan was to collide with the Daranian craft and explode themselves and their targets?

"There's no sign of them trying to overload their reactors," the first officer objected. "Surely they'd do that to take out another ship?"

"Maybe," Marel agreed uncertainly. He'd never encountered anything like this. The alien ships, all in pairs, were now targeting his ships and moving to intercept. What kind of soldier went into battle without weapons?

The answer was obvious: none. They *had* to have some kind of weapon.

So—what was it?

"Careful," he muttered to himself, as the first of his interceptors sped toward the spreading alien ships. "They're up to something."

And then the firing began. The two lead ships phasered blasts at the closest of the enemy ships. There was a brief flare of shields. "Report!" barked Marel.

"The alien ships' shields are standing," his first officer answered. "They're very strong from the prow," she added. "Built to take attack."

He nodded his comprehension of the report, and through narrowed eyes surveyed the images on the screen. The enemy still hadn't fired back, and there was no sign of any weapons. What was going on here?

The first of the twinned alien ships approached one of his interceptors. Marel concentrated on seeing what they were going to do.

Apparently, they did nothing. Each of the ships simply passed the interceptor by on opposing sides—

—leaving only minute wreckage, as the interceptor seemed to just disintegrate in space.

"What the hell *happened?*" Marel growled, frustrated, puzzled and furious. "What did they do?"

His first officer looked up, stunned. "I don't know," she

answered. "They didn't use any kind of energy at all. The ship just . . . fell apart."

"Ships don't just *fall apart!*" he exclaimed. "They must have done something, and I want to know what!" His eyes were riveted to the screen, when two more alien ships passed over and below a second interceptor.

Like the first, it seemed to simply fall apart as it fell, dissolving into tiny, indetectable pieces.

What was going on here? What kind of weaponry did these aliens possess?

And was there any defense against it?

Marel knew he didn't have very long to discover the answer to that. Phaser blasts seared across the screen again, but their energy was dissipated against unflagging shields. A third and fourth interceptor simply ceased to exist.

They were losing this battle; he was losing his men. And the aliens were simply plowing through his ships as if they didn't exist. Once they had passed, the ships *didn't* exist. . . .

Tork stood nervously, clenching and unclenching his hands as he watched the holographic representation of the battle above the conference table. The aliens had begun the fight, true, but they were being annihilated by the Hive forces.

Why did he feel so bad inside?

"It is never very pleasant to watch anyone die," Hosir told him gently. "I know; I'm very old, and I've seen most of my friends, colleagues, and family die." He gestured at the ongoing battle. "Even if they are aliens, and insane, it is still regrettable that they perish."

"Yes," Tork agreed. "I wish it had not come to this. If they had only been reasonable."

Hosir smiled. *"If snarks had wings, maybe you could train your breakfast to come to you,"* he quoted. "What is, is. That is another thing you learn with age. Regrets help no one, least of all the one who regrets. These aliens are what they are. We are what we are." He pointed again at the whirling images. "Because of that, this was inevitable."

Tork sighed. "And how many more times will it be inevitable?" he asked.

"That depends on the aliens in this new galaxy, youngster." Hosir sighed, too, a long, protracted sound. "To be honest, I am afraid it we may be compelled to repeat this every time. Still, let us try and speak of less violent matters. You are new to the Hivemaster status, and I know very little about you. Tell me about yourself."

Unable to tear his gaze away from the battle, Tork wrinkled his nose slightly. "This is not the time to speak of peaceful things."

"On the contrary," the oldster answered. "Now is the perfect time. *When wars wage without,*" he quoted, *"there is only peace within."*

"Actually," Tork couldn't help but reply, "the original reads: *When war is without, seek peace within.*"

"Does it indeed?" There was a hint of a smile on Hosir's face. "How could I have misquoted so badly?"

"It is not your fault, sir," Tork said quickly, thankful he hadn't caused offense with his unthinking reply. "It is just that . . . well, I am a scholar of the Texts. I have been researching them for some time."

"And you've found . . . errors?" asked Hosir, obviously being deliberately provocative.

"Not that," Tork said, aghast. "Merely . . . some small changes."

"Indeed?"

Hosir seemed to be genuinely interested in hearing what he had to say, unlike most of the elders. Tork had been afraid that his research might have brought him trouble. Instead, they had brought him the badge of a Hivemaster. "You no doubt recall the time of the Two Hundred and Third Hive," he said.

"Not personally," Hosir answered, laughing. "I'm not quite *that* ancient. But I know all the stories of the mutineers, and their overthrow, of course. And their attempts to change the Texts and alter our Great Design. But nothing came of it."

"Not exactly," Tork answered. "You see, I studied the

commentaries from the early Hives—Two Hundred and Four through Seven specifically."

Hosir's nose twitched. "Not many now read those commentaries," he said slowly. "They've been considered obsolete and generally pretty foolish for fifty millennia. I hope you have not been too influenced by them."

"Not the commentaries," Tork agreed, with a bark of derision. "I assure you, they are just as foolish as legend has it. No, what interested me is the way the scholars quoted the Texts. Their versions are very similar to ours, but in some cases they differ slightly. As in the quote you just used. Now, it seems to me that the ancient scholars were much, much closer to the Texts than we are, and would therefore have known them better. To misquote them—and to do so quite consistently—is hard to believe."

"And you chose to believe instead?" prompted Hosir.

"My conclusion was that there have been some minor alterations to the Texts over the millennia," Tork answered slowly. "Nothing large, nothing significant, but changes nonetheless."

"An intriguing suggestion," Hosir said dryly, "and not a popular one, I would wager. So, how is your research progressing?"

"Not too well," admitted Tork. "Being a Hivemaster is virtually a full-time occupation. And, with the Great Design now so close to fulfillment . . ." He spread his hands helplessly.

Hosir nodded, and then directed his gaze across the table. Tork followed suit, and saw that Dron was watching them closely. As soon as he realized he had been seen, Dron looked away.

"I wonder if that is why you were *made* a Hivemaster?" mused Hosir. "So that you wouldn't have time for your research?"

Tork couldn't follow this. "I am sorry, I do not understand."

Hosir gave a throaty chuckle. "In my youth, I was a bit of a rebel, too," he confessed. "I am not shocked by your

56

suggestion, though I'm sure that many in the Hive would be. Perhaps you have been kept deliberately too busy to continue your studies. It is worth considering, you know. After all, if the Texts *have* been changed, only the Hivemasters could have done the work. And I doubt the current Grand Master would want that fact known."

Startled by this, Tork exclaimed, "You cannot be suggesting what it sounds as if you are."

"Can I not?" Hosir shrugged. "I am old; perhaps I am too old. Perhaps my words get away from my brain." His nose wrinkled. "Or perhaps you are too young to be dedicated completely to the truth." He patted the youngster on the shell. "Think about what I have said. And then think about what you will do about it."

Kira glanced up as her board registered an incoming message from Bajor. It had been pretty peaceful on the station for the past few days—if she ignored two fights in Quark's, one smuggling arrest, and several minor breakdowns. It had seemed even quieter since O'Brien and his engineers had been spending most of their waking hours working on the *Defiant,* trying to get it spaceworthy once again. It was strange not to see him fiddling with the systems here in Ops.

This was probably nothing but a routine call, but Kira felt a little tense as she punched the command to bring the call up on her screen. Her worries faded as she saw Shakaar's face. "Shakaar!" she exclaimed in delight. She had fought under his superb leadership as a freedom fighter while Bajor had been occupied by the Cardassians, and now sadly saw far too little of him. "I haven't heard from you since you won the election! By the way, I haven't cong—"

"This isn't a social call, Nerys," he said tightly, and Kira stopped talking. There was pain in every line on his handsome face. "Can I speak to Captain Sisko, please? It's most urgent."

"Ten seconds," she promised, recognizing the urgency in his voice. She glanced up at Sisko, who was conferring with

Dax in low tones at the science station. "Captain," she called. "First Minister Shakaar is calling—extremely urgently for you."

Sisko sighed. "If it's not one thing . . ." he muttered. He strode across the room to her panel. Kira moved aside to give him access, but remained close enough to hear what was said. "First Minister, it's always a pleasure."

"Not this time," Shakaar said bluntly. "I've just received a distress call from Darane Four. They're under attack by some unknown alien species and need help desperately. I've already dispatched what ships I can spare, but . . ."

"Understood," Sisko answered. Kira could see the tension grip him as he spoke. "I'll do what I can. We'll contact you again when we're on our way. Sisko out." he cut the line and turned to Kira. "Tell O'Brien that the *Defiant* is leaving now," he ordered. "Assemble the crew. I'm going to punch through a request for aid from Starfleet."

Kira knew she had to state the obvious. "Captain, the *Defiant* is still not repaired. According to O'Brien's last report, there's still only partial shields, and the weapons aren't on-line."

"I'm aware of that, Major," Sisko said softly. "But do you want us just to sit here and do nothing?" She shook her head vehemently. "Neither do I. Tell him we launch in fifteen minutes, and he can do whatever work he's able to in transit. But, battle-ready or not, we launch."

CHAPTER
8

THE BATTLE WAS faring far worse than Marel could ever have feared. So far, over twenty of his small fleet had been annihilated by the aliens' peculiar weapon, and none of the enemy's ships had been even damaged. The intruders were well protected, and the few Daranian ships were not well armed. This had never been considered a dangerous system, and the need for defense had seemed slight.

What he would give for a single dreadnought right now . . .

But this was not the time for wishful thinking. Marel called out to his first officer: "Order Red Flight to attack the six alien ships on heading one zero nine mark four. I want two ships to go for the head-on assault, and the other four to try from behind. Tell Red Leader to single out one of the intruders and attack it with all of their firepower."

She nodded. "An idea?"

"A hope." In fact, it was more of a wish, but Marel had little else to try. In all of the attacks, the intruders had always flown in pairs, a precise distance apart. Whatever their weapon, perhaps it required two ships for it to be effective? In which case . . .

He watched the schematics as Red Flight whirled to meet the targeted enemy craft. Marel tensed, as he saw two of his ships flying directly for the three pairs of alien vessels. The other four of his ships boosted, spun, and came whipping in from the rear of the aliens. All four opened fire on a single ship.

"Their shields are overheating," his first officer reported. "If they can keep this up just a short while longer . . ."

There was a burst of white light from the screen. "One alien down!" she called, elated. Then, grimly: "Two of Red Flight are also destroyed."

They were bad statistics, but Marel felt a little happier knowing that the intruders could be taken out. "And the destroyed ship's partner?" he snapped.

The first officer studied her screen. "It's . . . pulling away," she reported. "Red Leader is initiating pursuit."

"No!" Marel ordered. "Let it go. Tell him to target another ship instead." His hunch had been correct, then— the enemy *had* to fight in pairs. "We only need to destroy one of each duo to stop the attacks. Order all units to so target their attacks. We can beat them," he added, trying to sound a lot more confident than he felt. They had destroyed one enemy ship—at a cost of almost two dozen of their own. At this rate, the battle wouldn't take long—and his forces would be utterly annihilated. . . .

Pakat glanced up from the projection, grimly. "One of our ships has been destroyed," he reported to Dron. "Its partner is returning to the Hive."

"How soon will the next flight be ready?" Dron asked.

"Very shortly," the Defense Master answered. "Two time units at most. The natives cannot possibly destroy many more of our ships."

Dron nodded his understanding, and then turned to Boran. "How soon before we can commence extractions?"

"In slightly less than three units," he replied. "The generators are almost at peak. The fields are beginning to be generated. As soon as we are in orbit of this world, we can start our work."

"Good." Dron studied the projection of the battle again. "The fewer of our youngsters who die, the better." He clenched his fist, as if clutching at the planet ahead of them. "And the aliens will pay for this attack of theirs."

"Give us full power," Sisko ordered as he took the command chair on the *Defiant*.

O'Brien sighed. "I wish I could, Captain." He shrugged. "Eighty percent's about the best you'll get. And there's still no weapons on-line. Fontana's working on them right now, but I can't promise anything."

"I know, Chief," Sisko said gently. "Whatever's humanly possible, I know that you'll accomplish. But we *must* try to help."

"Aye," O'Brien agreed. "We'll do all that we can."

"Helm ready," Dax reported. "Course plotted and laid in."

Sisko nodded, and glanced around the bridge. It was a lot tidier than before, with most of the circuit boards replaced, and all of the nonrepaired material removed. "Then let's go," he said simply. "Warp as soon as we possibly can."

"Understood," Dax assented. She tapped in the codes, and the umbilicals attaching the *Defiant* to *Deep Space Nine* were retracted. Dax nudged the ship away with the thrusters, and then switched to impulse. They streaked away from the station, which hung in view on the main screen.

Sisko wondered with a pang whether any of them would make it back again. There was so much still to be done. And there was Jake, waiting there. . . . Would he see his son again? Shrugging off the depressing thoughts, Sisko tried to concentrate on the mission. Even without weapons, there had to be something that they could do to help out.

Didn't there?

Startled by the sudden chime that shattered her train of thought, Sahna answered her comp. Harl's face floated out from the screen. Disappointed, she said, "Harl . . ."

"Yes, I know you were hoping it was Tork instead," her friend said, his nose twitching. "Sorry it was just me. You have not managed to reach him yet and tell him about your predicament?"

"No," Sahna answered. "He is in a meeting with the other Hivemasters, and cannot be disturbed."

"Well, I know why," Harl informed her. "The Great Design is under way, Sahna. We are ready to begin Phase Two."

Sahna stared at his image. "How can you know that?"

He gave a barking laugh. "I have just had my Determination," he informed her. "I am now a proud processor. Imagine that. And I have been told that we are in emergency working conditions. Preparations have begun. You know what this means, don't you?"

Icy dread clutched at her shell. "Yes," she said softly. "I knew that we were approaching our target star. We must now be preparing to mine it for everything we need."

"Exactly. And Tork and the other Hivemasters are in session because there are aliens on this world. They are refusing to allow us to take what we need."

Sahna let that thought sink in. "Then we are at . . . war?" she asked, using the unfamiliar word.

"Yes." Harl's face twisted in anger. "Those bastards have finally done it, Sahna. They're planning to wipe out an alien civilization to take what we need. And Tork has obviously gone along with their plans. Now what do you think of his lofty morals?"

Sahna felt the shock of Harl's accusation sinking into her stomach. She could not believe that Tork would ever agree to anything immoral, let alone the destruction of a race of alien creatures. Harl had to be wrong. He had to be! "I do not know," she said, finally. "But I will discover the truth." She stood up, determined to act. "I shall go to the Hivemasters' chambers and demand to speak with Tork."

"They'll never allow it," Harl replied.

"They will have to kill me to stop me," Sahna said simply. "I must know the truth."

Harl hesitated, and then nodded. "You are brave, Sahna.

Listen, there is one here I am assigned to work with who shares my views about the Hivemasters. We are evolving a plan to create a little trouble."

"Harl!" she protested, afraid for her friend. He was so hot-tempered, and if he wasn't careful, he might do something very foolish. "You are an adult now," she admonished him. "And can be punished for your actions, instead of merely being reprimanded."

"I know that," he answered. "I am not stupid. I will be careful. Take care in your turn. And . . ." He grimaced again. "I know how hard it is for you to think ill of Tork, but you *must* be prepared to see that he may have already changed. He is a Hivemaster now."

"He is a Hivemaster now," Sahna agreed. "But he has been Tork all of his life. He will not change." She lowered her head slightly. "But I, too, am not stupid. I will hear what he has to say, and I shall make my own decisions."

Harl nodded. "Be strong," he said, and then cut his transmission.

Her head whirling, Sahna left her small apartment. It was not far to the chambers, and she could make it in two units or less. It would give her time to decide what she would say to Tork—if she was allowed to see him. Despite her words earlier, she was not sure that she would be allowed to see him.

And then what would she do?

"What can you tell me about Darane Four?" Sisko asked Major Kira quietly, as he stood beside her. "Is it likely to be defended?"

"Hardly." Kira's face twisted as she brought back her memories. "The place was originally a Cardassian slave camp. It's rich in deposits of many metals. The Cardassians shipped Bajorans there to work in the camps and then die. We finally liberated the planet, but we were unable to bring every prisoner back to Bajor." Kira paused and took a deep breath. "There were over four hundred thousand prisoners, many in poor health. The provisional government sent what medical supplies we could manage to help out, along with some able-bodied volunteers. The former slaves became farmers and colonists." She grimaced. "Until now, it was actually shaping up pretty well. Darane's soil is good for crops, and almost anything can grow there. Bajor's been importing food from them, and the colonists have done pretty well for themselves." She sighed. "They've got a few ships, Captain, mostly old and many obsolete. They wouldn't stand up well to a spitting match, let alone a firefight."

Sisko had been afraid of that. "Shakaar said he was sending what aid he could."

"And I'm sure he has," Kira agreed. "The problem is that it isn't much. You know we don't have many ships, Captain. If this invader is serious, they could wipe out Darane without even working up a sweat." She slammed her fist down on her console. "Dammit, and we don't even have our weapons capability! We're walking into a war zone without any protection! What can we do?"

"I'm not sure, Major," Sisko admitted. "But whatever we can do, we shall. We can only pray that it doesn't result in a shooting match." Trying not to allow the worry in his heart to show on his face, Sisko walked slowly back to his command chair and sat down. From all reports, the situation was not good, and it didn't look like it would get any better.

If only it didn't get any worse!

"What are they doing now?" Marel stared at his screen, puzzled. The battle—if you could use such a term for this one-sided fight—was trickling out. Most of his ships had been destroyed by the enemy. They had managed to take out six of the aliens, but that was all. In the past few minutes, six heavy interceptors had arrived from Bajor. Their firepower was much greater than that of any of Marel's ships, but they were just as vulnerable to the enemy weapon. Two of the new arrivals were already floating dust.

And now this!

The huge alien intruder had slowed considerably. It was

approaching Darane IV now, within a few thousand miles. It looked like a huge, predatory fish attacking a smaller, ball-shaped prey. Marel didn't know what was going to happen, but it didn't take a genius to guess that, whatever it was, it wouldn't be good.

"I'm picking up energy readings from the craft that are off the scale," the first officer called in alarm. "They're powering up some incredible stuff in there, sir! Energies like none I've ever seen."

"Prophets!" swore Marel. To the communications officer, he added, "Get through to Worin and the Council. Tell them that they'd better get everyone off Darane that they can!" He stared in shock and horror at the enemy vessel. What was going on?

The two spread wings started to move. It looked like an unhurried folding of the wings to envelop the planet, but Marel knew that the process only seemed slow because of the scale. Those wings had to be moving at incredible speeds. The intruder was starting to enfold Darane in its terrifying embrace!

"Power levels rising," the first officer said, choking. "Whatever they're going to do is about to start. . . ."

As Marel stared helplessly at the screen, the undersides of both wings started to glow with power. Crawling, flickering tubes of incandescent light slashed across the metallic surface. The power buildup was enormous. The lights glowed, writhed, and burnt their way across the wings. Then, like some student science experiment on static electricity, the bolts suddenly snapped across the intervening space from the enveloping wings and into the planet's atmosphere.

"Prophets . . ." Marel breathed in horror.

Slashing across the skies of Darane, the blinding bolts of light finally connected with the surface of the planet. Wherever the beams touched, huge clouds of dust, smoke, and vapor rose. The clouds then started to rise toward the enveloping ship above the planet.

"They're . . . boiling away the surface," Marel gasped.

"Those beams are destroying Darane!" Helpless, enthralled, appalled, the command crew stared at the ghastly image on the screen.

Beams of light, of destruction, lanced from the intruder, tearing into the surface of Darane. Wherever the beams touched, boiling columns writhed upward and were suctioned off toward the predator somehow by the incalculable energies involved.

Darane was being annihilated, while they watched, unable to do a thing to save their world or their people.

CHAPTER
9

AT THE MINE site in Formax, the blasts of energy burned the ground, searing through hundreds of feet of soil to the rich mineral deposits below. Several hundred miners were incinerated in the deadly beams of light, the few grams of metal in their vaporized bodies being added to the metals being siphoned off into space. The ground cracked, shook, and collapsed under the barrage of energy. The old tunnels collapsed, and more people died in the devastation. The mine supervisor barely had the chance to scream before she, too, burned away. She had been standing three miles from the impact point, but the bare shadow she left on the desiccated soil vanished as the earth trembled and imploded in the wake of the attack.

Similar scenes of devastation occurred all across the surface of Darane IV as the planet died.

Worin was beyond panic now. His mind had almost overloaded on mental and emotional pain. His world was being murdered around him, and there was nothing he could do about it. The various monitor screens showed devastation after disaster all over the peaceful planet he had governed only this morning. The high-intensity energy beams were tearing the world apart, as they sought out metals, minerals, and anything else the invaders wanted. Worin wasn't even bothering to try and cope with the death tolls, because thousands were added every minute. Some died in the barrage, others when the superheated atmosphere burned them down. Others died in the earthquakes caused by the beams.

So few had been able to escape this incredible devastation. Whatever spaceworthy craft there had been on Darane had been filled to capacity and sent off into space. The invaders would probably massacre the survivors as they fled, but perhaps some would stand a chance of escape.

And, hopefully, somehow, extract revenge for this genocide.

"We have to get out of here!" one of his aides screamed, barely audible over the terrifying roaring outside. The air that had boiled away into space had created a vacuum. Hurricane-level winds whirled across the planet as nature tried to fill that void. The winds were ripping apart what few buildings and structures the earthquakes and energy rays hadn't managed to destroy.

"And go where?" Worin yelled back. "There's nowhere left to escape to. And no ships left to flee in."

The aide was beyond thinking logically, however. He simply bolted for the closest door, running for his life. For a second, Worin considered following him. But what was the point? Out there or in here, he would still die. It didn't matter any longer.

There was the familiar hum of a transporter beam, and for a brief second hope flared within the minister. Somehow, they were being rescued! Maybe it was the Federation at last, or—

His heart fell as he realized that the targets of the transporters were not the survivors. In a shimmer of light, blocks of computers, equipment and anything still intact were vanishing.

The invaders weren't content to destroy the inhabitants of Darane IV. They were even robbing the corpses as they died. . . .

"No!" Worin screamed, shaking a futile fist at the sky. It was pure white now, as energy bolts arched from horizon to horizon, dismantling everything in their path. The ground shook beneath his feet, sending him reeling against one of the now-blank walls. In a shower of exploding glass and mortar, that collapsed. Worin's dead body was briefly buried under half a ton of brick and steel before the energy arcs played across it, vaporizing everything.

"Heart of the Prophets," breathed Marel. His mind refused to function as he saw the destruction of his homeworld. "This is *genocide*. . . ." Sections of the crust of Darane were breaking apart as he watched. The inner magma of the planet surged free, spurting up in great geysers of boiling rock. "Nothing could survive that. . . ."

He finally broke his gaze from the screen and stared into the shocked faces of his bridge crew. They were even more affected than he was, he realized. Every one of them had lost families, friends, and neighbors in the holocaust. As Darane seethed, cracked, and bubbled, everyone and everything they knew must surely have perished.

Marel tried to concentrate. The intruder was still sucking the last dregs of whatever it wished. The energy fires were still blazing, but there was no atmosphere left to conduct the great discharges any longer. Incandescent blasts continued to rip through the heart of Darane.

"Enough!" he announced. It was impossible to help his world any longer, but perhaps it was not too late to extract some measure of vengeance. Turning to his first officer, he ordered, "Set course for the closest of those portals you discovered on the intruder. Maximum speed." Turning to his engineering officer, he added, "I want all warp drives to be overrun. Throw the damn dampers away. And I want the containment fields down-powered."

None of them had to ask him what he meant. And,

thankfully, not one of them questioned his orders. As they moved to obey, he saw only the desire for revenge in their otherwise bleak eyes.

Marel collapsed into his seat, drained of everything save the desire for revenge. Perhaps his phasers could do no damage to the alien craft. Well, they'd see what a starship with its warp core breached might do when it crashed into the intruder. . . .

Satisfaction filled Dron's being as he watched the projection of the target planet that hovered over the conference table. As anticipated, the energy beams were boiling away the much-needed metals and chemicals of the dying world. The comp was scrolling facts and figures faster than anyone could possibly read as the tally was taken of the resources obtained. The transporter rooms were taking all the intact machinery they could find for future salvage. And the botanical receptors had rescued billions of units of plants and edibles.

The processing of this world was going well.

Dron glanced up as he realized one of the messengers was standing beside him. "What is it?" he asked, annoyed at being disturbed in this moment of triumph. "Can you not see that I am busy?"

"My apologies, Grand Master," the female answered, bowing her head obsequiously. "There is a female at the chamber door who insists she must speak with Hivemaster Tork with great urgency."

"Send the fool away," snapped Raldar, looking up from the projection. "You know we are not to be disturbed whilst in session."

"Wait," Dron ordered, as the messenger started to turn. "This female—would her name be Sahna?"

The messenger bowed again. "Indeed."

Dron smiled slightly. "Then by all means you had better pass on her message to Hivemaster Tork," he told her. "And tell the Hivemaster that he is excused his duties for the moment to speak with her." The messenger bowed again and hurried away. Dron smiled once again, this time at

Raldar. "She has no doubt come to tell Tork that she has been assigned to Team Two," he explained. "Tork will then need to save her." Dron tapped his fingers thoughtfully on the edge of his shell. "He will have to come to ask for a favor from me. I have been watching him as this . . . recovery operation has been taking place. He did not look happy. I have a strong suspicion that he will attempt to block our next procurement. If he is in our debt, however, this will prevent him from an outcry."

Raldar inclined his head. "A wise plan," he murmured.

"I know," Dron agreed. He turned his attention back to the holographic projection. "Now, to business. I see that the operation is thirty percent accomplished—in so short a time. I think we shall have to publicly commend Boran and his team for their magnificent work."

The rape of Darane continued.

"We're approaching Darane Four now," Dax called from her console. "We can drop out of warp in two minutes."

"Understood," Sisko answered. He had been monitoring all the information he could from Bajor; all transmissions from Darane had died out more than twenty minutes earlier. None of what had come through, though, was good. It sounded as though the invader was annihilating everything and everyone in its way. Sisko slapped his comm badge. "Sisko to O'Brien. Chief, tell me something I want to hear."

O'Brien's voice floated back. Sisko could hear the strain in it. "Well, the good news is that shields are up to eighty percent, Captain. The bad news is that it'll be at least two more hours before Fontana and I can get the weapons systems back on-line. The circuit boards here were really riddled."

"All right, Chief," Sisko said, trying not to sound too disappointed or worried. "I know you're doing your best. Can you return to the bridge? I know I'm going to need you here. Sisko out." He stared at the screen thoughtfully, weighing his options. With the shields almost back up to strength, at least they had some protection against whatever the aliens were using as weaponry. But without firepower, they weren't going to be able to sway the course of the battle much.

Which left diplomacy—if that had a chance of working. If he couldn't make the aliens listen, then there would be little option but to run for cover, tail between his legs. And he *hated* that option. It would look as if he were abandoning his responsibilities, and the situation was appalling enough without that.

Dax glanced around from the navigation console. "Approaching Darane," she reported. Even she looked tense.

"Full impulse," Sisko ordered, focusing all his thoughts on what was about to happen.

Dax's hands flew across the panel, and there was the subtle shift in engine thrumming that signaled change. "Full impulse," she reported. "Switching main screen."

All eyes on the bridge were drawn to the screen as it sprang to life. There was a collective gasp of horror at what they all witnessed.

Darane was virtually invisible, with the intruder vessel draped about it. Bolts of celestial lightning ravaged the smoking, blackened core of the murdered planet. About thirty percent of its mass was gone, either to the ship or boiled off into space.

Sisko managed to swallow and called out, "Life signs?"

Julian, looking pale and shaken, managed to turn back to his station. His fingers shook as he fought to gather readings. "On the planet . . . none," he answered, his voice haunted. "I can't get any readings from the intruder."

"I'm picking up several hundred ships," Kira called from her post. With weaponry off-line, she was staffing the science station with Julian. "Most of them are fleeing the planet. Hard to say how many survivors made it, but there can't be a whole lot."

"There's still some fighting going on," Odo added. "I'm reading eight alien vessels, unfamiliar configuration. And . . . three Bajoran craft."

"On screen," Sisko ordered. Almost anything had to be better than watching the destruction of Darane. The picture shimmered and was replaced by one of four of the alien's dartlike craft speeding toward two of the defenders. As Sisko watched, he heard the turbolift door hiss open.

"Bloody hell." That was O'Brien's voice.

The first two alien ships caught up with one of the Daranian ships. The lone vessel was pouring everything it could into phaser power, but the shields of the attackers held firm. As the bridge crew watched, the two aliens passed on either side of the Daranian ship, which seemed to simply disintegrate into dust as they passed.

"Chief, what are they using?" Sisko demanded.

O'Brien was already at the closest sensor post, striving to get readings. "Give me a minute, Captain," he said. "Two new weapons in two weeks . . ."

Sisko dragged his eyes away from the screen. "Dax," he said grimly. "Try and raise the invaders' ship. I have to try and talk to them."

"Got it," O'Brien said, with a trace of satisfaction in his voice. "I've been trying to figure out what they were doing since we got the first pictures of the battle from Bajor," he explained. "I had an idea, but my readings just confirmed it."

"So, what is it?" growled Sisko impatiently.

"Monofilament."

"What?"

O'Brien spread his hands, fingers extended. "Monofilament," he repeated. "Wire only a few microns thick—virtually invisible and undetectable. But aligned molecules. The result is an incredibly tiny thread that can cut through anything at all with virtually no resistance. These aliens have made a sort of web out of it, stretched between two of their ships. They just fly past their target and the monofilament slices it apart."

Kira scowled. "But why won't shields stop it?"

"Because it's too thin," O'Brien explained. "It's probably out of the shields' sensor range. It's only a couple of atoms thick, and no shields I know of can stop a couple of atoms from getting through."

"Can ours?" asked Odo.

O'Brien snorted. "Not even at full strength. And we've only got eighty-two percent right now."

"That's not very reassuring," Odo answered.

"It's the best I can do," O'Brien informed him. "But I have reconfigured the sensors to detect the nets."

Kira looked thoughtful. "Now we know why the enemy attack only in pairs. They need two anchors for the monofilament, to keep it tense."

"Right," O'Brien agreed. "It's fantastic technology. There have been experiments with the stuff before, but nobody's been able to stabilize monfilaments that thin. They generally just break apart." He shook his head admiringly. "I'd love to take a peek at how they do it. They're marvelous engineers."

"And bloody killers," Kira growled. "Look what they've done to Darane."

"Oh, they're killers all right," O'Brien agreed. "I was admiring their technology, not their actions. It's a damned shame to pervert science like that."

Dax glanced up from her panel. "I've managed to patch through to that . . . ship," she announced. "The person in charge is a Hivemaster Dron, and he's reluctantly agreed to speak with you, Captain."

"Has he?" asked Sisko softly. He felt a burning rage in the pit of his stomach at what these intruders had done. "Then put him on the main screen. I think we all want to see him."

The picture of Darane being ripped to ruins faded, to be replaced by that of Hivemaster Dron. Sisko's right eyebrow rose slightly as he studied the alien.

It was impossible to judge his size just from the picture, but he looked vaguely humanoid. Actually, Sisko realized, what he most resembled was an armadillo. The most obvious thing about Dron and the other aliens he could glimpse behind the Hivemaster was that they all had segmented shells covering their backs and skulls. They were all varying shades of gray and brown, and none wore clothing of any kind. Their arms were long, with four thin fingers. Their necks were thick, their heads long. They had snouts, with two slit nostrils in the front, and large, expressive eyes. Small tufts of spiky hair protruded in clumps all across their non-shelled skin.

"What is it?" asked the Hivemaster, clearly annoyed.

"I am Captain Benjamin Sisko of the *U.S.S. Defiant,*" Sisko replied, trying to keep his anger under control.

The alien peered at him, and then wrinkled his nose. "Another alien species," he complained. "How many of you *are* there in this system?"

That wasn't quite the response Sisko had expected or hoped for, but he wasn't about to get sidetracked. "Hivemaster," he said firmly, "call off your ships."

"They are *not* attacking," Dron snapped. "They are *defending.* The criminally insane inhabitants of this world attacked us."

"That's not what I heard," Sisko replied coldly. "Nor is it what I see. You have destroyed Darane and killed almost half a million people."

Dron's snout almost rippled with muscular spasms. "That is *not* what occurred. You have been misinformed."

It was more than Sisko could bear. "Your ship is sucking the shreds out of Darane's dead husk!" he cried. "You're trying to tell me that you didn't do it?"

"That is not what I claim," Dron replied. "We have absorbed the planet, yes. It is necessary for our survival. But the fighting was begun by the inhabitants of this world. Captain Sisko, we offered them safe passage away and even aid in leaving. They refused our offer and attacked us." He spread his arms wide in a very human gesture. "We had no choice but to retaliate."

Sisko wasn't going to argue semantics while there were still people dying. "Call off your ships," he repeated. "Allow us to aid the survivors."

Dron's snout twitched again. "I would be more than happy to comply," he agreed. "But only if you will guarantee that the attack on our Hive will cease. If you do so, we would be glad to help you collect survivors."

"I don't think we'll need your aid," Sisko answered, only just managing to contain his fury. "But I will make certain that you are not attacked."

Dron inclined his head. "Then I shall have my defenders withdraw, Captain." He turned to give an order to one of his fellows. "It is done," he reported. "You may collect your peoples."

Sisko nodded, and made a chopping motion with his hand. Dax cut the link, and the picture of Dron vanished, to be replaced again by the smoking wreckage of Darane. "Start scanning for survivors," Sisko ordered the command crew. "See how many need assistance." He stared at Bashir. "Doctor, I suspect a great number of them will need considerable medical help."

"My teams will do what they can here," Bashir replied. "And I'll organize DS9 to prepare for refugees."

"Can you *believe* that creep?" Kira snarled, as she started the scans Sisko had ordered. "Claiming that *Darane* started this?"

"I believe that Dron really thinks that," Odo answered her. "Or, at least, wishes us to believe that he really thinks that."

Kira glowered at Sisko. "Are we just going to allow them to get away with what they've done?" she demanded.

"No," Sisko replied softly. "I promise you, they will be held accountable for every death they've caused. But this is not the time to start a fight. We still don't have weapons capabilities, and even if we did, I doubt we could fight a vessel like that."

"So we just do *nothing?*" Kira cried.

"No." Sisko gave her a very firm stare. "We help the survivors. *Then* we think about retaliation. Do you understand me, Major?"

It took a great deal of willpower, but Kira finally managed a very tense, curt nod. "Yes, Captain."

"Good." Sisko deliberately turned away from her. He hated having to confront Major Kira—especially when a large part of his own mind was crying out in the same pain as hers. But the living came first. The dead could wait.

"Captain!" Odo looked up from his panel. "I'm reading signs of a dangerous engine overload from the *Morvan Falls*. Its engines are going critical."

Bashir paled. "They must have had a malfunction."

"No malfunction," Odo contradicted him. "The crew has done this deliberately. They are moving in toward the intruder on a collision course."

"A suicide run," Sisko exclaimed. "They're on a suicide run." He stared at the image of the Hive on the screen. What would happen if they succeeded?

CHAPTER
10

TORK HURRIED OUT of the meeting room, relieved to be leaving the scenes of death and destruction he had witnessed. His conscience ached terribly with the strain of what he had seen. *Had it been necessary?* He still couldn't answer that. But he strove to bury his doubts as he went to meet with Sahna. Today had been her Determination, that much he knew. But why had she come to take him from such an important meeting?

And why had Dron allowed it?

Then Tork saw Sahna, standing nervously, her fingers running up and down the edge of her shell. It was obvious to him that she was in serious emotional pain. There was a tic below her left eye. "What is it?" he asked, concerned and protective. "What is wrong?"

"I just spoke with Harl," she answered, the tic more pronounced. "He told me that we have attacked an alien world and killed its inhabitants. Is this true?"

Tork's snout twitched in concern and anguish. "Yes," he conceded. "It is indeed true."

She looked at him in anger, shock, and betrayal. "How

could you allow this?" she cried. "You, of whom I thought so highly? How?"

It didn't help Tork's emotional state that he had been pondering much the same question. "They attacked us first," he explained. "Their ships began the fight. We only retaliated after that."

"And their planet?" Sahna gestured behind her wildly. "I am no fool, Tork. Processing has begun. Servos have started their operations. Phase Two is beginning. That can only mean that the Hive has processed the alien planet."

"Yes," he agreed again, reluctant to meet her accusing stare. "Their world is processed. We have almost everything from it that we needed."

"And its inhabitants?"

The fury of the question was like a knife between his plates. "Most are dead. The survivors are being allowed to leave unmolested."

"How generous!" Sahna cried. "What happened? Did even Hivemaster Dron's bloodlust get sated?"

"They were all insane," Tork answered, trying to quell his own doubts also. "They were dangerous. They refused to leave their world peacefully. Sahna, they *lived* on the dirt of a planet, and would not go! We could not reason with them."

"Is that any reason to slaughter them?" she asked, with a cold fury.

"No," he admitted. "No, it is not. But I could think of nothing to do that would save them, or stop Dron. I did not know that this would happen. Nor did many of the other Hivemasters. Dron told only those he could trust, I am certain. The rest of us were caught with our shells open, unprepared. I am sorry, Sahna. I need time to think this through. I want to do what is right, but I am becoming more and more uncertain what that is."

The anger in Sahna's eyes faded slightly. "I knew that you would never support such evil deeds," she told him, stroking the edge of his shell. "And I am sorry if I was too harsh on you."

"No," Tork replied. "You are not as harsh on me as I am

79

with myself. This is a terrible situation, and I must find some way to honorably resolve it. I promise you that I shall do something—although at this moment I do not know what it is."

"You are a good person, Tork," Sahna said, the affection in her voice unmistakable. "And I only wish that I could support you in all the ways that you need."

"You always have," he said gratefully. "And I am certain that you always will." This reminded him of his earlier thoughts. "Today was your Determination!" he exclaimed. "I had almost forgotten. Today you have become an adult."

"Yes," Sahna agreed, and there was no mistaking even further pain in her voice. "And it is the most wretched day of my life."

Fear stabbed at his stomach. "What do you mean?"

"My Determination was that I should become an astronomer—"

"Which you desired!"

"Indeed. But . . . I am to be on Team Two."

Tork was devastated by this news. There had always been this possibility, of course, but he had always refused to face it. He and Sahna were *meant* for one another. The Determination would have to reflect that and place them both together. And now—this, on top of everything else. Tork didn't have to say a word; Sahna knew what was going through his mind, because it had to be going through her own as well. She gripped his hands.

"I know that it is terrible," she said, as gently as possible. "But it is the Determination. It has been decided."

"Yes." Tork spoke dully. He felt as if the shell had been ripped from him, leaving him naked and utterly defenseless.

"Harl believes that you will try to get the Determination changed," she added. "But I know that you are too honorable to abuse your powers in such a way."

"Then I wish I were *not* so honorable!" Tork cried. "To avoid losing you, I would almost go so far as to request a reassignment."

Sahna stroked his shell gently. "But only almost."

"Yes." Tork sighed. "It would be wrong of me to question the Determination. It would seem that we are destined to be apart, always." He shook his head in bewilderment. "If there were only *something* I could do!"

"You can be brave," Sahna informed him. "I am as shattered by this as you, my love, but we must both be strong. We have to face our destinies and do the best we can for the Hive. If it must be apart, then no matter how difficult it is, we must bear it."

Tork sighed again. "I have much to bear," he told her. "And, saddened as I am by this news, there are more urgent calls on my attention. There must be something that I can do to mitigate the next phase of the Great Design."

Sahna managed a wan smile. "If anyone can, it will be you. I have great faith in you—and great love for you. Remember that, always." She turned, and left the chamber swiftly.

"As if I could ever forget it," he murmured to himself. With a heavy shell, he turned and walked back to face his own destiny. Never before had he felt so alone, or so bleak.

Waiting for him inside the conference room was Hosir. Tork didn't want to talk with anyone, not even Hosir, at this moment, but he could hardly avoid it without being extremely rude.

"Bad news?" guessed the elder. He wrinkled his snout in sympathy. "Has your woman jilted you?"

"Not exactly," Tork answered. "She has been assigned to Team Two."

"Ah." Hosir nodded, and then scratched at himself below one of his plates. "And you, of course, are Team One. Well, what are you going to do about it?"

"What *can* I do about it?" demanded Tork, angrily. "The Determination has been made. And it is a basic of our life that the Determination is never wrong."

Hosir snuffled. "Yes, I suppose it is. Still, even if the Determination is infallible, it isn't omniscient. Think about that." He gave Tork a friendly pat on the shell and then wandered off.

What did he mean by that? Tork had no idea whether Hosir was making a point, or whether he was simply getting senile. Still, as depressing as the news about Sahna was, the most important thing to do right now was to try and figure out a way of alleviating the terrible pain that the next phase of the Great Design would cause to the inhabitants of this area of space.

If there *was* any way . . .

"Get me Marel," Sisko snapped at Kira. Then, to Dax, he added, "Move us closer to the *Morvan Falls*. We have to stop them." Finally, he whirled around to O'Brien. "Chief, get to the transporter room. Lock on to any life-forms aboard that ship and beam them over as fast as possible." O'Brien acknoweldged and ran for the turbolift.

This was all he needed right now! Sisko was finding it more and more difficult to keep his temper under control. The universe seemed to be filled with nothing but lunatics at the moment.

"On screen!" Kira called.

Sisko glared up as Marel's image faded in. The warrior looked aged and tired, which wasn't surprising. "Marel," he snapped. "Break off this suicide run. I'm having your crew beamed off now."

"No, Captain," Marel answered, with some hint of steel still in his voice. "This is my last chance to pay those murderers back for what they've done. Don't try and stop me."

"I have no option!" Sisko thundered. "If you attack the intruder, they'll annihilate whatever survivors there are from this massacre. Stand down, now."

"No, Captain," Marel repeated. "I'm sure that the survivors would agree with me. We have to strike back."

"Don't be a fool," Sisko exclaimed. "There's nothing to be gained by this attack. Right now, the important thing is to look after the living, not avenge the dead. That can come later."

Marel shook his head. "There is no *later*," he said simply.

"There is only now. Goodbye." He cut the transmission, and the screen returned to stars.

"Damn that man," Sisko muttered. "Major, what's he doing?"

"Still on a collision course with the intruder," she reported. There was both pain and pride in her voice. "He's not going out without a fight."

"That's what he thinks," Sisko said. Tapping his communicator, he called, "Chief? How's it going?"

"I'm trying to lock on, Captain," O'Brien's voice said from the air. "With that power overload, it's going to be difficult. I can only chance taking out half a dozen or so at a time."

"Then do it as soon as you can," Sisko ordered. He turned to Odo. "Any idea how long we have?"

The security officer scowled. "About four minutes, I'd say." His face twitched. "Those engines are really straining now."

Sisko nodded. To Dax, he called, "How close are we?"

"Three thousand kilometers." Her hands were steady on the helm. "Closing slowly. They've built up their own velocity quite well."

Kira spoke up. "When the ship explodes, will our shields be able to take it at this range?"

"We'll have to find out," Sisko replied. "Dax, use the tractor beam on maximum. Slow down the *Morvan Falls.*"

"Acknowledged." The Trill's fingers flew across her board even faster. Sisko leaned over her shoulder and adjusted the main viewer.

The intruder vessel filled the whole screen. They were approaching it in pursuit of the *Morvan Falls.* It had seemed impressive at a distance, but as they drew closer, it was breathtaking. The entire outer shell seemed to be smooth and polished. The lights of the stars reflected from the burnished metal—if it was exactly metal—creating a tinged reflection, with the light spinning off in rainbow hues. As O'Brien had commented, these aliens had an incredible technology. It was appalling that they couldn't apply it constructively.

"Got her," Dax announced. "But it may not hold. Tractor strength is only eighty-seven percent."

Sisko could see the tiny form of the *Morvan Falls* on the screen now. The vague glow of the tractor field that had enfolded it showed up thanks to the computer enhancement. The tractor lock *had* to hold.

"Transport commencing," Odo announced from his station. Then he shook his head. "The chief doesn't have much time."

"Tractor lock is weakening," Dax announced, striving furiously to establish a stronger link. "Those circuits still aren't back to normal, and they're starting to break down."

"Hold on," Sisko encouraged her—and the *Defiant*. "Hold on. Just another minute . . ."

The picture on the screen abruptly reverted to that of Marel, who was desperate and furious. "Sisko! Let us go!"

"I'm sorry, I can't do that," Sisko replied. "Prepare to be beamed over." He cut the transmission by hand.

"They're overrunning their engines harder," Odo announced. "It can't—"

His words were cut off as the screen exploded to white light, and then the dampening field closed down the incoming view. Dax slapped her hand down on her controls, cutting off the tractor beam.

The shock wave of the explosion, transmitted down the tractor carrier wave, slammed into the *Defiant*. Buffeted like an ancient sailing ship in a storm, the ship whirled, the inertial dampers striving to absorb and redirect the load. Sisko was sent stumbling against his own command chair, and he grabbed hold of it. The other bridge crew had all been seated, and managed to stay that way by grabbing any available handholds.

Then the blow faded, and the ship reverted to normal. "Report!" Sisko barked.

"Shields are holding," Odo announced. "Though we've lost several minor systems. The chief isn't going to be happy."

"Helm is responding to power again," Dax added.

"O'Brien?" demanded Sisko, slapping his communicator. "How many did you get off?"

"Eighteen, Captain," came the chief's voice. "It was all I had time for."

"Well done," Sisko told him. That meant another forty must have died in that futile gesture. *War is hell, indeed* . . . "Prepare to continue searching for survivors," he ordered.

As the crew moved to obey, Dax glanced up. "There's an incoming message from Hivemaster Dron," she said, surprised.

"On screen," Sisko ordered. He straightened in his seat. "What is it now?"

Dron's face looked slightly puzzled, if Sisko was reading him correctly. "Captain Sisko, I owe you our thanks. We saw what you just did. You probably saved the lives of thousands of my people."

"I didn't do it for you," Sisko replied. "I did it to prevent you from taking revenge on the survivors from your massacre."

"Whyever you did it," Dron answered, unperturbed, "you have our thanks. I am quite surprised by your actions." His nose twitched. "You do not live on a planet, do you?"

"No," Sisko answered. "We are from *Deep Space Nine*. It's a station in orbit about Bajor." He wondered if it was wise to give that information, but could see nothing to be gained by keeping the truth secret.

"Ah." Dron seemed happy with the news. "I had suspected that you were an intelligent person."

Sisko wondered what that was supposed to mean. "I'm also a very angry one," he replied, as calmly as he could. "Right now, my priority is to help the survivors back to Bajor. Once that is done," he leaned forward in his seat, "I promise you, I'll be back."

The Hivemaster nodded slightly. "Yes. We may have a great deal to discuss. I look forward to seeing you again, Captain." The picture broke up.

"I look forward to feeling my hands around his scrawny

neck," Kira muttered. "Can you believe the nerve of him? Making it sound like a social call?"

Sisko spun to face her. "Well, he'll be disabused of that notion very quickly," he promised. "Whatever Dron thinks, I aim to see that he pays very dearly for what he and his people have done to Darane."

CHAPTER
11

Gul Dukat turned away from his screens, thinking furiously. The science team on the *Karitan* had decided that these unknown aliens were using some kind of monofilament weapon, which had interested him greatly. The level of the invaders' technology was quite formidable.

There had to be some way to obtain it for Cardassia. . . .

Dukat had been completely unprepared to witness the destruction of Darane, however. Seeing the alien ship enclose and then demolish the world had been quite unsettling. Nothing was now left of the planet but a smoking, blackened core.

That was a weapon the Cardassians needed to obtain!

However, there was more than the seed of uncertainty in Dukat's mind. Could even they defeat a foe as powerful as this? He was certain that the aliens would never give over their technology willingly. It was bound to come down to a match of force, but Dukat could not be certain that the Cardassians would prevail in such a match.

And, if attempted and lost, such a war would presumably

end with Cardassia itself in the place of Darane IV. The stakes were very high indeed.

But the prize might be worth taking that risk.

The *Karitan* had intercepted the conversation between Sisko and the Hivemaster. Dukat had not been too surprised by Sisko's actions. He tended to be quite predictable—for the most part. And when he wasn't predictable, he was quite a formidable ally—or foe. Sisko had bought time to evacuate the refugees, and then aimed to return.

Was he, too, after the alien technology? The Federation preferred to barter for such things, so perhaps Sisko was returning to contact his superiors and arrange for negotiations. . . . It would be completely unacceptable for the Federation to possess this alien technology and for the Cardassians to be denied it, of course. That would affect the balance of power here far too much.

Dukat rose to his feet and glanced around the monitoring room. No one was paying any attention to him, which was as it should be. "Ral," he barked. "Take over monitor control. If any further communications from the *Karitan* come through, acknowledge only and then contact me immediately. I shall be in conference with the other Guls. For the *Karitan* and that alone you are authorized to disturb me."

"Understood," Ral replied, saluting. He marched across and took over Dukat's station.

Dukat nodded curtly, and then walked thoughtfully from the room. The next decision could not be his alone, but it would have to be made swiftly. The Federation could not be allowed to be the sole recipient of this alien technology. Better yet, the Federation should not possess it at all; it belonged in Cardassian hands.

Deep Space Nine was a shambles. The *Defiant* had escorted most of the refugee ships that had fled the destruction of Darane back to the station. Many of them barely made the journey, and Sisko had been forced to evacuate eighteen of the smaller, older vessels during the flight. The

Defiant had been crowded when it had docked. Now the several hundred smaller refugee vessels swarmed about the station, awaiting their turn at the docking ports.

Sisko had contacted Lieutenant Soyka on his way back, and he had managed to organize dozens of spare rooms. Others that had been unoccupied since the Cardassian departure three years before were being opened and prepped for temporary use. Everywhere one looked on the station, there was feverish activity.

Many of the refugees had nothing but the clothes they wore. Even so, they were the lucky ones. Hundreds were in need of medical help, and Bashir had fled to the infirmary as soon as he could. He and his teams were working like dervishes, trying to get at least the most serious cases stabilized. Even so, there were hundreds waiting, with temporary bandages covering scar tissue, gashes, and sometimes even the stumps of lost limbs.

Those survivors who were at least mobile tried to find rooms and stay out of the way, but it wasn't easy. They were tired, scared, sick, and angry. There was no way that they could forget what had happened to them, even for a moment.

Shuttles were also arriving from Bajor with whatever medical staff and supplies Shakaar had managed to obtain. It wasn't much, but it was a help—and it added to the congestion. As Sisko made his way to Ops, the cries, the despair, and the tears of the refugees gathered around him like a cloud. He couldn't afford to let his anger and sympathy affect his judgment, and he tried his hardest to steel his heart against reacting.

It wasn't easy.

Reaching Ops at last gave Sisko a little quiet. Only the essential staff were here, and the noise seemed muted compared with the rest of the station. Kira and Dax were already at their posts. O'Brien, of course, was nowhere to be seen. He was either helping to prep more rooms for the refugees or else already back at work on the *Defiant*. Lieutenant Soyka nodded to Sisko, and then took a science station out of the way.

"Contact Starfleet," Sisko ordered him. "I want to speak with Admiral Noguchi immediately." He turned to Kira. "I think you'd better speak to Minister Shakaar," he said gently. "Tell him everything that's happened."

"And then what?" Kira asked pointedly. "He's bound to want to know what we're going to do." She didn't have to add what Sisko could read in her eyes: *And so do I.*

"Tell him that we're going back as soon as the refugees are unloaded from the *Defiant*. We're going to talk with Hivemaster Dron."

"Just *talk?*" demanded Kira.

"What would you have me do?" Sisko asked mildly.

The tone should have warned her off, but it didn't. She glared at him. "Wipe them out," she said bluntly.

"With what?" Sisko asked. "Even if the chief gets the *Defiant*'s weapons systems back on-line, I very much doubt we could take out that starship of theirs. And I'm not at all sure that we should, even if we could."

Kira gave him a filthy look. "They *massacred* Darane!"

"I don't need to be reminded of that," Sisko answered. "But who is *they?* Is it every inhabitant of the Hive? That ship is enormous; it must contain a population of millions, if not billions. Are they *all* guilty? Or was the attack planned and executed only by the elite? Until I know for a fact which it was, I am not going to sanction genocide."

Conflicting emotions warred across Kira's face. Finally, though, she managed to neutralize her expression and give a very tight nod. "I'm sorry, Captain," she said, through gritted teeth. "You're right, of course. Genocide is not the answer."

"Thank you." Sisko managed a weak smile. "But I'm sure you expressed an opinion a lot of people must hold by now. Probably one that Shakaar will have. Do your best to see that he understands mine, please."

"Of course." Kira turned, and Sisko could see the tension in every muscle of her lithe body. It wasn't easy for her to control the urge to strike back.

It wasn't a lot easier for him to restrain the same urge.

"I have Admiral Noguchi for you, sir," Soyka called out.

"I'll take it in my office," Sisko replied. He felt almost as though he were fleeing Ops and accusing eyes as he headed for his room. As the doors hissed shut, he hurried to his desk and tapped in the *accept call* code. The ancient, wrinkled face stared back at him. "Admiral."

"Captain," Noguchi replied, inclining his head slightly. "You have something to report?"

"Yes." Sisko sighed. "I have to report the destruction of Darane Four, and the deaths of a great number of its inhabitants. I'll be transmitting complete recordings, Admiral, but thought you should hear this immediately." He gave a brief report of all that had happened. "I'm getting ready to return to the Hive," he finished. "Hivemaster Dron has agreed to a meeting."

Noguchi's face seemed to have grown even more lines while Sisko had been talking. "And what do you aim to do, Captain?" he inquired.

"Discover who is responsible for this massacre," he answered. "How long will it be before I can expect backup?"

Scowling slightly, the admiral answered, "Seven days."

"A week?" Sisko tried not to make it sound like a reprimand. "Isn't that a . . . long time?"

Noguchi nodded. "As you know, we don't like to keep too many large vessels in your sector, Captain. It makes the Cardassians rather nervous. Normally, the *Enterprise* would have been much closer, but . . ." He spread his hands. Sisko knew all about the recent destruction of the *Enterprise*-D, of course. "The next closest vessels are the *Farragut* and the *Pike*. I've had both rerouted to you. The *Farragut* will arrive in seven days, and the *Pike* in nine. That's the best I can do, Benjamin."

That wasn't what Sisko had been hoping to hear. Knowledge that there was a starship close behind the *Defiant* would have boosted morale. Especially his. "And how about our allies, sir?" he asked carefully. "Any chance of help there?"

"The Klingons are being rather . . . difficult at the moment," Noguchi answered politely. "They will not be able to spare aid. The Cardassians, of course, have three fleets in your vicinity, but they also claim they can spare no ships."

"Marvelous," muttered Sisko. "So, it's entirely up to me, then?"

"I have tremendous faith in you, Benjamin," Noguchi answered. "How are repairs to the *Defiant* progressing?"

"At last word, we had no weapons up and running," Sisko informed him. "I imagine that will be rectified as soon as possible, but it does mean that at the moment my most powerful weapon is diplomacy. I'd have preferred something considerably stronger."

Noguchi nodded. "Yet you have always been very capable at talking. I am sure you will do everything possible in these less than encouraging circumstances."

"I don't have a lot of options, do I?" asked Sisko.

"No," agreed Noguchi. "And for that I am truly sorry. You are in a very difficult position."

"Then I'll simply have to work harder to extricate myself." With a sigh, Sisko signed off. Not good news. Not good at all. Seven days . . .

Who knew *what* the invader would be up to in seven days?

He clambered to his feet, wishing he had time for a shower and some rest. Right now, they were luxuries he simply couldn't afford. He returned to Ops, and caught Major Kira's eye. She didn't look at all happy. "What's wrong now?" he asked gently.

"Shakaar is . . . less than overjoyed with my report," Kira informed him. "He is also less than happy with what we've done so far. He seems to share the majority opinion on Bajor."

Sisko sighed. "Which is that we should annihilate the invaders?" he guessed.

"Something like that."

"Well, I'm afraid I'm going to have to disappoint him— and the rest of your planet. At the moment, I doubt we could eliminate a fly using the *Defiant*'s weapons." He tapped his communicator. "Sisko to O'Brien. Give me some good news, Chief. I *really* need it."

There was a slight cough, and a muttered oath, and then O'Brien's testy reply: "Weapons are up, Captain. We've got about forty-percent capacity right now."

"Thank you, Chief," Sisko said sincerely. "That's the best news I've had all day."

"And," O'Brien added, "the refugees are almost all evacuated. I've just got a systems check to run, and we can launch again in . . . oh, fifteen minutes, I'd estimate. Fontana and I can work on the weapons systems in flight."

"Chief, you're a marvel." Sisko nodded to Kira. "Major, Dax . . . get Odo again, and meet me on the *Defiant*." He managed a tight smile. "We're going to practice our diplomacy."

"I'm not so sure about that," Harl said, staring at the comp. "It seems potentially dangerous to me."

"Well, of *course* there will be some risk," Tukh agreed, scowling. "But this is *rebellion*, right? We aim to show the Hivemasters what we think of their plans. We *have* to take some chances."

"I know that," Harl replied, trying not to let his anger get the better of him. Tukh was on his side, after all. "But sabotaging the drones seems to me to be an indiscriminate method of striking at them. Someone might get injured."

"Afraid?" asked Tukh, sneeringly. "You're not truly committed to change, are you?"

"No one can say that about me," Harl said. He felt like slamming his companion's head against the nearest metal wall. "But I want to be certain that when I strike, it will harm only the Hivemasters. We are not at war with our fellows."

"I know that, of course," agreed Tukh, obviously attempting to placate him. "But we have to get attention. Sabotaging the drones in this sector while they are hard at work will draw a lot of notice."

Harl considered it. While the drones were replicating feverishly, it wouldn't be too difficult to cause a glitch in their programming. But there were an awful lot of workers around, and too many chances that one or more might be injured if something unexpected occurred. "No," he decided finally. "It's a good idea, but too risky. We'll have to find some other way of striking." He handed the comp back to Tukh. "This is not the way."

Scowling, Tukh accepted the comp ungraciously. "I think you're wrong," he complained. "But . . . have it your way."

"Good." Harl moved off to his next workstation, ignoring his companion in rebellion.

Which was decidedly a mistake. As soon as Harl disappeared from view, a wide smile crossed Tukh's snout. "It doesn't matter what you wish," he said softly. "The sabotage will take place." He glanced down at the comp he held carefully. It had Harl's palm prints all over it, and he had been the one to use the keys to access the details of the sabotage.

Once Tukh set the destruction in motion, it would be Harl who would be blamed for the resulting explosion. And Tukh was quite certain that there would be casualties. He'd already selected three victims who would be in the processing area when the drones exploded.

With three victims and such a visible act of sabotage, Harl was bound to be arrested, tried, and convicted, just as Security Master Raldar had ordered.

Pleased with his planning, Tukh set off to finish his task.

CHAPTER
12

GUL DUKAT STOOD stiffly at attention in the quarters of Gul-Tar Keve. The suite of rooms was very spartan, even by Cardassian standards. This would not have been so remarkable had Keve not been the effective ruler of the Cardassian Empire. Not technically, of course—theoretically, Cardassia Prime was ruled by a Citizens' Council that was elected into power.

Practically speaking, the Council was no more than a figurehead for Keve and the military. They held the power, and power was everything.

Despite this, Dukat was impressed that Keve eschewed almost all the trappings of power. His suite of rooms was larger than most, naturally, but he had more support staff in attendance. There were few furnishings beyond the utilitarian desks, monitors, and seats. There were no artworks of the sort that many of the lesser military loved to show off in their own quarters. Even the food for Keve's table came from a standard-issue replicator. Keve had always claimed that his position was one of responsibility and not privilege.

Dukat sometimes believed that. More often, he believed that Keve believed it.

"At ease," Keve finally barked, looking up from the report he had rather too ostentatiously been studying. It was the oldest *I'm in charge and you're not* trick in the book. Even the humans used it. "I've studied your reports and recommendations, Dukat. Incisive, interesting, and egotistical as ever."

"Thank you, sir." Dukat inclined his head slightly. There were questions he was dying to discover the answers to, but there was no way he was going to ask them. It was up to Keve to announce his plans—or keep them bottled up, as he often did.

"Your recommendations are—provocative," Keve added, standing up. He was a thickset, elderly figure, slightly shorter than Dukat, and he walked with a pronounced limp, the result of an old war wound. Or, at least, so he claimed.

Dukat said nothing, knowing this was merely a conversational gambit. Keve was trying to get him worried and nervous. With others, these tactics often worked, but Dukat had served under the Gul-Tar for too long. He knew all of his affectations and mannerisms.

Keve, knowing that Dukat knew this, tapped the computer screen. "You propose taking the Home Fleet to the Darane system and investigating this alien vessel further."

"Yes, sir," agreed Dukat. Now was the time to explain his reasoning. "The First Fleet is needed to protect our borders from Dominion infiltration. The Third Fleet is several days distant. The Second Fleet is monitoring events on the Klingon frontier. Only the Home Fleet could reach Darane in time to contact the aliens."

"True," agreed Keve. "If that were our priority." He glowered at Dukat. "The Home Fleet is needed precisely where it is: at home. Your request is denied."

Dukat scowled back. "Then we are to do nothing about this potential threat?" he asked, feigning surprise. "That is a little . . . puzzling, sir."

"I didn't say we're doing nothing." Keve hobbled out

from behind his desk. "I've contacted Gul Gavron and ordered him to investigate."

"But, sir!" protested Dukat. "The Third Fleet—"

"—is several days away, I know," agreed Keve. "It's a pity, but there's nothing else to do. And I know that Gavron doesn't have your . . . shall we say *devious?* . . . mind, Dukat, but there's no help for that."

"Sir," Dukat pointed out cautiously, "I was the one who made the discovery of this alien Hive. I monitored and reported on it. By rights, this assignment should be mine."

Keve waved a hand dismissively. "By rights, by rights," he echoed. "You *have* no rights that I don't allow you, Dukat, and never forget that!"

"No, sir," Dukat agreed, casting his eyes down to the floor. "I apologize if I have disappointed you."

"You haven't disappointed me," Keve answered, a slight smile on his face. "On the contrary, you've rarely pleased me more. Given the information that you have, your report and recommendations are perfect. If things were not as they are, I'd have given you permission to go hunting. I'm glad to see that you're so keen on getting the alien knowledge to help the military."

Dukat looked confused. "I'm sorry, Gul-Tar," he said. "Did I omit something from my analysis then?"

"Nothing you could have known about." Keve appeared to consider for a moment; then he said, "Come here." He led the way to his one affectation, the wall-sized window looking out over the capital. The view of the city from here was breathtaking, looking down on the myriad buildings and complexes below the Citadel. Dukat could see why Keve had this window: it breathed power. Far, far below, tiny forms scurried about their business. Up *here* was where the heart of the Empire lay. "It looks peaceful, doesn't it?" Keve asked him a moment later.

"Very," agreed Dukat. "In a productive sort of way, of course."

"Of course," Keve said dryly. "But that is merely the surface. Scratch that view and you will find any number of malcontents and troublemakers."

Dukat frowned. "There have always been those who dislike the power that the military have, sir," he objected. "But they are a minority; they are hardly worth *you* being concerned about them. They can't get along with one another and have no organization at all."

"Until recently," Keve told him. "Now the resistance to the military is growing daily. Unrest is spreading." He grimaced. "Three days ago, a shipment of arms was intercepted and stolen on its way to the Bavroma spaceport."

Dukat looked shocked. "I hadn't heard about that," he replied.

"Of course you hadn't," Keve responded. "That's not the kind of news I allow to get out." He scowled out at the city below. "Sooner or later, there will be an insurrection. My sources indicate that it will be sooner. *That's* why the Home Fleet stays here." He laid an arm on Dukat's shoulder. "And why you do, too. I need good officers close to me, officers I can trust. Let Gavron go after this alien vessel, and seek glory. You will remain here with me, and we shall begin to hunt for traitors. You will be my right hand, Dukat. Isn't that more important than the mission you desired?"

Much more, Dukat thought. He'd know all along about the arms theft, and had planned his "recommendations" very carefully. Keve had done precisely what Dukat had hoped he would—removed the Third Fleet from consideration and strengthened Dukat's own grip on power. By seeming eager for this mission, Dukat had made certain he wouldn't go on it. Let Gavron get the glory—if he could. Dukat rather suspected that these aliens had a few more tricks to play yet. It would be much better if Gavron was the one to fall in battle against them. Then Dukat could leap in to save the day. . . .

Dukat gave a smart salute. "It is my duty to serve where I am most needed, Gul-Tar," he said. "And it is also my pleasure."

"Good," Keve said, waving a dismissal. "I knew you'd see the sense of it."

Indeed I do, thought Dukat as he bowed and made his way from Keve's quarters. *Indeed I do.*

This time out, the *Defiant* felt right. Sisko sat back in the command chair, feeling more at ease. O'Brien, Fontana, and the other engineers had worked miracles on the ship's systems. Sisko's own tallies on his seat arm showed that shields were back to ninety-five percent, that engineering was on full, and that life support was functioning perfectly. Only the weapons systems remained in need of drastic work—which was where the chief and the lieutenant were right now—and weapons were already up to sixty percent.

Sisko felt a whole lot better returning to the Hive with at least a few teeth he could bare, should it prove necessary. Diplomacy first, of course. Sisko hadn't needed Admiral Noguchi's orders to know that. But if diplomacy failed, it didn't hurt to carry a big stick and be prepared to use it.

He still didn't know what to make of these aliens. They seemed to vacillate between making sense and making war. They claimed that the Daranians had been "insane"—but what did they *mean* by that word? Still, Hivemaster Dron had agreed to talk, and perhaps that would lead to a better understanding of what the Hive was after. His first directive as a Starfleet officer was to seek out new life—although this one seemed to have sought them out. It was important to understand the members of this species before he made judgments about them.

Still, it was hard not to judge them yet, given the countless lives they had taken.

But at the moment, Sisko had far too little information to build on.

"Incoming message, Benjamin," Dax said softly, obviously bothered about interrupting his train of thought. "It's from Shakaar."

"Thanks, old man." Sisko managed a wan smile. "I'll take it in the ready room." He had been expecting this call for a while now, and still wasn't certain what he'd say. When he was alone, he activated his screen. "First Minister," he said politely. "What can I do for you?"

Shakaar was no fool. He had been Kira's leader in the resistance, and Kira had the highest regard for him. Sisko, in turn, valued Kira's opinions and was certain that Shakaar probably lived up to everything that the major claimed of him. The first minister raised an eyebrow. "Well, Captain, I assume that asking you to wipe out these murderers isn't likely to get me anywhere, is it?"

"No, it isn't," agreed Sisko calmly. "Though I do understand the request."

"I thought you might." Shakaar rubbed the back of his neck, looking suddenly very tired. "And I'm equally sure you understand that I'm being pressured constantly to make certain the Federation destroys the Hive."

"Kai Winn," guessed Sisko.

Shakaar managed a mirthless laugh. "That was too easy, Captain. Yes, of course she's demanding it. Loudly, frequently, and publicly. Anything to embarrass me, naturally."

"I'm not totally surprised," admitted Sisko. "You have my sincere sympathies."

"Well," Shakaar finally asked, "what do you plan on doing?"

"Talking to them," Sisko informed him. "Discovering what they want here. What their plans are. And who is responsible for what they did to Darane."

"And then?" Shakaar leaned forward eagerly.

"I'm not sure," admitted Sisko. "But I will promise you this: Whoever is behind the destruction of Darane will pay for it. You have my word."

There was a slight pause, and then Shakaar nodded. "That's good enough for me." He managed a real smile. "Nerys holds you in very high regard, Captain, and I hold *her* in high regard. I am happier with your assurance."

"Thank you." Sisko inclined his head slightly. "I will do my best to live up to my reputation."

"Understood." Shakaar nodded slightly and then cut contact.

Leaning back in his seat, Sisko stared up at the ceiling for a few moments. At least Shakaar wasn't pressuring him too much. That was about the only positive aspect of this entire mission. He knew that Shakaar must be under tremendous pressure back on Bajor, but he had the wisdom not to try and pass that along. He was definitely shaping up to be a very good first minister, unlike the previous ones Sisko had been forced to deal with. As long as the backstabbing so common in Bajoran politics didn't get to Shakaar, he'd probably be the best thing to happen to the planet since the Cardassian withdrawal.

Meanwhile, Sisko still had to do something about the Hive.

Right on cue with this thought, his communicator beeped.

"Sorry to disturb you, Captain," said Dax's voice. "But we're about to enter the Darane system."

"On my way." Sisko collected his thoughts and returned to the bridge. Taking his seat, he said: "Put Darane Four on visual as soon as you can, Dax." He wanted to see what had happened to the planet in the few hours since they had last left it.

"Aye, sir," Dax acknowledged, concentrating on her instruments.

While he could do little but wait, Sisko tapped his communication badge. "Sisko to O'Brien. Chief, how's it going?"

There was a brief pause, and then O'Brien's reply. "All phasers are now on-line, Captain. I'd appreciate the chance to run another diagnostic before they're used, but if you need them, I'm pretty sure they'll be fine. Photon torpedoes will take us about another half hour or so."

"Thank you, Chief," Sisko said gratefully. "That's excellent news. I won't bother you until you're finished. Sisko out."

Phasers back on-line . . . Sisko hoped he wouldn't be needing them and that this whole mess could somehow be resolved peacefully. But he couldn't envisage Hivemaster Dron agreeing to punish himself and the other guilty parties for the destruction of Darane. Sooner or later, he felt that this would end up as a shooting war. The best Sisko could manage would be to make it later.

"Darane on screen," Dax announced.

Sisko and the bridge crew had been prepared to see the smoldering ruins of the planet. It still hung there in space, gases venting from the charred core.

The alien ship had changed, however. It still hung above the planet, but the enveloping wings had once more straightened out. That wasn't what surprised Sisko. It was the activity down the center of the Hive's axis.

There was a definite gap of some kind, with space showing through in several points. They were still too far away to make out any details beyond that, but every instinct in Sisko's body told him that whatever was going on spelled trouble in the worst way.

"Dax," he said urgently. "What's happening? Is the Hive breaking up?"

She didn't reply for a moment, instead turning all the sensors on the craft. Behind him, Sisko could hear Odo tapping frantic commands into his own panels. Finally, Dax sighed. "I don't know what's going on," she announced. "We're still not close enough for a good scan. But I'd say that whatever is happening there is no accident."

"What do you mean?" asked Sisko, moving to stand directly behind her.

"That line is much too straight and regular to be accidental," she pointed out. "If there were a problem, it would look more chaotic."

"Maybe," agreed Sisko. "Keep scanning. Let me know the second you discover anything." He turned to Kira. "Try and contact the Hivemaster," he said. "Let him know we're coming and that we expect to be allowed on board to talk." Then he turned to Odo, who was scowling over his own equipment. "Anything, Constable?"

The changeling glanced up. Though he had never quite mastered the art of duplicating a human face precisely, he had definitely got the hang of looking worried. "It's difficult to say," he answered. "I've been scanning the rest of the system, on a hunch. There's a Cardassian science ship hanging about at the extreme limits of sensor contact."

Sisko snorted. "I might have guessed that they're monitoring the whole business."

"And doing nothing to help," agreed Odo. "I'd expect no more of them. But this means that they probably witnessed the battle—and the alien capabilities."

He didn't have to finish that thought. Sisko nodded. "So we can probably expect a Cardassian delegation to try and join these talks soon?"

"That's what I'd predict." Odo scowled. "It won't make your job any easier."

"I'll be happy if it simply doesn't make it harder," Sisko admitted.

"Captain," called Dax. "I'm getting some very . . . odd readings from the Hive." As Sisko hurried to join her, she explained: "I'm getting a preliminary sensor scan from the ship now. There are thousands of small mechanisms on the skin of the Hive, and probably even more inside the vessel."

"Repairing the break?" Sisko hazarded.

"No—*creating* it." Dax looked up, her strong face shrouded in puzzlement. "They're splitting the Hive in two."

CHAPTER
13

NONE OF THIS was making sense of any kind to Sisko. Why would the Hive apparently be destroying itself? There had to be something here that they were all missing. Tapping his communicator, Sisko called, "Sisko to O'Brien. Chief, you want to take a look at what's happening with the Hive right now?"

"I'm on my way to the bridge anyway," came O'Brien's response. "Be with you in a minute or so."

Sisko stared at the screen. They were still too far away to make out details on the Hive, but in his mind, he could see the mechanisms running over the ship. Why were they trying to break the Hive in half? Had something gone wrong? Or was this somehow planned?

"I've spoken to the Hivemaster," Kira announced. "He's given me a set of beam-down coordinates."

"Did he sound at all worried?" asked Sisko.

"No. More bored and put-upon, if you ask me."

So whatever was happening to the Hive wasn't a mistake. He'd never have sounded so calm if his world was breaking apart. Sisko nodded. "I'll be taking just a small team,

Major," he said softly. "Would you be very offended if I left you here in command?"

Kira's eyes sparkled. "It's probably the best idea, Captain," she answered sincerely. "I'm not sure I could restrain myself from killing somebody down there."

Sisko managed a small smile. "I may have similar trouble," he confessed. "Dax, you'll be with me. Odo, you too."

Odo inclined his head slightly. "Why me? Not that I mind accompanying you, but surely the chief would be more logical?"

"To check out the technology?" Sisko guessed. "Maybe. But this is in effect a police action. I think you'd be of much more use in that. Plus, you have quite an uncanny knack for seeing through lies and bravado."

"It comes from associating with Quark too much," Odo complained. "I'll be happy to help out."

The turbolift doors hissed open, and O'Brien emerged. "Good grief," he muttered, witnessing what was happening on the screen. He hurried to the science station and began his scans.

The *Defiant* was closing fast on the Hive now. The ship was growing slowly on the forward screen, and some details finally started to emerge on the ship's hull. The machines at work there varied greatly in size, but they all seemed to be moving with feverish activity. Whatever their purposes, they were busy little mechs.

"Chief?" prompted Sisko.

O'Brien glanced up from his readings and shook his head slightly in bafflement. "You've got to admire their technology," he finally offered. "They're ingenious little murderers." He gestured at the main screen. "They're disassembling parts of the structure, to split the Hive into two."

"We can see that," Sisko observed. "But *why?*"

"Beg your pardon, Captain. I wasn't clear." O'Brien replied. "They're splitting the ship into two—into two *ships*. Those mechs are taking the first ship apart very carefully, and then reproducing the part that's been lost. It's a mechanical equivalent of an amoeba splitting into two—and obviously for the same reason. They're breeding."

Sisko stared at the screen in shock. *"Two* ships," he repeated. "They're making a second Hive?"

"Right, sir," said O'Brien. "And a heck of a lot faster than I'd have believed possible. I'd say that in two or three days tops there will be two Hives sitting there in space." He shrugged. "Now we know why they demolished Darane. They needed the spare materials for the split."

"And if one ship can destroy a planet," Kira offered, "two should be able to demolish a star system."

Sisko nodded. Kira had made the most important point. "Then we'd better insure that they do nothing of the kind. How long till we're in transporter range?"

"Two minutes," Kira answered.

"Fine. We'll contact you every half hour. If you don't hear from us for any reason, then contact Starfleet and inform them." Sisko gave her a grave look. "And then use your best judgment. Do you understand me?"

"Perfectly." Kira stood up, ready to take the command chair. "I'm not going to start shooting up the Hive without good cause, I promise. But if anything happens to the three of you, that may just be good cause."

"Look after my ship and crew," Sisko ordered. Then he rested his hand on her arm. "Like Shakaar, I trust you, Nerys."

"I won't let you down," she promised.

"I know." Sisko turned to Dax. "Well, old man, time to get moving." Dax and Odo fell in beside him as he headed for the turbolift. *Now,* thought Sisko, *we discover just how good a diplomat I really am.*

The stars were as magnificent as they had ever been, but Sahna could not bring herself to look upon them. Ever since she had been a youngster, she had loved only two things: the stars and Tork. Now she had lost the latter, and was cutting herself off from the former.

Her life could hardly be more miserable than it was now.

"Sahna?" It was her old tutor, Bree. She was a little bowed by age, but her eyes and spirits were as bright as ever. "What's wrong? Are you ill?"

"Ill?" Sahna sighed. "In my soul, yes. Very ill."

Bree came closer, and stroked the edge of Sahna's shell. "Want to talk about it? We oldsters have little left to enjoy in life but talk."

"You are not old," Sahna replied.

"Flattering, but not true," Bree answered with a *whuf* of amusement. "And have I not always taught you to be a scrupulously accurate observer?"

Sahna almost managed a smile at that. She gestured out of the observation window. "Those stars are old; you are not."

"Cheat." But Bree was amused. "Now, if you feel up to it, can you not tell me what troubles you?"

Composing herself, Sahna discovered that she didn't know where to begin. Finally, she said, "Life is so *wrong.*"

Bree snorted again. "That is a statement I have heard many times from youngsters. Let me tell you something: It rarely gets any more right as you age. Now, what ails you?"

"My Determination was today."

"Then I should think you would be very happy," Bree objected. "I recall my Determination Day quite clearly. Malko and I shared that evening a good meal, a bottle of *tling,* and a bed. It was a lot of fun."

"I shall be sharing nothing," Sahna replied, wrinkling her snout. "I have been assigned to Team Two."

"Ah. And the only male for you is on Team One, eh?" Bree shrugged her shoulders as much as she could, given her arthritis and the extra weight of her aging shell.

"Yes."

"Well, the split isn't final for two days," Bree pointed out. "You could have quite a busy time with him before that."

"I do not simply want to mate with him," Sahna answered. "I wish to be One with him."

"Take what you can get," suggested Bree. "Then, later, there will be another to take his place."

Sahna simply couldn't accept this cynicism. "I do not want another; I want only Tork."

"Maybe now," agreed Bree. "But you will come to your senses later."

Did everyone get this jaundiced with age? Sahna shook her head. "That is not necessarily true. But, even if I did wish only to mate, it would not be possible. Tork is a Hivemaster, and is currently very occupied with the Great Design. He would have no time to spare for mere mating."

"Then he is a very foolish male." Bree snickered to herself. "Anyway, if he is a Hivemaster, he could get you reassigned to Team One."

Sahna was shocked. "That would be an immoral use of power, and Tork would not agree to such a thing."

"You youngsters," Bree snorted. "It is done all the time, believe me. I knew Dron when he was younger, and some of the abuses of power he has managed over the years would shock you."

"Tork opposes such abuses," Sahna pointed out. "How could he then indulge in them? Besides which, there are heavier weights on his shell."

Bree wrinkled her snout. "Heavier weights than mating on a young male's mind? *That* is something I do not hear very often. What concerns this prodigious individual that you love?"

Sahna took a deep breath, knowing she was violating a confidence—and knowing that she could not stay silent. "The planet that was just absorbed," she said slowly. "There were inhabitants still upon it."

"What?" All traces of humor had vanished from Bree's elderly face now. Instead, there was anger and grim attentiveness. "You are sure of this?"

"I am." Sahna bowed her head. "Tork himself confirmed this to me. There were thousands of sentient beings on the world that we destroyed."

Bree's face was twisted with anger and horror. "Sentient? You are certain of this?"

"I am. Tork informed me that they were insane and refused to leave the planet, despite an offer of assistance. They then attacked our ships, which were forced to defend themselves."

Chittering angrily under her breath, Bree scowled, obviously deep in thought. Then she looked up again. "Insane or no, the Hivemasters had no right to kill them. They should have been removed by force if necessary, but not killed."

"I agree," Sahna informed her. "The guilt of what we have done hangs heavily on my shell."

"And this youngster of yours," snapped Bree. "This prodigy of morality, he did *nothing* at all to stop this massacre?"

"He wanted to," Sahna explained, desperately seeking to rebuild Tork's image in the older scientist's mind. "But he is new, and did not know what to do or say. He is consumed with guilt and anger also."

"And so he should be." Then Bree seemed to realize how distressed Sahna was. She stroked the edge of the younger one's shell. "If you say he is a good person, then I am certain he will do what he can. The problem is that Dron will not allow it." She wrinkled her snout in disgust. "As I told you, I knew that one when I was younger. Even then he was devious, a liar and a manipulator. I doubt he has changed at all in the decades since. You can be certain that he has plans for your youngster. No matter how moral and clever your One-to-be is, he will not be a match for Dron."

"Then there is nothing to be done?" asked Sahna in despair.

"That was not what I said!" snapped Bree angrily. "You are a scientist, child. There is always *something* that may be done in all circumstances. The point is to discover the *best* way to do things. If what you say is true—and I can see by your distress that it is—then there will be plenty of people who, like us, will abhor what has happened. We *cannot* allow this to happen again."

"But how can we change things?" asked Sahna miserably. "The Hivemasters are in command. They make the decisions."

Bree snorted again. "For now, perhaps."

With a shock, Sahna realized what her elderly mentor meant. "You are speaking of mutiny," she whispered, almost too afraid to say the word.

"I am speaking of *sanity,*" Bree argued. "If the Hivemasters make decisions that go against the beliefs of the Hive, then they should be Masters no more. Is that not logical?"

"It is also treasonous," Sahna gasped. "Since the Two Hundred and Third Hive, there has never been a rebellion against the authority of the Hivemasters. And the Two Hundred and Third Hive lost."

"Then it is high time someone questioned the authority of those fools and murderers," Bree snapped. "It may be that we shall lose also. But I will not stand by and accept the murder of even the insane as justifiable."

Sahna gazed at her mentor with new respect. "And nor shall I," she said, quietly but firmly. "What has happened is appalling and wrong. A repetition of it must be prevented at all costs."

Bree tapped her on the shell. "You have courage, my child," she said approvingly. "Nurture it; you are likely to have great need of it in the days ahead. Now, it's a fine night, and I am going to talk a little treason, so you'd better keep yourself busy while I am gone. You will have to cover for me, child." She winked. "Get those young eyes of yours back to observing, and make plenty of notes for the both of us, eh?"

The room in which Sisko, Dax, and Odo materialized was completely unremarkable. It was clearly the anteroom to somewhere more interesting, but contained only small tables and some very odd-looking pieces of furniture.

Along with two of the armadillo-like aliens, both armed with slender, rifle-like weapons. Though neither had the devices pointed at any of the arrivals, they were clearly there to prevent any trouble that Sisko or the others might offer.

"I will inform the Hivemasters that you have arrived," one of the guards announced as he exited the room. The other guard said nothing and barely glanced in their direction.

Sisko decided that the best thing to do was to return the silent treatment. He glanced at Dax and then at one of the odd pieces of furniture. It resembled a long, stiff board that was inclined backward at about a fifteen-degree angle. About two feet from the floor was a hornlike projection. There were several of these odd items about the room. "What do you think that is?" he asked her.

"Probably a chair," she answered. Smiling at the silent guard, she gestured. "Look at those shells of theirs. Wonderful for protection, but I doubt they can sit down. They must use these boards to lean against, and the protrusion to rest upon."

"That makes sense," Sisko agreed. "But a bit uncomfortable for me, I'm afraid. I think I'll remain standing." He wandered across to the doorway, but could see only a short corridor through it. The three visible walls were blank.

Then at the far end, an iris opening appeared. The guard who had remained with them turned at the slight mechanical sound, and then gestured with his weapon. "You may proceed," he announced.

"Thank you," Sisko said politely. He led the way to the iris, and then stepped through.

They were now inside a much larger chamber. In the center of the room was a large table. Around it were more than a dozen of the odd chairs, and most were occupied. At the head of the table was the alien Sisko recognized as Dron. "Hivemaster," he said politely.

"Captain," Dron responded, inclining his head slightly. "Please, will you and your companions join us?"

"Thank you." Sisko crossed to the table, where room had been cleared for them. There was nowhere to sit, but Sisko didn't feel like resting at this moment anyway. "You will forgive my manners if I get right to the point of this meeting?" he asked.

Dron spread his arms. "If you wish, Captain. We have no desire to alarm you or offend you."

It's too late for that, Sisko thought, the image of Darane in his mind. Aloud, he said, "We could not help but notice as we approached that there is considerable work going on on the skin of the Hive. My engineer tells me that this seems to be aimed at splitting the Hive into two separate, complete Hives."

Dron inclined his head again. "Your engineer is quite perceptive. That is indeed what is being done."

"May I ask the reason for this?"

"The reason?" Dron appeared genuinely puzzled. "Surely that is obvious, Captain? We are doubling our chances of survival. When the work is completed, we shall have two Hives, and our population is to be divided between them. Each Hive shall then go on its separate way."

"And where will this separate way take them?" asked Sisko.

Dron tapped commands into the computer pad that lay on the table before him. "I will call up the schematics for you if you wish, Captain," he answered. "We do not intend to hide anything from you. Ah."

There was clearly a holographic projector beneath the surface of the table, for a very detailed map of the local area sprang into being. One star was marked in red, and he recognized it immediately as Darane.

"That is where we are now," Dron said. "When the fission is complete, the two Hives will move in separate directions." He tapped in further commands, and the red ball of light split in two. Each then started to move across the projected starscape.

Dax leaned forward, her eyes narrowed as she watched the simulated motion. "Benjamin," she said softly. "One of those Hives is going to head into Cardassian space. The other . . ." She took a deep breath. "The other is aimed at Bajor."

Sisko turned to face Dron again. "And what will these Hives do?" he demanded. "Is what happened to Darane going to happen again?"

"Absorption?" asked Dron. "That was necessary to begin the fission. And once it is accomplished, we shall need to gather new materials to restock the two Hives. Further planets must then be mined."

"Mined?" Sisko echoed, appalled. "You're talking about the destruction of more planets." He jabbed a finger at the projection. "You're telling me that you aim to demolish Bajor!"

CHAPTER
14

APPARENTLY UNABLE TO comprehend what the fuss was about, Dron blinked. "If that is the name of the planet, then, yes—we aim to absorb Bajor next."

"You can't do that!" Sisko exclaimed, striving to keep his temper in check. "Billions of people live there. You can't condemn them all to death!"

"We are condemning no one, Captain," Dron replied. "We do not wish to harm any living being, no matter how insane they may be. We are quite prepared to wait a reasonable length of time until the planet has been evacuated before it is absorbed. Would three of their days be sufficient?"

Sisko could hardly believe what he was hearing. "Three days?" he echoed hollowly. "To evacuate an entire planet?"

"We could wait longer," Dron said, obviously believing he was being generous. "As many as seven, should it prove necessary."

"You can't be serious," Odo snapped. "You expect the Bajorans simply to pack up and leave their homes?"

"Homes?" Dron appeared to be puzzled again. "It is only

a planet. Why would they not agree to leave it if it is necessary to our survival?"

"Because they *live* there!" snarled Odo. "The planet is their home."

"That is absurd," one of the other Hivemasters broke in. "I, ah, I am Makarn, Science Master," he added. "It is simply not possible that any, ah, sane race would choose to live on the surface of a planet."

"Quite," agreed Dron. "After all, Captain, did you not tell me that you are all living on a space station?" He smiled. "And do you consider yourself sane or not?"

Sisko shook his head slightly. "It is true that we all live on a space station," he agreed slowly. "But that alone is no decider of sanity. We have all also lived on planets, and may yet do so again."

"There is no reasoning with such creatures!" exclaimed another of the Hivemasters. He glowered at Sisko. "Clearly, they are not completely civilized or intelligent."

Dax stared back at the alien until he flinched and looked away. "Is that your sole criterion for determining mental state?" she asked mildly. "Whether a person lives on a planetary surface or in space?"

"Not entirely," Dron replied smoothly. "But it is quite obviously the basis for such a judgment. No sane person would subject himself to the vagaries and hazards of an exposed world."

"That's a very far-flung accusation," Sisko commented. "And, since obviously none of you have lived on the surface of a planet, it smacks to me more of prejudice than fact."

"I *told* you they were incapable of reason," the angry Hivemaster broke out again.

"Pakat," Dron said admonishingly. "They are still our guests for the time being. Please do not be so rude to them." He turned back to Sisko. "My apologies, Captain, but Pakat is the Defense Master. It is his responsibility to keep the Hive safe. He takes his duties very seriously."

"Ah." Sisko stared at Pakat, determined to remember his face. "And it was you, then, who led this massacre?"

"Defense," Pakat corrected, with as much dignity as he could. "We were attacked first."

"No," Sisko answered. "You began the engagement by attempting to steal what does not belong to you—a world belonging to an intelligent species. As a representative of the United Federation of Planets, I have to inform you that this alone makes you the aggressors in our eyes."

"We're not interested in your warped moral perspectives," Pakat snapped.

"Captain," Dron said hastily, "how can anyone *own* a planet? Or a star? Or a comet? They are simply resources, to be utilized to their fullest. The inhabitants of the world we absorbed were not using it, and we needed it. Why, then, the accusation of theft?"

Odo growled, "You just don't understand, do you? You can't simply take a planet because you want to."

Dron spread his arms. "We did not *want* it, we *needed* it. And we need more planets for further raw materials. We shall take them as we must. It is not theft. It is survival."

Sisko was feeling very frustrated. It was quite clear that they were simply not getting through to these Hivemasters. Their attitudes and philosophies were fundamentally different from anything Sisko had ever experienced before. "Perhaps what is needed here," he suggested, "is better understanding of each other's point of view?"

Dron inclined his head. "How do you mean, Captain?"

"We don't seem to be comprehending one another," Sisko answered. "Perhaps what is needed is that we spend some time together in trying to see the other's perspective."

An elderly Hivemaster spoke up. "Ah, I begin to see," he commented. "I am Hosir, Master of very little at the moment." He moved forward. "Perhaps if you were to visit with us for a while, and see the Hive itself, with one of us as your guide, you would better understand what we believe in."

"Precisely," agreed Sisko. "Perhaps you would be good enough to honor us by showing us around?"

Hosir snorted. "I can barely walk across the room without pain, Captain. I would be a poor guide, believe me." He gestured at a younger person beside him. "Might I suggest Tork instead? He is a very capable young man, and possessed of both great knowledge and great enthusiasm."

"No!" Pakat exclaimed. He glared angrily at the visitors. "This is obviously merely a trick by these creatures to study us for weaknesses. They have shown in words and action that they mean to attack us."

There was always one paranoid, Sisko reflected. "No," he said gently. "We genuinely wish to understand your people, and I think that this is the best way to do so." He turned to Dron. "If you are worried that we are here to act as spies, then simply tell Tork not to show us anything to do with your war effort."

"We have no *war effort*," Dron said smoothly. "We do not attack; we only defend ourselves." He considered for a moment. "But your point is well made, Captain." He turned to Tork. "Will you be good enough to show our visitors about the Hive, Tork? Allow them to converse freely, and answer their questions to the best of your ability. But do not take them to the Defense areas."

Tork nodded, and Sisko saw a gleam of something in the young alien's eyes. Worry? Eagerness?

"I would be honored," Tork replied. "I agree that it is important that our motives and thoughts be correctly understood."

"Excellent," Dron said. "Now, Captain, perhaps we could offer you a little refreshment before your explorations commence?"

"Thank you," Sisko answered. "That is very gracious of you. Also, may I have your permission to contact my ship and inform them of what we have already discussed? I told them I would check in every thirty of our minutes."

"Of course, Captain." Dron inclined his head. "Do you desire privacy for this contact?"

"No," Sisko said. "After all, we are being open with one another, aren't we?" He smiled, and then tapped his communicator. "Sisko to Kira."

"Kira here," came back the major's voice. "Is everything okay, Captain?"

"We're fine," Sisko answered. "And we're about to get a guided tour, which may take some time. However, we do have some news that you may wish to pass along. The Hive is indeed undergoing fission, as the chief surmised. When it finishes this process in a couple of days, there will be two Hives. One will be heading into Cardassian space. The other will go toward Bajor."

There was no mistaking the tension in Kira's voice. "Are you saying what I think?"

"Yes." Sisko kept his voice as calm as possible. "Hivemaster Dron informs me that his people aim to . . . process Bajor next. He is willing to give your people a week to evacuate the planet."

"Captain, that's crazy!" Kira protested. "Those murdering—"

"That's enough!" Sisko snapped. "You have your orders, Major. Pass along the information to Shakaar and stand ready for further messages from me. Sisko out."

Dron blinked mildly. "Dear me," he murmured. "She sounds like a very excitable person. I do hope you can rely on her."

"I know I can." Sisko smiled without warmth. "And it's her home planet that you're talking about destroying next. I think she has every right to be excitable. Now, did you mention refreshments?"

Shakaar switched off his screen, rubbed the bridge of his nose, and sighed. Then he sat back in his chair, almost too numb to feel anything. Nerys had delivered what virtually amounted to a death warrant for Bajor just moments ago. Shakaar knew that he should be feverishly working on defense plans, evacuation plans, and the Prophets knew, maybe a dozen other plans, too. But for the moment, it all seemed utterly futile.

At this moment, there were thousands of refugees from Darane IV either here on the planet or else on *Deep Space Nine,* all seeking to regain some semblance of life. They had fled one destroyed world, and were now, apparently, sitting on another doomed world. Along with several billion other Bajorans.

And they were all his responsibility. Shakaar was their first minister, and it was up to him to cope with this overwhelming situation. But there was, practically speaking, nothing much he could do. Oh, the aliens had offered Bajor a week—a *week!*—to evacuate the population. Aside from the fact that the logistics of such an exodus were impossible even in tenfold the time, it really wasn't a viable option anyway.

Shakaar knew that the majority of the population would refuse to leave their homes, no matter what odds were against them. That left him exactly one option—to fight. But Bajor had never concentrated on arming itself again. In the resistance war with the Cardassian occupiers, the Bajorans had used light weaponry. They had nothing else. Now, three years after the occupation was ended, they still had very little in terms of planetary defenses. They had concentrated on rebuilding their wrecked world and shattered economy, not on preparing for war. They had all looked to their Federation alliance for aid in that quarter.

Aid that would now not be coming in time.

Shakaar knew that Captain Sisko and his associates would do everything in their power to defend Bajor, but, frankly, it was nowhere near enough against this alien Hive. The recent destruction of the *Enterprise* had left a large gap in the Federation coverage of this sector, and it would take too long for replacement vessels to arrive that might have the firepower to take on the Hive.

When the Hive came hunting for Bajor, everything that *Deep Space Nine* and the ground defenses of Bajor could throw at it would barely slow it down. Visions of the destruction of Darane filled his head. *That* would be the fate of Bajor. The Bajor he'd pledged to govern and protect to the best of his ability.

Dammit, he thought, *it just isn't fair!* Why was the fate of his world and his entire people now resting so heavily on his shoulders? What could he be expected to do? What was it that the Prophets required of him?

"Shakaar."

His head jerked up as he was startled out of his troubling

thoughts. For a second, he thought he'd imagined the voice, but then there was a movement in the shadows at the end of his office, and a robed figure emerged.

"Kai Winn!" he exclaimed in surprise. "How did you get in here? I gave explicit orders that I was not to be disturbed."

With the regal serenity that Shakaar was certain she practiced in front of mirrors when alone, Kai Winn glided across the room. She inclined her head slightly. "I am sure that you did, my child," she murmured, oozing sympathy and understanding. She could fake them very well, Shakaar knew. "But you are already disturbed, are you not? By your thoughts."

"How did you get in here?" he repeated, standing up and glaring down at her. He resented her patronizing attitude, and had never accepted her in the role of Kai—spiritual leader of all Bajor. She was perhaps one of the least spiritual people he'd ever met in his life. All she cared about was her own power.

"There are ways known only to the Prophets, my child," she finally answered evasively.

"And secret passages known only to the religious orders, I'll warrant," Shakaar snapped. "Well, you're here now, so say your piece before I have you escorted out—oh, very respectfully, of course."

Winn smiled serenely. "Of course," she agreed. "I did not think for an instant you would show the Kai less respect than she deserves. But I came to discuss your needs, and the needs of Bajor at this troubled time."

"What do you know of this *troubled time?*" he asked her.

"Only what the Prophets have seen fit to show me," Winn answered. Her hands appeared from the arms of her ornamental robes. One held a small scroll. "I have been studying the Third Prophecy of Andaki, and it is obviously about the crisis in which we find ourselves."

"With all due respect to the Prophets—" began Shakaar, but she cut him off with a gesture.

"Yes. Let us *all* show due respect to the Prophets." She glared mildly at him. "I understand your anger and frustration, my child, but this is very relevant. Listen." She unraveled the scroll and began to read from it:

"The land will be torn asunder as great wings hover.
Death will be on all who witness, and mourning on the
   lips of the few who survive.
Weep for the lost, the children, the land. Weep, for it
   and they are no more.

In that terrible day shall all my people be one.
Stand firm, for one shall protect you, and two shall
   convert.
In their faith, Bajor will be made whole."

She let the scroll roll up again, and slipped it back inside her voluminous sleeves. "Surely, my child, you can see what at least a part of this means?"

Shakaar considered himself as devout as the next person, but he knew that the Prophets always spoke in riddles. Many of the Prophecies were couched in obscure terms and subject to any number of interpretations. "The Third Book of Andaki is notoriously used by many unscrupulous and misguided individuals to predict the end of the world as we know it," he said. "I am surprised that you have joined their number, Kai Winn."

She didn't let the accusation annoy her. "It is so used by people who lack true insight," she answered calmly. "But to those that the Prophets have anointed, the book reveals many mysteries. Besides"—she allowed a fleeting smile to cross her face—"I can hardly be called misguided if I see the end of Bajor in the current situation, can I? After all, the Hive will be heading here next, I believe. And that will surely presage the end of the world if we do not act wisely."

"How did you hear about that?" he demanded. Someone must have informed her, despite his order for absolute secrecy.

"How I know is not important," she said. "What we are to do, however, is vital. Surely you can see that the first stanza refers to the destruction of Darane Four? That needs no interpretation, my child. The second stanza, however, is more difficult. *One shall protect you, and two shall convert."*

Shakaar regarded her suspiciously. "Even if I grant that the first stanza *may* be about Darane, I don't see what the second means at all."

"Of course you do not, my child." Winn spread her arms and smiled. "That is why I am here. If I cannot understand the Prophets correctly, who can?"

My pet draka *could understand the Prophets better than you,* thought Shakaar, but he was not foolish enough to say it aloud. Winn was cunning, and she clearly had something in mind for this meeting. "And what is your interpretation?" he asked.

"The one who stands firm is obviously myself," she replied seriously. "I stand firm as I always have in the faith of the Prophets. The two who shall convert . . ." She gave him a pitying gaze. "You are, I am afraid, one of those. Your lack of piety and trust in the Prophets is hardly secret, is it?"

"I do my duty by the Prophets," Shakaar snapped. "No one can say otherwise."

Winn shook her head chidingly. "None of us do *all* of our duty, my child. Even I sometimes fall short of what is expected of me. But we must all strive harder to obey the will of the Prophets."

"I don't see that your prophecy gives me anything to even consider," he replied, irritated at her fake piety. "And you still haven't told me who the second person is who must convert."

"The answer to both is tied to the other," Kai Winn informed him. "You alone, commanding the government, could never hope to stand against these murderous alien predators. If you stand with me, and the religious forces who follow me, then there is a better chance. To win the forthcoming battle, though, you will need further aid."

"From whom?" growled Shakaar. "The Federation cannot reach us, and the Cardassians would never agree to help. They have a Hive of their own to contend with. There is nobody else who can help."

"Oh?" asked a fresh voice. "I'm sorry to hear that I have been forgotten so quickly."

Shakaar spun about. He was going to tear this room apart to find that secret entrance when Winn was gone. Now, who could . . . ?

He stopped cold, staring at the tall, saturnine man who had stepped out of the shadows. "Jaro," he breathed.

Jaro's face broke into a smile. "It's good to see that I haven't been forgotten during my absence," he murmured, moving closer to the Kai.

"Forgotten?" Shakaar could hardly believe this. How could he have forgotten Jaro's abortive coup two year's earlier? "No, but we had hoped that someone had murdered you."

"Dear me, such hostility." Jaro shook his head in mock sadness. "No, I have been in retirement, preparing myself for the time my day would come again."

Shakaar's eyes darted from Jaro to Winn. They had worked together on the attempted coup, he knew, but nothing had been proven against the Kai. "Are you two attempting another takeover of Bajor?" he asked, almost laughing. "If so, you could hardly have chosen a worse time. In a week, Bajor will most likely no longer exist."

"This is no revolution," Winn said, trying to look shocked at the accusation. "Did you not hear my words? *Two* shall convert."

"Him?" Shakaar looked at the arch-traitor with loathing.

"I know it may sound a little difficult to believe," Jaro said smoothly, "but the Kai is correct. I am not here to fight you, but our joint enemies. I will throw in my forces and my weapons with yours. Working together, the three of us should be able to better defend Bajor than we could if we did not cooperate. Surely even you can see that, Shakaar?"

Fighting back his desire to throw Jaro out of the window or into a jail cell, Shakaar forced himself to think. "You want to help?"

"That is all." Jaro spread his hands and a smile.

"And afterward?" probed Shakaar. "Immunity? A place in the government? What is your price?"

"I have no price," Jaro answered. "I can see that you find this difficult to believe, but in this instance it is true." He raised his eyebrows. "May I be frank with you?"

"Please do," Shakaar said sarcastically.

Jaro inclined his head. "It is true that I think I am the best man for the seat you occupy. I always will think so. But that seat is of no use to either of us if Bajor no longer exists. Thus, while there is this threat to Bajor, I propose a truce between us all, so that we may join our efforts into a unified defense against the invaders. After we defeat them—*then* we can begin to fight among ourselves again. For now, let us forget all politics but the one aim of saving the world that we all love. What do you say, Shakaar?"

Shakaar considered his options. Much as he distrusted them both, Winn and Jaro both had valid points. Divided, their forces and efforts would be next to useless. Together . . . well, they might not win the upcoming battle, but at least they'd stand a chance. Shakaar made his decision. "I cannot refuse anyone whose wish it is to save our world," he replied, his heart heavy. "I accept your aid while the battle remains to be fought." *And I pray to all the Prophets that I don't live to regret this decision,* he thought bitterly.

Jaro grasped his forearm in greeting, and smiled. "Then we are, at least temporarily, on the same side."

"The one and the two," Kai Winn announced officiously. *"In their faith, Bajor shall be made whole,"* she quoted. "What can withstand us now?"

CHAPTER
15

"Do YOU REALLY think that this will do any good, Benjamin?"

Sisko blinked and then smiled slightly at Dax. "Old man, at the moment, I'm willing to grasp at *any* straws. Besides, I don't think these aliens are really evil."

"They're just very twisted," Odo observed. "They're willing to destroy Bajor and billions of people without even meaning them any harm." He growled. "How do you ever hope to reason with these people, Captain?"

"By finding some common ground," Sisko answered. "I refuse to believe we can't get through to them. This tour may show us what their culture is like, but I'm also praying that it'll show Tork what *we're* like. And, maybe, show us some chink in their mental armor that we can penetrate."

"An admirable goal, Captain," agreed Odo. "But I can't help feeling that it may be a futile one. These Hive dwellers show very little interest in logic."

"But Benjamin is right to try," Dax argued. "It may be the last chance that Bajor has."

"I agree," Odo admitted. "But I'd prefer a better one."

JOHN PEEL

"So would I," Sisko confessed. He stroked his chin. "Odo, thus far these aliens don't know that you're not one of us."

Odo's eyes sparkled. "And you'd like to keep it that way, eh? It might be a good idea at that."

At that moment, their guide came hurrying back down the short corridor toward them. Considering how short his legs were, Tork managed quite a respectable pace.

"We are ready to begin now," he announced. "I have reserved a travel tube strictly for our use. We can go wherever in the Hive you desire—with the exception of secured areas, I am afraid."

"We quite understand," Sisko said smoothly. "To be honest, what I'm most interested in is seeing what your people are like—what the Hive is like, in fact." He gestured at the walls of the corridor. "This is all we've really seen of the place so far. I hope it isn't all metal walls."

"Oh, no!" exclaimed Tork, aghast. "The Hive is a place of beauty and culture." He considered for a moment. "Perhaps an overview would be best to begin with." He ushered them along the corridor like a fussy mother hen. "This is really a remarkable privilege for me, to be allowed to show you around. You are, of course, the first aliens I have ever encountered."

They had reached the entrance to some kind of travel vehicle now, and Tork gestured for them to enter. Sisko had to bend slightly to do so, as it was built for the average Hive dweller, who was a good foot and a half shorter than he was. Inside was a small driver's position with a control pad and stick, and five of the boardlike seats. Tork moved to the controls, and glanced back at his passengers.

"I am sorry that you must stand," he apologized. "But it did not occur to us that you would find our seating uncomfortable."

"It's quite all right," Dax assured him. "This way, we'll be able to get a better view— assuming there is a view."

"Oh, yes," he assured her. "A very delightful one once we are out of the confines of the complex here." His fingers

126

rapped on the panel, and he seized the control stick firmly. "We begin."

The travel vehicle moved quite slowly to begin with, and then started to accelerate. The device was almost silent, save for a low hum of a motor.

Tork cleared his throat. "Please, feel free to ask questions," he told them. "I will be as frank with you as I can. We have very little to hide from you."

"Then why do you dislike people who live on planets?" asked Odo, getting straight to the heart of the matter. "It sounds like a mania to me."

"Not at all," exclaimed Tork, slightly shocked. "I had imagined that you understood the matter fully, since you live on a space station. Do you not find life in space so much better than it could ever be on the surface of a planet?"

"It's . . . different," Dax answered. "And it is possible to enjoy both. Surely your race lived on a planet once?"

"Of course," agreed Tork, "but we also were unicellular creatures once. We evolved through that, and on to further stages in life. Likewise, we have evolved beyond living on planets and into a more natural and fulfilling stage of life."

Sisko was starting to understand. "And you think that anyone who lives on the surface of a planet by choice is a lower form of intelligent life, then?"

"Is that not logical?" asked Tork. "It is natural progression: Life begins in the oceans, then moves to the land, then into space. To remain in any one place is counter to natural reason."

Odo snorted. "Then you'd have a hard time comprehending some life-forms in our galaxy."

"Right," agreed Sisko. "On Tirek Eight, for example, there is a species of highly intelligent squidlike creatures that spend all of their lives in the ocean. They have a tremendous civilization, one that has existed for sixteen thousand years."

Tork shook his head. "That sounds implausible," he admitted. "Though, of course, I accept your word that this civilization does exist. But it must obviously be an inferior one, and stagnant. Ah!" he exclaimed, before they could argue with him. "Now we emerge!"

The travel tube shot out of the featureless tunnel they had been traversing, and into the open. Sisko's eyes opened wide as he took in the view before them, and he couldn't suppress a gasp of surprise and admiration. He heard Dax give a similar exclamation, and stared raptly out of the large windows of the travel vehicle.

The view was panoramic and splendid. Sisko estimated that they were probably about a third of the way down the Hive's main axis, and a quarter of the way toward the center of the vessel. They were therefore looking down a long tube as they headed what he decided to call south.

The walls curved gently upward on either side of them, enveloping their "world" until they met together over their heads. Either there was artificial gravity inside the Hive, or else gravity was provided by rotating this inner core, because the Hive spread over every available surface.

There were buildings all around. They were constructed of crystal and metal, of many varying designs and heights. Towers, minarets, spires, and bridgelike structures abounded. Domes in different hues of the rainbow were scattered about, and walkways on the "ground" and at higher levels. It was like seeing the Promenade of *Deep Space Nine* multiplied a millionfold.

Spaced at irregular and pleasing intervals between the buildings were parks of varying shapes and contents. Trees and treelike growths abounded also in the cities themselves. There were vines and other climbing plants, and thousands upon thousands of floral sites. There were vast rivers running through all of this, and lakes and ponds. One river wound its way directly above their heads. Sisko could make out boats upon the surfaces.

There were vast tracts of what appeared to be farmlands, and in the distance . . .

"Are those *mountains?*" he asked in awe. They could create a view like this any day in a holosuite, but *this* one was real. What an engineering feat!

"Small ones," Tork apologized. "Beyond them is the ocean."

"You have an *ocean* in this ship?" Dax gasped in astonishment.

"The Hive is very large," Tork explained. "And we wished to preserve as many diverse habitats of our homeworld as we could."

Sisko shook his head. "This has to be one of the greatest engineering projects I've ever witnessed," he confessed. "And I've seen many."

"It was a great and noble work," said Tork with understandable pride. "And it is our responsibility to see that it goes on."

Down the central axis of the Hive were what looked to be small suns blazing away. To provide light and heat for the "world" within, clearly.

"Do they always burn?" asked Dax.

"No," Tork replied. "We maintain the illusion of day and night within the Hive. It was discovered that we function best when given regular light and dark cycles."

"It's much the same with us," Sisko observed. "Part of growing up as a species on a planet, I imagine," he added. "You retain some aspects of them even when they're long gone."

And then, above and below them, Sisko saw the dark line that was growing slightly wider all the time. The line where the Hive was splitting. Soon there would be two Hives— and then one less Bajor.

"Could we see what is happening where the Hive is being split?" Sisko asked.

"Of course," agreed Tork. "In fact, one of my friends is assigned to a station at the break." He pulled a small computer pad from a recess in his shell and tapped at it for a moment. "Sector one-two-seven-four," he announced. "If we visit there, I am sure he will be happy to show you what is being done."

"Fine," Sisko agreed. Perhaps, once they were there, he might get some idea of the strength and composition of the Hive. And, with luck, some idea of what he could do next.

Tukh worked quietly and efficiently, completing his task. The worker drones were now set to detonate on his signal—to be sent from Harl's comp. The three drones he had selected were all back at work again, after being "repaired" under Harl's authorization. All that was left was to insure that Harl would be somewhere near the blast zone without a good alibi for what was to follow.

Fingering the small tranquilizer dart he had stolen, Tukh headed for the maintenance dome where Harl was working. He quietly irised the door and glanced around the bay. There were two further drones in for repair, and he could see a shape hunched across one of them, intent on his work. Harl was very good with machinery and was allowed to work unsupervised for the most part, which was perfect for Tukh's plan.

Silently, Tukh slipped across the floor, checking as he went that the bay actually was empty. Then, he carefully ascertained that the lone repairer was in fact Harl. He wanted no last-minute errors here. . . . Perfect! The tranquilizer dart was in his fingers, and Tukh moved in swiftly. The dart slipped into a gap between Harl's shell plates, and then out again.

With a sigh, Harl collapsed forward onto the drone he had been repairing. He hadn't even looked up, so there was no chance Harl had seen who had attacked him. The drug would keep him insensate for about half an hour, which was more than enough time.

Pleased with the progress of his plan, Tukh exited the repair bay, irising the door closed behind him. He had Harl's comp with him, ready to transmit the lethal signal as soon as he was far enough away not to be affected by the blast.

Sisko couldn't restrain his admiration for the Hive. "How long have you been traveling?" he asked Tork. "The Hive looks almost brand-new."

"We have been scrupulous in checking for errors and in maintenance work," Tork answered. "The Hive has been in our care for two thousand seven hundred and sixteen generations. Each generation lasts about . . . two hundred of your years."

Dax raised her eyebrows, impressed. "Half a million years?" she murmured. "And since the start of the flight, you've never known any other world?"

"We need no other worlds—except as resources," Tork answered proudly. "The First Hive built well, and they knew that the Crossing would take this long. It is fortunate that we were not delayed, as we were getting close to the end of our supplies, which is why it was so imperative that we restock."

The only problem with "restocking," Sisko mused, was that it had involved the annihilation of Darane IV. "Magnificent technology," he commented. "But a lamentable use for it—to destroy worlds and kill people."

Tork looked pained. "That is not our intention," he protested. "We gave the people of that world a chance to leave. They responded by attacking us." He sighed. "Do you not weary of covering the same ground continuously?"

"I keep hoping that we can impress on you what your people have done," Sisko answered. "However you attempt to justify it, your Hive has murdered half a million people."

Tork glared at him. "Do you think I do not know that?" he asked. "I hear their screams in my head all the time. I am not without softer parts, Captain. I do care. But if the choice is between an insane alien species and the Hive, then my duty is clearly to the Hive. It has been that way since the First Hive created the Great Design, and it must remain that way for us."

"The Great Design?" echoed Odo. "That smacks to me of excuses, not reasons. What *is* this Great Design?"

The travel tube was passing through one of the small forest areas now. Sisko couldn't help admiring the beauty of the setting. Outside, adult and young members of the Hive were playing and enjoying themselves. There were no doubt lovers walking hand-in-hand, and parents playing the equivalent of baseball with their children. There would be elderly people, watching the young, envying their strength and agility. It was a serene and cheerful picture—if you could forget the darker side of the Hive's purposes for a moment.

"The Great Design was formulated in the beginning by the members of the First Hive," Tork explained, in answer to Odo's question. "We once lived on a planet, as you surmised. The star that was our sun was unstable, however, and showed signs that it was going to explode."

"A supernova," Dax muttered. "Your science was clearly advanced to be able to detect this so far ahead of time."

"Yes," agreed Tork. "We already had rudimentary space-travel capabilities, and had explored the stars and worlds closest to our own. None was fit for any kind of life, and we had run out of hope of simply moving our population to a safer world. Then the scientists of the First Hive evolved a brilliant idea.

"They proposed taking one of the rocky worlds in our system and converting it into a colony that would be able to travel between the stars. It was risky and audacious, but they were insistent that this was the only hope for our people. Eventually, it was agreed that they be allowed to try. Construction of the Hive took almost the full generation, but it was accomplished. Life-forms from our world were transported to the Hive, and then our population was evacuated. The Great Design began."

Dax frowned. "But according to our calculations, the Hive has only just entered our galaxy from intergalactic space. It shows that you have come from the direction of what we call the Magellanic Clouds. Why did you not simply seek a world in your own galaxy, instead of risking such a dangerous and lengthy crossing?"

"Because as work was under way on the Hive, we finally made contact with an alien species—the first we ever met until a few days ago. They were warlike and aggressive, and had conquered a large part of the . . . Magellanic Cloud. We were forced for the first time to build ships of war, to defend ourselves. We won some of the battles, but their strength was far too great for this to continue for long. They pressured us continually, and we knew that we could never hold out. We could not be assured of a refuge in our own galaxy, and therefore the goal was set to make the Great Crossing here.

"The Hive was launched, and began its journey. The enemy could not follow us, as their ships were not able to spend long periods away from fuel. The Hive gathers most of its fuel from the thinly stretched material between the stars and the galaxies."

"Hence the large wings on your ship," Dax commented. "They serve as collectors for the intergalactic gases, and no doubt condensers also."

"Correct," agreed Tork. "It is an efficient system that has lasted us well. Between stars instead of between galaxies, matter is more common, and we are gathering reserves. When the split is achieved, both Hives will be well fueled."

"And then what?" demanded Odo. "You have told us *why* the Great Design was necessary, but you still have not told us what it is."

There was a sharp *ping* from the control panel, and Tork glanced down. "We are arriving at the work area where Harl labors," he announced. "We shall be decelerating."

Sisko watched as the travel tube emerged from the forest and recreational area and into what was clearly an industrial complex. Huge machines were moving between the large buildings. Many of them carried flat plates, and others bundles of machinery or electronics. Some carried spars and beams, and others equipment that Sisko couldn't immediately identify.

The buildings themselves were obviously manufacturing these products, which were all heading toward the growing gap. The noise level outside had to be fairly high, but inside their transport tube, Sisko heard barely little more than a low rumble.

"It's very impressive," Dax remarked. "The raw materials are processed here and then converted into whatever is needed to construct the new Hives."

"Here, and in a thousand other factory complexes," Tork explained. "We will be coming closer to the work area. You may suffer some sensory discomfort, so please alert me if you do not feel well."

The travel tube finally drew to a halt beside a small platform, and Tork opened the door. As he had warned them, they were immediately assaulted by everything the tube had sheltered them from.

There was a rhythmic pounding, the sound of the workings of vast furnaces and engines in the complex they had passed. Transports whirled along the roadways, adding their quota to the noise. It was loud, but not unbearable, and a lot less than Sisko would have expected of such a complex and vast worksite.

There was an increased level of heat, and the smell of molten metals and burned earths from the foundries where the vast deck plates were being cast. Smoke and vapors curled about the buildings.

And none of this really impressed Sisko at all. He was too taken in by staring at the gap ahead of them.

They were probably a mile or so from the split in the Hive, but the gap itself was by now almost that wide. It was pure black, without any sign of the stars beyond. On either edge of the gap were legions of machines at work. Huge, spiderlike welding machines prowled the edge of the area, sparks and flames flying as they worked on melding the new materials with the old. As they passed, other machines scurried in, carrying the braces, beams, and other supports. Smaller welders danced along, fixing the beams into position. There were workers, some in environmental suits, busily measuring, moving, and fixing materials. Trucks crawled in bearing machinery, some of which was apparently movable, and some of which was clearly in place.

A vast army of workers and drones were frantically constructing the new material for the twin Hives. It was industry and purpose on a scale that Sisko had never before seen. Whatever else the inhabitants of the Hive might be, they were certainly engineers extraordinare. Too bad they needed O'Brien back on the *Defiant*. He would have adored this.

"It's very impressive," Odo grumbled. "Magnificent, almost."

"Thank you," Tork replied. "We are working at our fastest pace to create the two Hives. It will be accomplished in a matter of days."

"I can believe it," Dax said admiringly. "The work pace is tremendous. I assume you have force shields in place along the edge of the gap?"

"Yes, to protect the workers." Tork pointed. "On the edge itself, only the drones are allowed to lay the plates and weld them. The area is checked for leaks, and then the edge of the field is pushed further out. Those cone-shaped devices you see beside the workers are the generators themselves. Would you like a closer look?"

"If it would not interfere with the work, yes," agreed Sisko.

"It would be more than acceptable," Tork assured him. "My fried, Harl, should be in the maintenance dome a short way ahead of us. He will be able to explain much more than I can. Please, follow me, and do not stray. It is for your own safety. While the drones are programmed to avoid living beings, I am not entirely certain that they would recognize you as such. Our body chemistries are surely different."

"Yes," Sisko said with a smile. "I'm a trifle more thin-skinned than you, I suspect." They followed along behind Tork, who continually pointed out items of interest—from integration machines to the bioregenerators that would move in to begin planting and soil processing as soon as the metals had cooled. The outer skin was three layers thick, he explained, to guard against possible leaks into space, and reinforced with force generators to prevent meteorite impact.

"That's probably why the sensors couldn't get a good reading of the Hive," Dax commented to Sisko. "The layering effect would reinforce the screen shields and make readings difficult or impossible."

"It's all very impressive," Sisko agreed. "These people have a tremendous technology. It's a shame their sense of morality isn't as well developed."

Odo grunted. "I'm not sure that I agree with you, Captain," he said.

Sisko raised an eyebrow. "You're the one who is putting the most pressure on him, Constable," he pointed out.

"Because I have a feeling he's going to crack," Odo explained. "Tork is quite clearly uncomfortable with what his people have done. He knows what will happen to Bajor and probably Cardassia Prime, too. This does not sit well on his conscience." Odo inclined his head slightly. "I have a feeling that the pressure I'm applying may well pierce his sense of duty toward the Hive. He could come around to our point of view."

"I'd be very happy if he did," Sisko commented. "But will one Hivemaster on our side be enough? The others all seem dead-set on their course of action."

"If one can come around, then possibly more can be persuaded," Odo said. "You're the one who insists on using diplomacy to fight this battle, after all. What other options do we have?"

"None," agreed Sisko. "Keep up the good work, Constable."

"I shall."

They were now within several hundred yards of the gap. At this distance, the view of space beyond should have been stunning. Sisko was puzzled to note that the screens were opaque. It was as if a vast wall separated them from the gap and space. That was odd, because it was always simpler and more energy-efficient to make force screens invisible than to make them solid. Maybe it was to show the workers and drones exactly where the limit was? Or could there be another reason? A gnawing suspicion was starting to grow in his mind. He had assumed that the Hivemasters' view of planetary dwellers being insane was simply prejudice—but what if it was more than that?

He could hear the movement of the mechanisms behind

the screens, but absolutely nothing of their work was visible. Still, there was plenty to see on this side of the barrier. Trucks were drawing in materials, and the growing area of open floor created by the drones was starting to fill in with the walls of buildings or the outlines of where parks and even rivers would be. All the workers and machines were evidently following some sort of master plan worked out more than two thousand generations before.

It was astounding.

Tork had his small computer out again, and tapped into it. "Odd," he muttered.

Odo turned abruptly. "What is?" He seemed to be sensing trouble.

"I'm getting a reading from Harl's comp," Tork explained. "It is several units away from here, and he does not reply to my call."

"Maybe he's resting?" suggested Sisko.

"At this time of day? Unlikely." Tork's snout wrinkled in confusion. "Besides, his work area is that maintenance dome ahead of us." He gestured at the thirty-foot crimson half globe. "Why would he be over in the factory units?"

"Perhaps we should find him and ask," Odo suggested.

"That is—"

The noise of the work was suddenly overwhelmed by the sound of an explosion. Sisko whirled automatically to take in the situation. About half a mile away, one of the drones carrying welding gear was enveloped in an expanding ball of fire. Then the welding gases caught fire, and there was a loud *crump,* and then a flattened shock wave that slammed through the air.

Heat, smoke, stench, and screams all slammed into them at the same instant. The sound of the blast rang in Sisko's ears as he was hurled back into the closest wall. Around him, slivers of metal and crystal flew. He felt his skin slashed in several places, and then a terrific blow in his back as he slammed into the wall. Dazed, he tried to stay on his feet.

There was the sound of a second explosion, and then a

third. The shock waves flew through the deck plates, hurling Sisko and his companions aside. Flames and gases licked out from the machinery, enveloping the area as they expanded. The sound of shattering machinery and screams seemed to come from everywhere.

And then the force wall ahead of them died, showing the vacuum of space beyond, and all hell broke loose.

CHAPTER
16

SHAKING HIS HEAD to try and clear the ringing in his ears, Sisko managed to stagger back to his feet. He ran the back of his right hand across his forehead, and it came away sticky with blood. Not too much, though, so he tried to ignore it. His shoulders ached from the blow the wall had dealt him, and he felt slightly disoriented. Otherwise, he was in acceptable condition.

"Dax!" he called. "Odo!" And, as an afterthought: "Tork!"

"I'm here, Benjamin," Dax replied. She was beside the same wall he had hit, but about twenty feet away. She was cut and bleeding in several places, and there was a red stain on her left leg. Despite this, she was struggling to her feet.

Sisko hurried across to help her. "Rest here," he suggested, but she shrugged off the suggestion impatiently.

"I'll rest later." She glanced around the wreckage. "Have you found Odo or Tork yet?"

"I'm here," came Odo's voice. The shapeshifter abruptly grew into being from a puddle of liquid close by. "I'm sorry about revealing myself, Captain, but I automatically liquefied when I hit the wall." He was undamaged, naturally. It took a lot to injure the changeling.

"That's okay, Constable," Sisko answered. "This is something of an emergency, obviously. Can you see Tork?"

They all glanced around the area. Fires were still blazing, and an alarm was whooping in the distance. Strangely, all the screams had ceased. Sisko could see the stars through the collapsing barrier. There was no sign of any repair crew or mechs heading to check out the gap.

"Okay, more important," he snapped. "The forcefield's dropping. Dax?"

Whipping out her tricorder, Dax scanned the area. "It's down to five percent and failing, Benjamin. We've got to do something fast." She winced as she started to move. "Uh, could you give me a hand? I don't think I can make it alone."

Sisko gripped her around the shoulders and allowed her to lean on him. "My pleasure." He glanced back at Odo. "See if you can find Tork, or any other survivors."

"Acknowledged."

Concentrating on helping Dax limp over to the crackling force generator, Sisko could spare little attention for what was going on around him. There had been some kind of malfunction, obviously. One—no, more—of the transports had exploded.

But why weren't there rescue crews swarming all over the area? The Hive dwellers were so efficient at everything. What had gone so badly awry now? Well, he could worry about that later. Right now, the important thing was to prevent the generator from failing. If it went, then the atmosphere inside the Hive would be sucked out into space. There was no way of knowing how many this would kill—but the three of them would certainly be included. Sisko moved to tap his communicator to contact the *Defiant,* but it was missing. It must have fallen off when he'd been hit by the blast.

They reached the conical generator, and Sisko eased Dax against it. "Think you can figure it out, old man?" he asked.

"I can figure anything out," she replied, smiling through her obvious pain. "In time. Better hope I've got long enough." She started to use her tricorder to scan the machine, the first step in understanding it. "I'll be fine if you want to help Odo," she added, pointedly.

Sisko glanced at her and saw her communicator was gone also. She was lucky to have retained the tricorder, really. That left Odo. He nodded. "I'll be back soon."

"I'll be here," she promised. "If I can get this working again." She started to remove one of the panels. "Go."

He ran back the way they had come. Thick smoke was starting to descend on the entire area from all the fires. No doubt chemicals ignited by the blast caused these. The once-level roadway was buckled and shattered in several places, and there were now large chunks of metal protruding up from the floor, thrown there by the violence of the explosion. Sisko, Odo, and Dax had been very fortunate. But what about the workers who had been here? Where were they?

"Captain!" he heard Odo call. "I've found Tork—I think."

That didn't sound good. Sisko ran to join the Constable, preparing himself to see a shattered and perhaps unidentifiable body. Instead he saw—"What the blazes?"

"I believe it's Tork," Odo offered, rising from where he was crouched. At his feet was a circular object, about three and a half feet across. As he stared at it, Sisko realized what it was.

"He's rolled up in a ball," he exclaimed. All that was now visible of him were the plates from his shell, overlapped in a circle.

"A protective measure, no doubt," Odo growled. "Probably instinctive, in fact. All of them must have curled up when the explosion went off. It probably saved their lives."

Sisko nodded, and bent over what was presumably Tork. He rapped on the shell. "It's safe to come out now," he called.

"I've tried that," Odo remarked. "Nothing's getting through to him. He'll have to come out of this on his own."

"I doubt he can hear anything in that state," agreed Sisko. "And he may even take my tapping his shell for further trouble." He glanced around. "I guess he'll be safe enough here. There's no immediate danger from the fire. Let's see if we can find further survivors. Some may be in trouble." As he was about to hurry off, he remembered something. "Do you still have your communicator?"

"Of course," Odo replied.

"Contact the *Defiant* and get Kira to offer help to Dron. But tell her that on no account is she to beam anyone else over without permission. They'll have to use you to zero in on us. Both Dax and I have lost our badges."

"Understood." Odo tapped his communicator as he hurried off.

Sisko ignored that aspect of things. Strangely, there was still no sign of rescue equipment or crews arriving, though there had been plenty of time. What was going on here? He was starting to get what seemed like a crazy answer to that question forming in his mind. He started to scan the streets and wreckage for further signs of the curled-up balls that were the Hive dwellers. Now he knew what to look for, he could see several of them. Most were out of immediate danger, but some he had to grab and roll away from trouble and licking flames. Their shells were obviously tough, but he doubted that they could stand being baked.

After about ten minutes, he had cleared as many as he could see. The wreckage of several trucks still blazed, and the smoke was getting worse. He found two of the aliens quite obviously dead. One had been caught in the blast, and his or her body was charred and shattered beyond hope. The second one had a length of steel rod impaled and extruding a foot and a half from its back. Thankfully, there were no further casualties that he could detect. He'd need a tricorder to discover any others, and Dax had the only one.

He loped back through the throat-burning smog to where he had left her. Parts of the generator were scattered about, and she had her tricorder plugged deep within the generator's heart. Her left leg was extended stiffly behind her, and the trouser leg was even more soaked with blood.

Deciding not to mention this, he asked gently, "How's it going?"

"This is it," she replied. "The field is going to fail any second, unless my patchwork is right." Her head emerged from the machine, grimy and cut. She managed a wan smile. "Here goes." She tapped in the command signal on the main panel.

And the generator failed.

There was a shriek of air as it was sucked through the void in the field. Wind tore at them both, and started to drag off loose pieces of metal.

"I guess I got it wrong," Dax yelled over the din. She started tapping out further commands on the machine.

"You can't win them all," Sisko answered, holding on to the generator for support. The howling wind plucked at his clothing, trying to draw him up into the gaping maw above them. All around, small objects were clattering down the streets toward the empty space and stars beyond. "Better luck next time."

"I'd better win this," she replied, "or there won't *be* any next time." Her fingers flew as fast as she could manage, as she scanned the readouts. "Damn! That's what happened. I misdiagnosed the couplings." Given her medical condition, Sisko was hardly surprised, but he knew she wouldn't forgive herself. She managed to enter her new figures.

And the wall was back in place where it should be.

The wind died away, and all the debris fell back onto the ground with clashing and clatterings. Sisko smiled at her.

"Well done, old man."

"Thank you, Benjamin." Pale and weak, she slid down the side of the machine. Sisko caught her and lowered her the rest of the way to the ground.

"How do you feel?" he asked, concerned. The patch on her leg was wet with fresh blood.

"Marvelous," she said, and shook her head. "I have felt better."

Sisko glanced up and around. "Odo!" he yelled. "Get over here now!"

"Coming, Captain!" A moment later, Odo sprinted out of

one of the buildings, looking as fresh as he always did. He saw Dax lying on the ground and understood immediately. As he ran, he slapped his communicator. "Odo to *Defiant*. Lock in on my signal. Two to beam up immediately to sickbay."

Sisko jumped aside, to allow Odo to scoop up Dax into his arms. Then the transporter beam took hold, and in a sparkle of lights, both of them disappeared. Sisko stood watching the empty spot for a moment, and then he became aware of movement.

He looked around, and saw several of the Hive aliens hurrying along the roads. They were all pushing what looked like floating stretchers. "About time," he grumbled. "Where have you been?"

One of them glared at him. "We could not come in until the barrier was repaired," he snapped. "We came as fast as we could."

"Then why didn't anyone come to repair the barrier?" Sisko queried. "You were very lucky my friend could accomplish the task."

"The repair crew was on its way," the alien answered. "They could not reach here fast enough."

"Only *one* repair crew for the generator?" Sisko couldn't believe it. "Surely there are more?"

The alien gestured at the barrier. "Considering what lies beyond that?" he asked, shocked. "We are fortunate to have even one crew."

Sisko frowned. "But all that lies beyond the barrier is space."

"Exactly." The medic hurried on to help with the injured.

Sisko watched them at work, gathering up the fallen. All of the Hive dwellers who had been here during the accident were still curled up in balls, and had to simply be lifted onto stretchers to be moved. His suspicions were starting to clarify into certainty now.

They were afraid of space.

Two hours later, Sisko stood once again in the Hivemasters' assembly room. Much of the confusion seemed to have settled down by now, but there was still plenty of action going on. Sisko had quietly gravitated to the rear of the room while Dron took initial charge of the tidying-up operations and then handed the task over to Industry Master Boran, with clear instructions to get the work back on target once again.

Sisko was piecing the information he'd been gathering together in his head, and trying to work out exactly what was going on, and how he could use whatever information he got out of this visit to the best advantage. He was still musing over possibilities when Odo returned.

"Dax will be fine," the constable reported, handing Sisko a new communications badge. "She lost a lot of blood through her leg wound, but Dr. Bashir says we got her back in plenty of time. She'll just have to take it easy for a while."

"Which I doubt Dax will agree to," Sisko replied, clipping on his badge. He felt dressed again now. "Anything else?"

"Nothing that won't wait awhile." Odo stared around the room. "Has anything significant happened here?"

"It's hard to say. I'm not in the loop, so to speak." Sisko nodded at the small clutch of Hivemasters at the end of the room. "Dron and his senior associates are conferring about getting their construction back on-line."

"And how is Tork?"

Sisko shrugged. "No sign of him yet, but I think we'd have heard if he were injured. There is one significant thing, though." He blinked. "Ah—action, at last."

The group had broken up, and Dron proceeded across the room to join Sisko and Odo. "We owe you both our thanks," Dron announced, obviously for everyone in the room to hear. "Without your aid, the disaster might have been much worse. If there is any way we can repay you—"

"There is," Sisko replied, without expecting much. "Call off the move on Bajor."

"That, I am afraid, is impossible, Captain." Dron spread his hands. "Surely you realize that all our resources are being used up in forming the two Hives. They must be replenished, and Bajor is the closest suitable world. We have no option but to absorb it. I wish that it were otherwise, but it is so."

"I see." Sisko frowned. "I had hoped that our display of good intentions would influence your decision."

"Your help is very much appreciated, Captain, believe me," Dron informed him. "But we cannot change what must be."

At that moment, the door irised open and Tork hurried in. He appeared tired, drained, and still shaken, but there was a grim resolve in his eyes. "Captain!" he called loudly. "Captain, I cannot possibly thank you enough for what you did." He hurried across, and held out his hand, and then stopped in confusion. "My apologies. I was about to greet you as one of the Hive, and for a moment I forgot that you were not one of us."

"I'll bet," muttered Odo.

"You have, of course, no shell to stroke," Tork added. He looked about the room at his fellow Hivemasters. "But in all other aspects, you have proven yourselves beings with honor and great courage. I salute you as an equal."

There was a murmur of comment at this. Some of the Masters clearly didn't like the sound of that. The old Hivemaster, Hosir, stepped forward from the bunch.

"An emotion I second," he said. "Captain Sisko, Odo, and the unfortunately absent Lieutenant Dax have all acted well. They are clearly rational and compassionate beings."

Dron looked more than a little put out by this, and Sisko could understand why. He had been publicly endorsed by two Hivemasters, and Dron would look foolish if he refused to listen to Sisko's arguments now. Apparently at least two of the aliens were on his side.

"As I said," Dron said, catching the spirit smoothly, "we owe you our thanks. You are welcome here at any time you wish. Now, on to important matters." He turned and beckoned Raldar to him. "Security Master Raldar, you have something to report, I believe?"

"Indeed," agreed Raldar, bowing his head slightly. "My men have been investigating the explosions of the three drones that began this state of emergency. They have discovered that the drones did not explode accidentally."

"Really?" growled Odo. "You're saying that someone sabotaged them?"

Raldar scowled back at him, obviously irritated that an outsider should be commenting. "Yes, I am. And I believe we have uncovered the culprit." He gestured to one of the guards at the door, who then ushered in a young Hive dweller. "This is worker Tukh," he explained. "He was stationed close to the explosion site. He has relevant information the Masters should hear."

"Proceed," Dron decided. "Give your evidence."

"As you command." Tukh gave a low bow, not easy considering his shell. "One of my coworkers has been speaking treason in my hearing," he told the assembled Masters. "He spoke of creating trouble to bring dissent into the Hive and to attack the authority of the Hivemasters themselves. He works in the repair bays, and he recently completed work on the three drones that blew up."

There was a murmur of outrage from the council. "Who would dare do such an evil act?" demanded Premon. "What is the name of this deviant individual?"

"His name is Harl," announced Tukh.

CHAPTER
17

"No!" EXCLAIMED TORK, shaken and clearly disturbed. "I know Harl! He would never do such a thing."

Dron scowled, wrinkling his snout. "You claim that worker Tukh is lying?" he asked. "For what reason?"

"I do not know his motives," Tork answered, sounding more confident now. "But I do know Harl."

Raldar snorted. "And you claim he never spoke treason?"

This point told on Tork, who reeled as if struck. "He *spoke* a lot of things," he admitted slowly. "It is true that he has little love for the Hivemasters. But he loves the Hive itself. He would never do anything to endanger us all."

Raldar shook his head. "Four people lost their lives in this act of sabotage," he growled. "Machines and valuable resources were destroyed. Harl has been accused and must answer the accusation."

Odo stepped forward. "On what grounds?" he asked skeptically.

Raldar glared at him. "Who gave you the authority to intefere in this?" he demanded.

"I am the Chief of Security on *Deep Space Nine*," Odo

answered. "It is my task to uncover guilt and innocence. I would hardly do more than question a man on mere *hearsay.*" He gestured at Tukh. "Can anyone vouch for the truth of what this person says? Are there others who heard these threats of violence? Or is it simply his word against Harl's?"

"Well said," Tork approved. "Never has unsupported accusations been the base of a charge. Is there no more proof against Harl than this?"

"We have the culprit himself," Raldar announced, clearly annoyed by what was happening. He gestured to the guards. "Bring him in."

Tork gasped as his friend was escorted in by two guards. Harl's hands were manacled together. "Why is he being treated like this?" he demanded. "He is only accused, and not convicted. He should not be restrained."

Harl snorted. "It is too late for logic, friend," he said. "I have already been tried and convicted of this deed without proof and without being allowed to speak."

Dron held up his hand. "You are being allowed to speak now," he said dryly. "I see you are already availing yourself of the right. Now, answer truthfully: Did you commit this sabotage?"

"No," Harl said loudly and strongly. "I did not. He asked me to," he added, pointing to Tukh, "but I refused. He obviously went ahead and performed the deed himself, and blamed me for it."

"A counteraccusation," Raldar sneered. "It is only to be expected."

"There is also his comp," added Tukh. "I discovered it near the site of the explosion. It has only his handprints on it, and it was the one used to detonate the explosives."

Odo could stomach no more. Though he was only a guest on the Hive, his passion for justice would not allow him to remain silent any further. "Really?" he asked sarcastically. "Am I to understand that this young revolutionary here apparently used his own computer to trigger the bombs?" He turned to Harl. "That was terribly foolish of you, wasn't it? To use something that could be traced directly back to you so simply? You're either a very poor rebel, or *you*"—he gestured at Tukh—"are a very poor liar."

"You have no right—" Raldar began, but Hosir raised his own voice.

"He has *every* right. He was there and endangered by the blasts. Besides, he makes sense. I wish to hear him out."

"So do I," added Tork. "Please, continue."

In his element now, Odo did so. He glared at Tukh so ferociously the alien took a step backward. "You found Harl's comp at the site of the explosion, did you?"

"Yes," Tukh answered defiantly.

"Really?" Odo turned to Tork. "Do you have your comp with you?"

"Of course." Tork pulled it from the niche in his shell. "Why?"

"Just prior to the explosion," Odo reminded him, "you tried to contact Harl, didn't you? Where did your comp say that his comp was?"

Tork's face lit up as he realized what Odo was getting at. "To the west of the site," he answered. "Well out of range of the explosion."

Odo spun around. "And *you* found it *at* the site?" he growled. "I wonder how it got there?"

Tukh appeared shaken and confused. "You would say that he is innocent," he said to Tork. "He is your friend and probably your accomplice."

"Ah!" Odo crowed. "More accusations to cover a slip in your story, eh? That's not good enough. And another thing—you said that only Harl's prints are on the comp?"

"Yes," Tukh answered defiantly.

"How do you know that?" asked Odo. "You could not have tested for prints, could you? Besides, wouldn't yours be on it, too, if you found it as you claim?"

Tukh was clearly shaken now. "I suppose they would be, yes."

"Convenient." Odo surveyed the Masters. "And perhaps they were there *before* the explosion, too? So we have *two* sets of prints on the weapon—Harl's and yours. And you were the one discovered with the device, and which you claim you were turning in as evidence of Harl's guilt. Evidence you have no way of checking, surely?"

Raldar stepped forward. "You are simply confusing the issue," he snapped. "And you are harassing the witness."

"Witness?" asked Odo. "I'd say *suspect* would be a better word for it, wouldn't you?" He whirled to face Dron. "I think there is at least as much evidence implicating Tukh in this matter as there is against Harl. Wouldn't you agree?"

Dron clearly didn't want to make a decision about that. "Well," he hedged. "It does appear confusing."

"Confusing?" Everyone's eyes turned to Hosir, who was seated at the main comp in the room. "If you want to know what is *really* puzzling, I have just checked the Determination records, and I confess myself bemused."

"Ah, what?" asked Makarn, stammering slightly. "I do not see the, ah, relevance of the Determination records."

"You do not see a great deal, that is your problem," Hosir informed him cruelly. "I just looked up *witness* Tukh there. It seems from his Determination that he is not a worker at all." He feigned surprise. "It says that he was assigned to *security.*" He blinked mildly and then stared at Raldar. "That means he works for *you.* Odd that you did not know this."

"I was . . . reassigned," stammered Tukh, but the damage had been done. The other Masters in the room stared alternately at him and at Raldar.

"Really?" asked Hosir. "And who changed your Determination for you? Only a Hivemaster could do that." He stared at his fellows one at a time. "Anyone wish to confess to having changed Tukh's status for him?" There was dead silence. "I thought not."

Happily, Tork said, "I move that this matter be investigated more thoroughly. And that Tukh be taken to restraining cells for the time being. And that Harl be set free. And," he finished, glaring at Raldar, "that Security Master Raldar give a full and sufficient explanation for this to the assembled Masters."

There was a surge of agreement with his motions, which Dron cut short. "What you say," he commented smoothly, "is clearly only reasonable and just." He gestured to the guards, who struck the manacles from Harl and transferred them to the protesting Tukh. "Take him away. And you, Raldar, had better go as well. I shall want a full accounting of this from you at our next meeting."

Raldar was scowling deeply, and glaring at Tork, Odo, and Hosir in turn. Finally he nodded. "I obey," he growled in low tones and then stalked from the room.

Dron turned to survey Tork and then Odo. "It appears that this matter is more complicated than it first appeared," he said slowly. "I thank you for your help. I suspect it will take some time for the truth to emerge."

"I'm sure it will," Odo agreed cynically. "That's often the case in such matters."

Tork turned to Odo and Sisko with a smile. "Once again, I am in your debt," he said. "You have saved the reputation and life of a friend."

"It seems to be becoming a habit," Sisko replied.

"If there is anything that I can do in return," Tork said simply, "please name it."

"There is one thing," Sisko answered. "You have kindly shown us some of the Hive and answered many of our questions. I feel that I am beginning to understand your people. Now, perhaps, you will let me return the favor, so that you may start to understand mine?"

Tork's snout wrinkled. "I do not understand you."

"Accompany me back to Bajor," Sisko asked. "See how they live. Try and understand why they will not leave their homes." There was a collective gasp at this suggestion, and Tork was clearly shaken by the suggestion. "I'm sorry," Sisko said, feigning puzzlement. "Have I offended in some way?" He already had a good idea what the answer would be.

Dron moved forward. "What you ask is absolutely impossible," he explained. "Surely you must realize this?"

"I'm sorry," Sisko replied, determined to make him spell it out, "but I don't. *Why* is it impossible?"

When Dron didn't seem inclined to reply, Makarn stepped forward. "Ah, it is because we are too well adapted to our lives here inside the Hive. Everything that is, uh, outside is nonessential and counter to our well-being."

His earlier insight, Sisko realized, had been correct. He had guessed the reason for the nontransparent barrier, the lack of help, the reaction of the noninjured Hive members to no apparent threat. "You can't stand space," he murmured. "You can't be outside, or look outside."

Odo frowned. "You mean this entire species is *agoraphobic?*" he demanded.

"Yes," Sisko said. "They are. That's why they view planet dwellers as insane—they can't cope with the concept themselves, and declare the *idea* madness, instead of their response."

"That is not true," Dron blustered. "Our approach is rational. There is nothing wrong with any of us."

"Then prove it," Sisko said. "Open a window into space. Look on the stars."

Dron couldn't disguise his shudder of revulsion. "That's disgusting!"

"That's what I thought." Sisko glared around the room. "It isn't the planet dwellers who are insane," he said gently. "Has it occurred to you that you're the ones not facing up to reality?"

"You can't say things like that about us!" Pakat yelled. "We are not deviant in any way. Our way is the only true, evolved way to live."

Odo sneered, "Really? How evolved, how true a life can you have hiding behind walls built from flimsy logic and half truths? None of you has the courage to face the facts."

"I do." Tork swallowed and sighed. "I will go with you to see Bajor."

"What?" Pakat stared at his colleague in revulsion. "You will allow yourself to be deluded by these . . . aliens?"

"No," Tork answered gently. "This is my decision. The captain is correct: How can we understand the Bajorans if we are not willing to experience what they experience?"

Hosir laid a kindly hand on Tork's shell. "But you are badly affected by the sight of the stars," he said. "We all know that; you tried the experience once already, and failed."

"Then I will try again," Tork replied. He was obviously unhappy, but determined. "I cannot stand by and do nothing. Captain Sisko and his friends have proven their good intentions. Can we do any less?"

Sisko cleared his throat. "It's a brave decision," he said with genuine sympathy. "But is it a wise one? If you retreat into your shell again when you reach Bajor, then you will learn nothing. I may have underestimated how difficult it is for all of your people. Perhaps this is not a wise idea."

Hosir smiled slightly, and gave Tork a significant look. "It is not so for *all* of our people, Captain," he replied, without turning. "A small percentage of us can stare into space without ill effect. They are our astronomers."

Clearly his words meant something very significant to Tork. The alien's face lit up with delight and hope. "Yes," he breathed. He turned to Dron. "Grand Master, I formally request your permission to accompany the captain back to the world of Bajor, to study it and report back to the Hivemasters in assembly."

Dron had obviously been trying to understand what had been happening, and to turn it to his best advantage. He scowled at the request, but clearly needed to reply. "Are you sure that this is wise?" he asked, playing for time. "It may affect you very adversely."

"I know the risks," Tork answered with confidence. "I am willing to undertake them."

Dron glanced around the room, taking in the feelings of his fellow council members. "Then I have little option but to grant your request," he decided. "You will accompany the aliens, and report back to us as soon as possible. *If* you are able," he added, significantly.

"Thank you," Tork said. "I shall endeavor to serve the Hive to the best of my limited abilities." His snout twitched. "There is one further matter. The possibility is that I may indeed become incapacitated by shock. Therefore, I request a companion to aid me who will not be so affected."

"Do you have anyone in mind?" asked Hosir, before Dron could say anything.

"Yes," Tork said. "An astronomer named Sahna. I *know* she is unaffected by . . . agoraphobia."

Makarn looked shocked. "But she has only just passed her Determination," he objected. "She, ah, has been assigned to Team Two as an astronomer. The Determination cannot be wrong."

"But it could, of course, be changed at the request of a Hivemaster, for personal reasons," Dron said slyly.

Sisko wasn't following this exchange, but there was obviously some kind of power play going on here. Dron and Tork were clearly battling over something.

"This is not a personal request," Tork answered smoothly. "Such a request for change of Determination for selfish reasons would go against everything our society holds dear. As Makarn said, the Determination is infallible. But it is not omniscient." He smiled at Hosir.

"What is that supposed to mean?" demanded Makarn, frowning.

"Simply that the Determination is made on the best possible data available," Tork replied. *"At the time of Determination."* He looked around the room. "But the task of assistant to an ambassador to Bajor was *not* available at the time that Sahna took her Determination, so she could not have been appointed to the post. I believe that Sahna is the person best suited to the task and am willing to have her undergo a second Determination in order to prove it."

There was another round of shocked muttering in the room. "There has never been a second Determination," Premon protested. "It is without precedent."

"So is this situation," argued Hosir. "I, for one, move that we simply accept our colleague's recommendation. He is bravely risking his life and sanity to try and help in a difficult situation. One that none of us would volunteer to undertake," he added significantly. "His choice of assistant seems wise to me."

Dron didn't appear to be happy with the direction in which the discussion was going, but he was obviously not intending to lose control. "We do seem to be moving quickly in new directions," he commented. "But as matters are very pressing, I for one will agree to forgo a second Determination for this . . . Sahna. Unless anyone has any serious objections, therefore, I am inclined to agree with our young colleague's request. Is there any dissent?"

Though Makarn looked as if he might challenge the ruling, he subsided under one of Dron's withering glares. There was no other comment.

"Then it is agreed," Dron commented. He turned to face Sisko. "You will accept full responsibility for the safety of our observers?" he demanded.

"I will," Sisko agreed. "I promise you all that I shall do everything in my power to keep both Tork and Sahna safe."

"So be it." Dron turned to the Hivemasters. "I believe that is quite sufficient for one meeting. We all have our duties to attend to."

They all got the point of that message, and began filing out of the room, in clumps of two or three, all talking in low tones. After a moment, only Hosir, Tork, and Dron were left with Sisko and Odo.

Hosir clapped Tork cheerily on the shell. "I admire your courage, youngster," he commented. "Before you leave, stop by and see me. And when you return, I look forward to hearing what you have to say." He inclined his head at Dron, and then turned to Sisko. "Captain, it has been very . . . interesting. I hope that we shall meet again under less tense circumstances."

Sisko liked the old alien. He was craftier than he seemed, and was clearly playing some political games of his own. "Likewise," he commented. Hosir nodded and then left the room.

Tork bowed to Dron. "Thank you for your . . . wise decisions, Grand Master," he murmured. "I will endeavor to fulfill the trust you have placed in me."

Dron nodded. "Remember always that we serve the greater good of the Hive," he said. "Do not be swayed by emotion or appearances. Judge wisely, and return in safety."

Tork nodded, and then led Sisko and Odo outside. "I must inform Sahna of the Hivemasters' decision," he said. "We should be ready to go with you in less than one of your hours, if that is acceptable."

"That's fine, Tork," Sisko answered. "I'd better get back to my ship. Constable, would you be kind enough to wait here and then escort our guests to the *Defiant?*"

"Of course."

Sisko slapped his communicator. "Sisko to *Defiant.* One to beam back."

In the council chamber, Dron crossed to the other door and irised it open. Raldar stepped in, looking duly chagrined.

"I would hardly call that a clever scheme," Dron snapped. "Not only did you not succeed in placing the blame on Harl, but you even managed to implicate yourself in the business. What do you have to say for yourself?"

"It was the fault of that alien, Odo," complained Raldar. "If he had not interfered—"

"Then Hosir or one of the others would have!" exclaimed Dron. "At least take the blame for your mistakes honestly. Harl is cleared, and you yourself are seen in a poor light." He considered for a moment. "It might be better if that idiot Tukh were not around to create further problems."

Raldar nodded. "I fear that he might just take his own life out of guilt and remorse for what he has done."

"That sounds more than plausible," agreed Dron. The Hivemaster slumped onto a seat. "Perhaps we can then allow the matter to fade in memory, especially with the formation of the second Hive. There are more important matters to consider than one foolish worker with a grudge." He started tapping out commands on his comp. "The division will go according to plan. The Masters will be split between the two Hives. You will remain with me on Hive One. Pakat will be Grand Master of Hive Two."

"That was to have been my Hive!" exclaimed Raldar, angrily. "You had agreed—"

"That was before this fiasco," Dron snapped. "You have

shown yourself lacking in good judgment. If you redeem yourself—and I say again, *if*—then you will become my successor. Otherwise, you will become nothing. Do you understand me?"

Fighting to control his anger and disappointment, Raldar managed a curt nod.

"Good."

"And what of Tork?" asked Raldar, more subdued. "He has escaped both traps you laid for him."

"You have been listening at doors again, I see." Dron's snout wrinkled in irritation. "True, Tork has proven to be more . . . flexible than I had expected. Obviously Hosir favors the youth."

Raldar sneered. "Out of anger over losing the Grand Master post to you?" he suggested.

"He never desired it." Dron snorted. "Hosir is bright and cunning, but he lacks ambition and drive. Until recently, he has never gone against me in any decision. I think his shell has finally started to firm up. Hosir sees Tork as his protégé, and wishes to groom him to be everything that he never had the nerve to become." There was a thoughtful look on Dron's face. "Even if I do wish you to be my successor, you may face a challenge from Tork."

"He is barely more than a child!" protested Raldar.

"But an intelligent one!" thundered Dron. "And unless you show yourself to be cleverer than you have today, he will become the next Grand Master. You have to apply yourself."

Raldar bowed again. "As you say," he agreed, trying to sound submissive. "May I ask why you allowed him to accompany the aliens? Surely you cannot be thinking of allowing him to change your objectives?"

"Do not even think such thoughts!" Dron snarled. "The Great Design *will* go forward, even if we have to wipe out a dozen worlds! No," he continued in a more calm vein, "I allowed Tork to go for one simple reason. When the aliens cannot dissuade us from our course, they will obviously hold Tork hostage to try and force us to change our plans. They will threaten to kill him if we proceed. We will never allow such perfidious behavior to affect our destiny, and we will refuse. They will kill him. When they do that, Tork will become a martyr to our people. And he will cease to be a problem to you and me. Better a dead martyr than a live problem."

Raldar nodded. "You have thought it all out clearly," he said in admiration. "The Great Design will succeed."

"Of course." Dron stood up. "Now, I must rest. This has all been fatiguing. See to Tukh, and wait for my call. The time for action has come."

CHAPTER
18

IT FELT GOOD to be back on the *Defiant*. The Hive had been fascinating and even more than a trifle enviable. If only DS9 had some of the facilities that were available on that ship! Sisko smiled ruefully. Sometimes the spartan nature of *Deep Space Nine* made him wish that he were assigned to either a starship or a starbase. Then came a challenge such as this, and he knew he was where he was meant to be.

Still, he had several calls to make, none of which were likely to be pleasant. When he reached his ready room, the first one he placed was to Admiral Noguchi.

The old man managed a thin smile. "I hope you have good news to report, Captain."

"I wish I had, sir," Sisko replied. "The Hivemasters are still intent on making Bajor their next target, and nothing I've managed to do so far has convinced them to change their minds. However, one of the Masters, Tork, is accompanying me back to Bajor to study the situation for himself. I believe he is sympathetic, and I hope that I can win him over to our side."

Noguchi nodded. "But will one lone voice for us affect them?"

"Frankly, I'm not sure," Sisko admitted. "But there's very little hope otherwise."

"I understand, Captain." Noguchi drew himself up straight. "Then Starfleet's orders are clear: If you cannot persuade the Hive to change its plans, you must do all within your power to stop them. We cannot allow these intruders to devastate another planet—particularly not Bajor. Is that clear, Captain?"

"Perfectly." Even though he had been expecting the command, it still disturbed Sisko. "They are not a bad people, Admiral. I hope we can negotiate a peaceful settlement."

"So do I, Captain," Noguchi said fervently. "Starfleet wants nothing more than peace. But we cannot allow a planet-wrecking society to remain at large in this galaxy." He glanced at his padd. "Relief will not be with you any faster," he apologized. "This one is on your shoulders, Benjamin. I'm sorry."

"So am I, Admiral," Sisko admitted. "But it's part of my job." He signed off, feeling weary. That communication had been bad enough, but he was dreading the next one.

A few moments later, Gul Dukat's supercilious smile greeted him. "Captain! Allow me to congratulate you on your recent promotion. It couldn't have happened to a better human."

"Thank you, Dukat," Sisko answered. "But this is not a social call. I assume you have been briefed on the situation in the Darane system by your ship that's sitting here watching?"

Dukat inclined his head slightly. "You mean the tragic destruction of Darane IV and the appalling loss of life with it? Sadly, yes." He spread his hands. "I wish I could help, but complications have arisen, and there is little we can do but offer condolences."

"You'd better save them for your own people," Sisko told him, and was slightly pleased to see the smug expression wiped off the Cardassian's face.

"What do you mean, Captain?"

Sisko hedged for a moment. "Do you know what is happening to the Hive at this moment?"

Dukat glanced away for a few seconds, and then back. "It appears to be suffering some kind of splitting process," he replied. "My observers think it may be fissioning into two separate craft."

"Your observers are quite correct," Sisko confirmed. "In two days, there will be two identical Hives, each with the capacity and appetite of the first Hive."

"That is . . . unfortunate," Dukat answered. Then the point sank home, and he scowled into the screen. "Appetite? You mean that the two Hives will be seeking further worlds to plunder?"

"Precisely. One of the Hives is targeting Bajor."

Dukat clucked his tongue. "That's a shame. I assume that the Federation will be protecting their ally?"

"We will be doing everything that we can," Sisko extemporized. "What should interest you more is that the second Hive will be heading for Cardassia Prime."

That completely wiped the last vestiges of his smugness away. "What?" If it was possible for a Cardassian to look paler, Dukat managed that astounding feat. "Cardassia Prime?"

"Your hearing is excellent." Sisko leaned forward. "I wish we could offer you assistance, but under the circumstances . . ." He spread his arms. "Given their level of technology, Dukat, I'd strongly advise you to try and talk to these people to avoid a war."

"Thank you for your concern, Captain," Dukat managed to say, looking very pained. "But we know best how to look after our own interests. Thank you for this . . . information. Now, I believe I had better discuss this matter with my colleagues." The screen went blank.

At least I managed to shake him up a bit, Sisko thought. But the Cardassians were in a much better position to meet this threat head-on than Bajor was. Cardassia had three fleets stationed within two days of the homeworld at all times. Maybe they would stand a chance if it came down to a war with the Hive. Bajor had no such forces. The only things that stood between it and the Hive were the *Defiant* and *Deep Space Nine*. And there wasn't a great deal of firepower concentrated between the two of them.

He could put off his next call no longer. A moment later, he was looking into the troubled eyes of Shakaar. The first minister grimaced slightly.

"It's too much to hope for good news, I imagine," he said.

"I'm afraid so," agreed Sisko. "The Hivemasters remain firm in their intentions. However, I will be bringing one of their number with me back to DS9 and then on to Bajor. He is willing to listen to whatever you have to say. I think he is sympathetic to our point of view, and we may be able to win him over."

Shakaar nodded. "That, as you humans say, is the good news. I can tell from your expression that there is also bad, and that it probably outweighs the good."

"Yes," Sisko admitted. "Even if Tork is on our side, I am not sure that his fellow Hivemasters will agree with him that Bajor should be spared. They seem pretty set on making you their next target."

Shakaar sighed. "How can any race be so indifferent to the suffering they cause?" he exclaimed.

"They aren't indifferent," Sisko corrected him. "They do feel badly about the whole thing. But they're working on some Great Design, and feel that the needs of the Hive take precedence over the wishes of aliens."

"Wonderful." Shakaar shook his head. "So we're going to be attacked by a race that doesn't wish us any harm but will kill us anyway."

"That's about it," agreed Sisko. "Naturally, my people and I will do everything in our power to stop them, Shakaar."

"I know that, Captain, and we are truly grateful. We, also, will do everything in our power to stop the Hive. Let us both pray that our combined efforts will be successful." He terminated the conversation.

Sisko sighed and settled back. It had gone better than he'd feared. Shakaar, at least, was a very rational man, and didn't waste time or words on recriminations or foolish posturing. But there was no denying that this was a dire situation. And their only hope at the moment was one sympathetic alien who might turn out to be completely powerless in the end. . . .

Sahna was both elated and terrified. When Tork had broken the good news to her that they would not be separated after all, she had, at first, been thrilled. Her confidence in him had not been misplaced: he had salvaged their relationship without compromising his integrity. Now, however, as she stood prepared to accompany him to the alien vessel, she was having twinges of fear.

She had never been off the Hive before. None of her people had, as far back as the First Hive. To leave the comfort and friendship of her people, to risk her life with *aliens* . . . that was, quite frankly, scaring her. She did not know what to expect. The only thing that prevented her from panicking and backing out of this trip was Tork's confidence. He had to be as scared as she was, but he trusted and liked these aliens. They had saved his life, and the lives of others. That spoke well for them. They lived in a space station of their own, which showed their intellectual evolution.

But they *terrified* her. Aliens!

Sahna wished she could behave more like a scientist, to simply accept facts and not burden herself with emotional issues, but she could not. The idea of being out among the stars she loved was appealing. And she would be going where none of her race had gone before. She and Tork were pioneers. . . .

She wished it were someone else. But it was not.

Tork gave her an encouraging smile. "Courage," he whispered to her, stroking her shell affectionately.

"I will not shame you," she promised.

"I know that," he answered. "Ah, here is Odo now."

Sahna looked around the vestibule as the alien—the first she had ever seen—arrived. She couldn't suppress a shudder and a gasp as she saw him. "Forgive me," she said, attempting to excuse her lack of respect. "I did not mean to be rude. But you are so . . ."

"Ugly?" asked Odo. He bent his head to one side and studied her. "I am not offended. Others have thought me so before, and doubtless others will in the future."

"I am sure I must look as ugly to you," Sahna stammered.

"Not quite," Odo replied. "But I have the advantage over you. I have met thousands of alien intelligences and am beyond such reactions. Considering I am your first alien, I think you're doing rather well."

Pleased by his understanding, Sahna inclined her head. "You are very kind."

"Well," Odo said brusquely, as if embarrassed by the compliment, "I think it is time that we left." He looked at Sahna and then Tork. "Are you both prepared for this?"

Sahna swallowed nervously. "Will it hurt?" she asked.

"Not at all. There will be a momentary sense of dislocation, and then you will be on board the *Defiant*. It is a safe and not unpleasant experience." Odo tapped the badge on his clothing. "Three to beam over."

Trying hard not to panic, Sahna steeled her nerves for whatever was about to happen. For an instant, that was nothing at all. Then she felt a tingle throughout her body, and her vision seemed to shimmer. When this cleared, her surroundings were utterly different. She stood within a different chamber, on a slightly raised platform. Facing her were three beings that were clearly non-Hive. In rough shape and appearance, they resembled Odo, but she realized that there were minor and possibly significant differences.

"Welcome to the *Defiant*." The one who had spoken and stepped forward was tall and dark in coloring. This must be the Sisko, of whom Tork had spoken. Her guess was confirmed when Tork stepped down and greeted the man.

"Thank you, Captain Sisko. May I present Sahna? She is my assistant and my One-to-be."

"I'm pleased to meet you, Sahna." Sisko smiled at her, and gestured for her to leave the platform. "Please join us."

"Thank you, Captain." Sahna followed Tork, staying

close to him. These aliens were strange-looking and puzzling to her—and at the same time exhilarating. An alien species! No, several, if what Tork had said was accurate.

Sisko finished the introductions. "This is Major Kira, and this is Chief O'Brien."

Sahna bowed her head to each in turn. Kira was also tall, but her nose structure was odd. She also wore some form of ornamentation on one ear, perhaps for some ritual reason. She was, judging by the shape of her unshelled body, a female. O'Brien was stockier, and she guessed probably male. It was difficult to be certain with alien races. Could she judge them by the standards of the Hive?

"Let's go to the bridge," Sisko suggested. "Then we can get under way for *Deep Space Nine.*"

Sahna followed along as a part of the group, trying to absorb as many details of the craft through which she passed as she could. The alien named Kira fell in beside her.

"So," Kira said, "You're Tork's One-to-be? Does that mean you two have a relationship, then?"

Sahna bowed her head. "Yes. As soon as is possible, we are to become One." She wrinkled her snout. "Do you have similar ritual arrangements?"

"Yes," answered Kira, laughing. "We call them *marriages.*"

"Ah." Sahna nodded. "Interesting."

"Here we are." Kira gestured for Sahna to precede her through an open doorway. Unlike the Hive, these doorways slid aside instead of irising open.

Moving on the bridge of the ship, Sahna stared about in amazement. It looked very complex and busy. It was also very cramped and dark, compared to her workspace on the Hive. She realized that space on this small craft was at a premium, but did it really have to be so small? She realized she was judging the aliens again, and clamped down on those thoughts.

There were several workstations, most of them staffed by the same kind of humans as she had already met. The far end of the room was taken up by a large screen, which was at the moment completely blank.

"I'm afraid we don't have chairs to fit you," Sisko commented as he led them across the bridge. "I'm having some fabricated for the quarters you'll be assigned on *Deep Space Nine,* though. Meanwhile, I hope you won't be too uncomfortable here."

"This will be fine, Captain," Tork said politely. Sahna could tell that he felt rather confined in the room also, but he was being polite. The aliens were trying their best, after all.

"Good." Sisko moved to what was obviously a chair designed for his body and sat down. It was weird seeing an intelligent being bend like that without snapping a limb! "Helm, set course back to DS9. Warp five."

"Acknowledged," the helmswoman answered.

There was the briefest flare of sound from whatever powered this ship, and then it settled back down to the background hum again. "Are we moving, Captain?" asked Sahna.

"Yes," Sisko replied. "The inertial dampers keep you from realizing it, though."

"Fascinating," she commented. "Your technology is truly amazing."

Sisko laughed. "I had thought the same of yours."

Inclining her head, Sahna agreed. "We both have some unique aspects to our lives, I suspect." She glanced up at the screen hungrily. "Is it possible for me to view the stars? I am excited to be out here among them, Captain. I have never been in space before."

Sisko glanced at Tork. "I've kept the screen blanked out in case of . . . problems," he replied carefully and politely.

"And I appreciate the thought, Captain," Tork answered. "But I must get used to the sight of the stars." He looked toward the screen. "This is only a representation, is it not? Perhaps, then, it will not affect me as strongly."

Proud of her male, Sahna said, "And I am with you, my love. I will try and give you strength." How many other males would dare so much as he?

"Very well," Sisko agreed. "But if it does prove to be too much for you, I'm switching it off." He moved to one of the panels and tapped in a series of commands. "Get ready," he warned them. "Screen is coming on-line . . . now."

The blankness vanished slowly, and gradually images started to form. The background was dark, and then thousands of points of light came into view.

The stars! And she was among them!

Beside her, Tork gave a strangled gasp of shock and terror. She whirled to him in concern. He was rigid with fear, but he had not curled into a ball. Sahna could see the tension in every line of his face and body, and his hands were clutched into claws. He was shaking and sweating, but he was fighting off the worst of it.

"I am so proud of you," she whispered in his ear.

Tork managed a very strained nod of his head, but he was spending almost all of his powers of concentration on fighting the terror that was ripping at his soul. This was a fight she could offer only emotional support for; he would have to wage this war alone.

Glancing around, Sahna saw that Sisko was watching with concern. "He is all right," Sahna informed the captain. "It will get better for him soon. This representation of the stars does not seem to be as hard on him as the real thing."

"I'm glad to hear it," Sisko replied, removing his hand from the screen's controls. "As long as you are sure."

"I am." She stared greedily back at the screen again, drinking in the view. It was magnificent! "Is it possible to change the angle of view?" she asked. "I should like to see what the Hive looks like from the outside."

"Of course." Sisko manipulated the controls again.

Slowly, the picture shifted. He was doing this out of concern for Tork, she was certain, and she felt grateful for this. Tork was still rigid, but he seemed less tense now. He really was getting acclimatized to the view. On the screen, the stars shifted, and then the Hive moved into the image. When it was centered, the picture stopped.

They were receding from the Hive quite quickly, and the beautiful shape was getting smaller and smaller as she watched raptly. Her home, and the home of her people for thousands of generations! No Hive dweller had ever been this far away in all of history. She felt a pang of sickness, wishing to be back. But that was swallowed up in her sense of wonder. What further marvels lay ahead of her?

She was on the adventure of a lifetime. The only cloud over it was the possibility that it might end with the destruction of an inhabited planet if the Hivemasters had their way. . . .

CHAPTER
19

"ROM! ROM! WHERE are you, you lazy good-for-nothing?"
Quark scanned his stockroom angrily.

"Here I am, brother!" Rom popped out from behind a
stack of crates, carrying a barrel of Romulan ale. "I was
just—"

"Well, don't," snapped Quark. "This is no time for such
frivolities. Put that thing down and listen to me."

With a grunt of relief, Rom did as he was asked. "What is
it, brother?" he asked anxiously. "You look worried."

"Of course I look worried, you idiot—anyone with half a
brain would be worried." He glared at Rom. "That's why
you're *not* worried, of course." He handed across a padd.
"Here, go and take inventory in storage room nine."

"Room nine?" Rom looked confused. "But you told me
never to go in there!"

Quark sighed, then growled, "And now I'm telling you to
go in there. Can't you do *anything* I tell you without
argument?"

"Of course I can, brother," Rom said quickly. "Uh . . .
isn't room nine where you store your armaments?"

"Special orders!" Quark yelled angrily. "Special orders— remember that. I've put the access code on the padd so you can get in."

Rom wisely didn't mention that he already knew it. "Of course, I get it!" he exclaimed happily. "You're going to be selling arms to the Bajorans for their upcoming war."

"How perceptive." Quark's voice dripped sarcasm. "Of course I am. Then we're getting out of here, fast."

Rom frowned. "But why, brother? Rule of Acquisition Number Thirty-Five states—"

"Don't start quoting the Rules to me!" snapped Quark. "I knew them backwards before you'd learned to stop drooling. 'War is good for business.' Rom, think for a minute— assuming it won't overload your wiring. *Why* is war good for business?"

After considering the question, Rom's face lit up with a smile. "Because we can sell weapons to both sides, and medical supplies to the survivors. At vastly inflated prices."

"Right." Quark replied through gritted teeth. "Now, when the Hive reaches Bajor, they aim to take the planet apart for its minerals and whatever else they need. What can we sell *them* that they can't just take?"

"Uh . . . nothing?" Rom guessed.

"Right! And the Bajoran race will be wiped out, won't they? So they won't be buying anything. There's no profit to be made in genocide. And once Bajor is gone, the odds are that these aliens will swallow the station next. *That's* why I'm getting out of here. You can stay if you like."

Rom thought about this for a moment. "No, I think I'll come with you."

"Lucky me," Quark snapped. "Now, go and check the inventory. I'm expecting some important customers for everything there later today."

Nodding over and over again, Rom scurried away. Quark watched him go with a sigh. Then he straightened his jacket and headed back to his office to place a call. It was time to reserve seats on the first shuttle out of here after his business was concluded.

Sixteen calls later, he wound up calling Ops. The face of

Lieutenant Soyka stared back at him. "Quark," the officer said. "Is there something I can do for you?"

"Yes." The Ferengi could barely control his temper. "You can tell me why nobody wants to sell me a seat on any ship leaving this station."

"Ah." Soyka tried to look sympathetic, but failed miserably. "That would be because Captain Sisko left strict orders that you were not to leave the station."

"What?" Quark was almost apoplectic. "How *dare* he? He has no right to restrict my movement. I'm not a Federation citizen! I want to speak to him immediately."

Soyka shook his head. "Sorry, Quark. He's not on-station right now. But I'll tell him you called and ask him to get back to you. Okay?"

"No, it is *not* okay!" Quark yelled. He felt like breaking something, but the only objects close at hand were much too expensive to destroy. "Did he say *why* he won't let me leave?"

"Something about rats and sinking ships, I think," Soyka answered. "Again, you'd have to ask him." He paused. "Have a nice day." The screen went blank.

Quark squealed in frustration.

"We have to be ready for war," Jaro insisted. He gave Shakaar a placating look. "I understand how much you loathe the idea, but it is being forced upon us by these aliens."

Shakaar muttered something under his breath, and then moved across his room to join Jaro and Kai Winn. She was seated at the conference table with a regal expression on her face.

"I understand necessity," Shakaar replied. "And I've ordered all Bajoran forces mobilized. If the Hive starts to move in our direction, then we'll be prepared to launch an all-out strike to try and stop it. Though the Prophets know we've very little firepower, even with all of our forces combined."

"You're still thinking defensively," objected Jaro. "We have the forces now. We could strike while the Hive is still fissioning. Hit it while it is weak. We stand a better chance of destroying it now than we would if it were in orbit above our planet."

"I don't believe so," Shakaar said once again. "Besides, Captain Sisko thinks that he may be able to persuade these aliens not to attack."

"He *thinks*," scoffed Jaro. "And you are willing to risk the fate of Bajor on what some outworlder *thinks?*

"I'm more Bajoran than you are," snapped Shakaar. "I don't recall ever hearing of any of your exploits against the Cardassians during the Occupation."

Jaro shook his head slightly. "I am a man of thought, and not of crude violence."

"Really?" Shakaar snorted. "For a man of thought, you seem to have amassed quite an array of weaponry. Photon cannons, short-range strike craft . . ." He glared at his opponent. "And the fate of Bajor does *not* rest on an outsider. After all, Captain Sisko is the Emissary of whom the Prophets speak—isn't he, Kai Winn?"

Without missing a beat, Winn replied, "So many think, Shakaar. I, myself, am open-minded."

I'm sure you are, Shakaar thought. "Well, to try and foil the *Emissary's* plans would run counter to the Prophets' will, in that case. And none of us would wish to do that. Would we?" He glared from one to the other.

"No," Winn finally replied. "We would not." She gave Jaro a mildly reproving stare. "Perhaps our colleague has been a trifle hasty in his urgings. But it was done with the best interests of Bajor at heart, I am sure."

"Of course," agreed Shakaar. "But for the moment, I think that the best thing we can do for the safety of Bajor is to pray that Captain Sisko's plan succeeds."

"A noble sentiment," agreed Kai Winn.

Jaro simply scowled and turned away.

Sahna couldn't take her eyes away from the screen as the *Defiant* prepared to dock with *Deep Space Nine*. The station looked so *small*, but she had to keep reminding herself that these people didn't have the same needs or philosophy as hers. To them, she supposed, the Hive must look huge and wasteful.

Tork stood beside her, his eyes fixed on the screen also. Only the tension in his body and the haunted expression in his eyes told her that he was still under a great deal of strain. Otherwise, he was covering up his fears quite well.

"Secure docking clamps," Sisko ordered, and then: "Stand down."

The crew began to power down their systems, and Sisko rose from his command chair to join Sahna and Tork.

"I trust this experience was not too traumatic," he said politely.

"It was . . . tolerable," Tork managed to say. "I was not as stressed as I had feared. Perhaps it is possible, after all, to overcome this agoraphobia."

"With sufficient incentive, I believe it is," agreed Sisko. Turning to Sahna, he asked, "And how did you find the trip?"

"Exhilarating," she confessed. "To be able to move so swiftly through space, to journey from star to star in so short a time. Captain, this freedom of yours is quite intoxicating."

Sisko smiled. "I've often thought the same," he admitted. "Sometimes I just long for an excuse to get away from DS9 and out into space again. Come, let me show you to your quarters. You can relax awhile there before we travel down to Bajor and you meet with their representatives."

"Thank you," said Tork. "That would be greatly appreciated. I am a little fatigued."

Following their host, Sahna once again stared all around as they left the *Defiant*. Many of the corridors they traversed were quite deserted. Aside from the ugliness of the decor, she could almost imagine that she was back within the Hive again.

From time to time, though, they passed other beings. Most of them were either human or Bajoran—thanks to Major Kira's conversations on the way here, Sahna had learned that the nose ridges were quite distinctive for the Bajorans. She felt rather proud of herself for being able to distinguish between the two, given such a small distinction. Then she saw one being who was clearly neither. He was a tall, hefty-looking individual, a dull gray in color, with a bare head and a large scowl on his face. Like the humans, he wore clothing. When he was past them, Sahna asked curiously, "What kind of a being was that?"

"That?" Sisko smiled. "That was Morn. He's most likely on his way to Quark's. He spends most of his life there."

"What is a *Morn?*" Sahna asked.

"To be honest, I'm not entirely sure," replied the captain. "He's the only one of his kind I've ever seen."

"Oh." Sahna was astonished that there might be species on the station that Sisko knew so little about. "How many different alien races are there on *Deep Space Nine?*"

"It varies a lot," Sisko answered. "At least thirty, I'd say. Sometimes as many as a hundred."

Sahna looked shocked.

"I'm sure you'll get used to it," Sisko laughed. "The first hundred aliens are the hardest to spot. After that, it gets really easy."

They reached the rooms set aside for Sahna and Tork. They adjoined one another, and Sisko showed them how to open the doors and to order food and drink on the replicators. It seemed to be straightforward enough.

"I have to go to Ops now," Sisko informed them. "We'll be going on to Bajor in a few hours, if you feel up to it."

"Thank you, Captain," Tork replied. "I am certain we will be fine with a little rest."

"Good." Sisko paused in the doorway. "I've had the shutters over your windows closed," he added. "You can open them if you desire by ordering the room computer to perform the task. I thought it better that way."

Tork inclined his head. "Your thoughtfulness is most appreciated, Captain." He watched as Sisko left, and the door closed. Then he turned to Sahna. "What do you think?" he asked her.

"Think?" She wrinkled her nose in amusement. "It is hard to know *what* to think. There has been so much that is new. But I think that you are right about these aliens, Tork:

they are a considerate and intelligent species. In fact, I like them."

"Good." Tork eased himself into one of the chairs that Sisko had had fabricated for them. "So do I. They are fascinating, are they not?"

"Yes." Sahna stroked his shell in concern. "Now, how do you feel? I know how difficult this has all been for you."

"I am as well as can be expected," Tork answered. He could not lie to her. "I do feel uncomfortable, but I know that what I do is for the best. We must correctly evaluate this planet Bajor. I could not live with myself if the world were destroyed needlessly."

Sahna was glad to hear this. "Perhaps we will be able to convince them to move," she said, gently. "They do seem to be intelligent. At least as intelligent as our ancestors were when they made the move into space. Surely they will listen to reason?"

Tork smiled at her. "They have brought us here hoping to convince *us* that their way is best," he reminded her.

"But they are bright," she objected. "So we may be able to win them over to our side."

Tork's snout wrinkled. "I do not feel that this Sisko is a person who changes his way so simply," he replied. "He is a decisive person, and a very strong one. I wish I possessed one-tenth his conviction and courage."

"Do not speak like that!" exclaimed Sahna. She took his hand in hers. "What you have already done took more courage than I ever hoped to see in one lifetime."

Tork smiled gently and glanced over at the shuttered window. "Perhaps you should open the portal. I know how much you hunger for the sight of space again."

She hesitated. "Are you sure?"

"Yes," he answered. "I must get used to it if I am to function on Bajor. I would rather not, of course, but it is my duty." He took a deep breath and steeled himself. "Open the shutter."

"Very well." Sahna crossed to the computer, and tapped the command key that Sisko had shown her. "Computer," she ordered. "Open the shutter."

"Affirmative," the computer replied. With the faintest of hisses, the steel shutter slid aside to reveal a view of the stars. From where she stood, Sahna could see a faint glow off to one edge of the window. She glanced back at Tork, who stood stiffly, his face a mask.

"I can manage," he gasped. It was clearly a struggle, but there was nothing that she could do at the moment to aid him. Sahna nodded, and then moved forward, drawn irresistibly to the glow.

As she neared the window, a new object resolved itself. She stared out across space at the globe she could see. It was small, but quite distinct. She could make out vague whiteness across the blue disc. It had to be the planet Bajor that she was observing.

It was the most beautiful thing she had ever seen in her life.

Hanging in the blackness of space, the tiny globe seemed so small and fragile. Yet it was a planet that bore all the comforts of life—rivers and seas, flowers and animals. And people and cities.

Sahna did not care what decision the Hivemasters made about this world. She knew only one thing.

To destroy such a work of beauty would be the gravest crime that anyone could ever commit. Whatever the Masters decided, whatever even Tork decided, she was absolutely clear in her own hearts. Bajor must not be harmed.

CHAPTER
20

"So what do you think of our visitors, Major?" Sisko steepled his hands and stared across his desk at Kira. She was standing at attention and looking even more uncomfortable in that pose than usual.

"Personally?" She shrugged. "I like them. Sahna seems like a nice person, and Tork is clearly trying to control fears that are almost tearing him apart. As a species, though, how can I have anything but disgust for them? They destroyed Darane Four! I had friends there, people I grew up with. They're dead because of these murderers."

Sisko nodded, empathizing with the struggle inside her. "And how do you resolve this?"

"How *can* I?" she asked. "All I can tell you, Captain, is that I know my duty. If the Hive does come for Bajor, I'm going back to my world to fight for it. I don't care what you or Starfleet think."

"I understand, Major," Sisko replied. "But I can't allow that. Nor, I suspect, will your government. You're their liaison on this station, and you can't simply desert your post when you feel like it."

"It's not simply *feeling,*" argued Kira. "I have to be where I can do my people the most good."

"Your place," Sisko said carefully, "is where *your people* say it is. And they want you here, Major." He stood up, and walked around his desk to join her. "Nerys, believe me: I understand how you feel. When my wife was murdered by the Borg, I wanted to go out and hunt down every last Borg in existence. But I came to my senses. I've even been able to deal with my grief and my loss. But you cannot abandon your post simply because of personal feelings."

"You lost a wife and friends to the Borg," Kira agreed, with sympathy. "I may lose my *world* to these invaders. It's not really the same thing."

"It's *exactly* the same thing," Sisko insisted. "The scale is different, I'll grant you, but the principle is the same. Nerys, we're both officers. When we put on our uniforms, we assumed duties that go beyond our personal desires. We have responsibilities. Yours is here and now to *Deep Space Nine,* as is mine. I promise you, I will do all that is in my power to safeguard Bajor, but I need to know that you'll be covering my back. I'm pretty certain that Bajor needs you here, but I'm absolutely certain that *I* need you here."

He could see her struggling between her logic and her heart. There was nothing more he could say to persuade her, and he simply waited. Finally, she nodded.

"You're right, Captain," she said tightly. "I should be here, not on Bajor. Whatever you need of me, I'll do." She sighed. "But I can't help wanting to be there."

"Good." Sisko touched her shoulder. "I appreciate the difficult decision you've made. Now——"

He broke off as his desk communicator beeped. "Yes?" he growled, irritated at being interrupted. "What is it?"

"Sorry to disturb you, Captain," came Dax's voice. "But there's someone here to see you. He claims it's urgent."

Sisko sighed. "Who is it?"

"Vedek Yarka, sir."

Sisko winced. He'd had dealings with Yarka before. The Vedek was a deeply religious man with his own agenda to pursue. He was absolutely convinced that Sisko was the Emissary promised in the writings of the Prophets, and the savior of Bajor. His first inclination was to ask the man to go away. On the other hand, Sisko couldn't afford to alienate any of the Vedeks, especially at a time like this. "Send him in," he decided, reluctantly.

"That sounds like my cue to leave," Kira said. "My sympathies." She had little time for most of the members of the religious orders, outside of the late Vedek Bareil. She nodded to Vedek Yarka as he entered Sisko's office, and the door closed behind her.

"Vedek," Sisko said in greeting.

"Emissary," replied the monk. He bowed his head, and then smiled slightly. His gray beard looked even more grizzled than usual, and his eyes showed lines of stress. "It was good of you to see me. I know how important your time is, especially now."

"Well, what can I do for you?" Sisko asked, getting directly to the point. "The upcoming crisis, I imagine."

"Naturally," agreed Yarka, in his deep, sonorous tones. "Kai Winn has been to see Shakaar, and has adduced a quotation from the Third Prophecy of Andaki as her reason. I believe she has seriously misinterpreted the text."

Sisko spread his hands. "Forgive me, but I'm not an expert in your holy writings, Vedek. I doubt I can be of help in any dispute the two of you may have."

"I understand that," Yarka agreed. "However, the text she used is one of the Emissary prophecies, and should be correctly applied to you."

"I was afraid of that," mumbled Sisko.

"Listen, and see if you do not agree that it is most apposite to this time of testing we are undergoing." Yarka held up his head and hands, and recited:

"The land will be torn asunder as great wings hover.
Death will be on all who witness, and mourning on the
    lips of the few who survive.
Weep for the lost, the children, the land. Weep, for it
    and they are no more.

In that terrible day shall all my people be one.
Stand firm, for one shall protect you, and two shall
   convert.
In their faith, Bajor will be made whole."

He looked sharply at Sisko. "You see the significance, of
course?"

Sisko wasn't sure how to reply. He knew that many of the
writings of the Prophets had been truly inspired in some
strange way. The aliens who had created the stable wormhole that was used for travel between the Alpha and Gamma
Quadrants lived outside of time. They had, however, some
measure of interest in the people of Bajor, and had sent nine
orbs to guide the Bajorans. Some of the orbs were lost to the
Cardassians, but others still existed in temples on Bajor.
Sisko had experienced communion through those orbs with
the wormhole aliens. He knew that Kira had seen visions of
the future through them. Given that the wormhole beings
lived outside of time, such prophecies had at least a
smattering of scientific plausibility behind them.

On the other hand, many of the writings of the Prophets
were couched in obscure and sometimes deliberately confusing phrases. Many of them might apply to almost anything, with the right slant placed on them. It was an old trick
used by oracles the galaxy over, so they could claim to be
always correct.

"It certainly sounds like the first part might apply to what
happened to Darane," he said cautiously. "But I have no
idea what the rest of it may mean."

"I understand that, Emissary," Yarka said smoothly.
"Kai Winn is claiming to be the one referred to in the
second stanza, but it is quite clear to me that *you*, Emissary,
are the one it must mean. 'One shall protect you.' That is
what you do, is it not?"

"It's what I try to do, yes," agreed Sisko, wondering how
he was going to talk his way out of this one. "But it could
mean almost anyone. Look, I don't wish to be rude, but I
am very busy with this crisis, and—"

"I understand," Yarka replied. "I shall be brief. I do not

know who the other two referred to in the prophecy are. But it is clear to me that in this hour of crisis, you are Bajor's only hope. Only through your faith can this crisis be averted. It is up to you to find the meaning of the prophecy, Emissary. It is my task only to bring these words to your attention. I am confident that, through you, Bajor will be saved." He bowed again. "And now I have taken up enough of your valuable time. I shall leave you to ponder the meaning of the Prophets. And I shall thank you for what you will do. Good day, Emissary." He gave another bow and swept from the room.

That was just perfect. As if he didn't have enough problems to contend with, now he was being made the object of another obscure prophecy. Sisko sighed. Maybe he'd believe more in these Prophets if they only spoke to him in English instead of riddles!

Her sense of wonder sated, Sahna turned from viewing Bajor back to Tork. He was tense, and clearly forcing himself to look, but he had not succumbed to his fears. "How do you feel?" she asked him gently.

"As well as can be expected," he said, managing a feeble smile. "But I have proven that it is possible to endure what was once considered unendurable."

"*You* can endure," Sahna corrected him affectionately. "You are the bravest person I know, Tork."

"If I can do it, then anyone can," he replied. "I have no great strength here, Sahna. I have only necessity to drive me. Perhaps this fear of space is not as ingrained in our race as we had thought. Perhaps it is simply that we have always given in to it, instead of challenging it."

Sahna considered the idea. "It is possible," she agreed. "By giving in to our fears, we strengthen them. By standing up to them, as you have done, we prove that they are not in command of our lives."

"I wish I felt better about winning, though," he joked. He moved to the seat, and lowered himself onto it. "At least I am gaining some control over one of my troubles. And the others help me to distract my mind from what I see."

Sahna frowned. "You refer to the problem about Bajor?"

"Partly." He gave her a very odd look. "Sahna, I am troubled, and there is no one to help me in this struggle in my soul."

She moved to his side and rubbed his shell. "I will always help you," she vowed.

"But in this matter, there is little you can do. I wish you could help me."

"I can do at least one thing," she informed him. "I can listen to you. What is it that distresses you so?"

Tork gathered his thoughts for a moment, and then nodded. "It will do me well to unburden myself, even if you cannot solve my dilemma," he agreed. "Shortly before we left the Hive, Hosir summoned me to talk with him."

"I know of Hosir," Sahna said. "He used to be the Security Master, did he not?"

"Yes. When Dron became Grand Master, however, he appointed Raldar to that post, and had Hosir made merely a Hivemaster in name, without purpose." He grimaced. "This conversation with Hosir was very short and troubling. He entered some technical data I do not comprehend into my comp, and then said only one thing to me that I cannot get out of my mind." He paused, deeply troubled, and then continued. "He asked me a question: 'How do you know that the Two Hundred and Third Hive's rebellion failed?' And he refused to say anything more."

It didn't make sense to Sahna. "Of course the Two Hundred and Third Hive's rebellion failed," she said, puzzled. "We all know that. It is in our records. It is part of the sacred texts."

"Exactly." Tork gave a deep sigh. "So then why did Hosir ask such a foolish question? Unless it is not as foolish as it sounds?"

Sahna shook her head. "I cannot say. But perhaps I can help you understand the data he gave you. May I see your comp?"

Fishing it out of his shell, Tork tapped in the commands to bring up the data. "Here." He passed it to her.

Glancing it over, Sahna scrolled the screen several times

back and forth. As Tork had said, it was in some obscure computer code. Yet, there was a little that she could understand. "Most of it is very opaque to me," she admitted. "But I can read portions of it. It appears to be some kind of computer command sequence."

"That I had already surmised," Tork replied. "But to what? And why? And why should Hosir give it to me?"

"He may not understand its significance, either," Sahna pointed out. "These codes are very old, in a form of logic we have not used in a thousand generations. But some of the data is quite clear. I can make out astronomical readings here. I have studied the old texts from the first Hives for data on our home system, and this is written in the same kind of coordinates. . . . And yet it is not *completely* the same." She sighed. "Perhaps back on the Hive, with access to my computers, I could decode this. Here, I can tell you no more." She passed him back his comp.

"Astronomical data?" mused Tork. "Why would Hosir wish me to have this? And what significance does it have to do with his question?"

"The data is old," Sahna offered. "Possibly dating before the Two Hundred and Third Hive."

He smiled. "That is a link," he agreed. "But astronomical data from so long back can have no bearing on our current troubles, can they?"

"I do not know," Sahna admitted. "As you say, I cannot help you further."

He stroked her shell fondly. "You have already helped me a great deal. What comes next is on my shell." He sighed. "I do not look forward to this trip to Bajor, but it is my duty. I will do whatever is needed." He smiled again at her. "Would you mind if I rested awhile? I am worn out from my struggles."

"Of course not," she answered. She glanced back at the window. "Shall I close the portal?"

"No," he answered. "I must get used to the sight."

She considered a moment further. "I am not tired," she said. "I am too excited. Would you mind if I left you to explore a little?"

"Of course not. But take care. These aliens might be friendly, but we do not know all of them. Perhaps it would be best to ask Captain Sisko for an escort?"

"A wise idea," she agreed. It had already occurred to her. "Rest, now. I shall be careful." She crossed to the computer. "Computer," she asked, turning it on. "May I speak with Captain Sisko?"

"One moment."

In far less than the promised time, the screen lit up with Sisko's face. "Sahna," he greeted her. "Is there a problem?"

"No, Captain," she answered. "It is merely that I should like to look at your fascinating station while Tork rests. Is it possible that you could supply me with an escort? Preferably one who knows science? I have many questions to ask."

"I know just the person," Sisko answered. "She'll be with you shortly."

About five minutes later, there was a buzz at the door, which Sahna answered. She discovered a young human-looking female there. She had long hair, clipped back behind her head, and curious rows of spots running down her face and neck.

"Hello, Sahna," she said cheerfully. "I'm Jadzia Dax."

"Hello." Sahna looked back, and saw that Tork was resting, his eyes closed, his body less tense. "Shall we leave him in peace?"

"A good idea." Dax led the way outside, and the door closed automatically behind them. "So, what would you like to see?"

"Almost anything," admitted Sahna. "But I should very much prefer to talk with you."

Dax laughed. "That sounds like the perfect cue for the Promenade," she answered. "Let's go."

She led Sahna to a marvelous place. They stood together beside a guardrail, looking down on a long, curved row of stores and peoples. Sahna was astonished and delighted by the variety of goods and aliens that she could view from here. And if she tired of those, she could simply turn about and look out of large windows and at the stars. It was almost too much to take in, and she laughed almost drunkenly.

"Such a place of wonders!" she exclaimed.

"It is, isn't it?" agreed Dax. "And yet, I've seen things that makes this place look dull and boring."

"I am sure you must have," agreed Sahna, wistfully. "I have studied astronomy since I was a child, and yet I never expected to *experience* any of it. Now, here I am. . . ." She sighed. "I do not want this to stop," she admitted. "Please, tell me about some of your experiences."

Dax smiled. She had an idea that it would take quite a while to answer even half of Sahna's questions.

"Forgive me for pointing this out, Captain," Kira said as patiently as she could, "but isn't time of the essence here? Bajor only has another four or five days before the Hive arrives."

"You're forgiven," Sisko replied with a smile. "That's quite correct, of course."

"Then why are we just sitting here doing nothing?" Kira demanded. She gestured at the screen on her workstation. "Dax is just chatting with Sahna, and Tork is catching up on his sleep."

"I know it *looks* like we're doing nothing," Sisko replied, "but that isn't the case. Sahna seems very eager to learn about what it's like to live on a planet. Dax is the perfect person to make her understand. After all, she's 'lived' many more years than the rest of us combined. I think there's a good chance Sahna is already in favor of letting Bajor alone. As for Tork . . ." He turned to Bashir, who was hovering close by. "Doctor?"

"The medical scanners in his room show that he is under a great deal of stress," Bashir explained, frowning. "I'm comparing his readings to those of Sahna, who seems to be pretty well adjusted, so there may be a percentage of error here, of course. If he were human, I'd say he was hovering on the brink of mental exhaustion at best, and dementia at worst." Bashir paused, then resumed in a more cheerful tone. "Sleep is the body's way of attempting to cope with stress and it's showing some effect already. I believe that an hour or so more of sleep will do wonders for him. After all, going down to Bajor will be quite traumatic for him. We want him as relaxed as possible before we start."

"So, as you see, we aren't doing nothing," Sisko added. "In an hour, we'll wake Tork and head down to meet the government. Hopefully, both Tork and Sahna will be sympathetic and we can sway them." His face became grim. "Believe me, I know how important this is to all concerned. I'm just trying to give us the best possible chance of success. After all, we won't get a second chance to try and save your world. We have to do what we can with this."

Kira nodded her understanding. "I just hope it's enough," she said.

"So do I, Major," agreed Sisko. "So do I."

CHAPTER
21

"Now what is it?" yelled Keve. He glanced up from his desk and winced. "Oh. Dukat. It's you."

"Yes," agreed Dukat. "Gul-Tar, the situation with the Hive has become worse. Sisko has informed me that they aim to target Cardassia Prime when the split of the Hives is complete. According to the captain of the *Karitan*, that will be in approximately one day."

Keve considered the news for a moment. "I agree, that's not good news," he snapped. "But Gavron and the Third Fleet will intercept this Hive before it could possibly reach Cardassia. So what's the problem?"

Dukat sighed mentally. "The problem is that the Third Fleet may not be sufficient to stop the Hive. I strongly suggest that we have the Home Fleet intercept—"

"No!" Keve thundered. He rose to his feet. "Dukat, I can understand that you want only what is best for Cardassia, but you don't see the larger picture." He slammed his hand down on the reports on his desk. "There have been antimilitary demonstrations in three provinces. In one case, I was forced to quell the protest before it developed into a riot. My agents inform me that unrest is growing. I *need* the Home Fleet where it is. Without it, the traitors would feel more secure in their demands and attacks. We cannot afford that. The Third Fleet should be more than sufficient to subdue or destroy this alien Hive."

"And if it is not?" Dukat asked, pointedly.

"Then I will turn over command of the Home Fleet to you, and you can have the second shot at the damned thing," Keve snarled. "Would that make you happy?"

Bowing slightly, Dukat said, "It is what would be best for Cardassia, Gul-Tar."

"And not bad for you personally, if you're the man who saved our planet, eh?" Keve remarked sourly. "Oh, I know you're thinking of the homeworld first," he said before Dukat could protest, "but I know you well enough to know that you're also after something for yourself. I'll have the orders drawn up, ready for implementing if the occasion should arise. Now get out of here, and let me deal with this rebellion problem."

"Of course." Dukat bowed again, and then left the room. Outside, he paused for a moment to ponder the exchange, and then hurried to his private quarters. Once there, he activated his communications unit and then tapped in a series of commands. Good—he was still unmonitored. His safeguards were paying off. Then he keyed in the private line to Feron Mulak's home.

Mulak's startled face looked back at his a moment later. "Dukat!" he exclaimed. "I was not expecting—"

"I know that," Dukat said smoothly. "I also know that you're the brains behind this so-called revolt against the military."

"I assure you—" Mulak began.

"Assure me of nothing," Dukat interrupted. "I'm not a fool, and you know that. As I say, I know you're the one behind the planning. Not the front man, of course. And I have not told the Gul-Tar what I know."

Mulak scowled, and then looked thoughtful. "I assume that means you want to make a deal."

"Perceptive." Dukat smiled. "That is indeed what I

propose. The military rule of Cardassia is coming to an end. We all know this, especially, I think, Keve. My concern here is that there be a speedy transition of power with the minimum amount of bloodshed and disruption. To that end, I do believe that I can help you."

"And why would you do that?" asked Mulak.

"Because in the new *civilian* government, you will need someone in charge of the military, naturally."

Mulak laughed, short and sharp. "And you know just the person for that post, I imagine. All right, Dukat: I'll bite. What do you propose?"

"An alliance," Dukat answered smoothly. "We can be of great help to one another, you and I. . . ."

Sisko had wondered if the runabout would pose a problem for Tork, but the alien had taken his specially prepared seat without a murmur. Sahna reclined beside him, their hands entwined in the classic pose of lovers from many cultures. "You're sure you'll be okay with this?" he asked again.

Tork smiled tightly. "Captain, I know what to expect now. I am getting more adjusted to the sight of the stars. I promise I will do my best."

"We can't ask for more than that," Sisko replied. He took his seat beside Kira. "Are we ready?"

"Affirmative," she replied, running the final checks on flight status. "Ready when you give the word."

Sisko looked back one last time. Dax, seated beside the aliens, gave him a reassuring smile. "Okay, let's move out."

As Kira tapped in the commands, the runabout came up to full power, and then the airlock ahead of them opened to reveal space. It was a strain for Sisko not to look back at Tork again, especially when he heard the sharp intake of the alien's breath, but he had to trust that things would be well with him. The trip to Bajor was too far for a transporter, and the runabout was the only way to get them there.

The craft gave a slight tremor as Kira took it through the open lock and then out into space. "Everything's fine," she reported. "Estimated flight time of twenty minutes, Captain."

"Excellent." Sisko smiled. "I'm going to talk to our passengers, Major." He rose and went aft to take the seat beside Dax. He gave Sahna an encouraging smile, which wasn't really needed. The female alien was enthralled with the view out of the windows. Tork, on the other hand, seemed understandably tense. But he was not catatonic, which was an improvement. "How are you feeling?" he asked sympathetically.

"Terrible," Tork confessed. "But I trust the feeling will pass. If not, I probably shall." He swallowed. "Captain, perhaps now would be a good time for us to continue our conversation. It would help to take my mind off my distress."

Sisko nodded. "I agree. You were going to tell me about the Great Design."

"That is correct." Tork made an effort to gather his thoughts. "When the makers of the First Hive constructed the Hive, they were not simply planning that we flee our world. They had an aim in mind. Since we had to leave our home galaxy, they had aimed us for this one, not knowing precisely what we should find here. But they believed that we would find worlds that contained at least primitive life.

"The Hive is constructed so that it can reproduce itself, as it is now doing. The First Hive decided that when we reached our new galaxy, the best way to insure the survival of our race was by duplicating the Hive. To do this, we would need to absorb the resources of a planet. It would have to be one with life of some kind, because we would need the vegetation and other lesser life-forms to replace those that had died during the journey. The Hive is an integral mix of technology and the biological sciences, Captain. It was designed to maintain a stable population for the journey and to contain the resources necessary for their survival. There would, of course, be some attrition over the millennia, and this would need to be replaced when we reached our goal.

"Once the Hive splits, these resources will need replenishing again. Once more, we must have one target world per Hive. When they are absorbed, both Hives will be at their peak again. The Great Design then calls for one of these Hives to return to intergalactic space and make the crossing to the galaxy that you term Andromeda. Once there, it will repeat the fission process. The other Hive will remain in this galaxy, and every thousand years or so will absorb another world and then fission. This will insure the survival of our species."

Dax frowned. "At the expense of native species to our galaxy," she pointed out. "Tork, what your First Hive proposed is highly immoral. You steal the life-forms and the resources of other species to propagate your own. How can you even try to justify such behavior?"

Tork shook his head. "The Hive must survive. Dax, would you not do *anything* to insure the survival of your race?"

"No," she said firmly. "I would not advocate the genocide of another species, for one thing. Which is what *you* propose to do."

"Tork," interrupted Sisko, "do you yourself feel that you have the right to murder others for your own purposes? People who have not threatened you?"

"No," Tork admitted slowly. "But we *were* threatened. And attacked. The Cardassians attacked us without provocation, and then so also did the Daranians. We were justified in defending ourselves."

"Defending, yes," agreed Sisko. "But you didn't have to destroy Darane and annihilate its people to defend yourselves. You could have simply stopped their ships."

This had clearly occurred to Tork, because there was pain on his face as he replied. "I know, Captain," he agreed. "I deeply regret what was done. And I wish that there were some way to spare Bajor. But I cannot see any. The Hive *must* survive, and this way is the way of the First Hive. They overcame the insanity of living on a planet and migrated into space. Their wisdom and courage has always inspired us."

"Their achievements were tremendous," agreed Dax. "The Hive is a magnificent creation. But has there never been any who questioned the Great Design?"

"Oh, yes," Tork replied. "We do not suppress thinking. The Two Hundred and Third Hive, for example, led a terrible rebellion. They wanted to alter the Great Design and to take the Hive itself in a new direction."

"Alter it?" asked Dax, intrigued. "In what way?"

Tork's snout wrinkled. "We do not know. The rebellion failed, and their plans never came to blossom. They were expunged from our historical records." He sighed. "It was a time of terrible strife and bloodshed. The leaders of the failed revolt were callous beings, unconcerned with everything but their own plans for the Hive. They ruthlessly executed their foes, but were in turn overthrown, and justice was restored."

"And this is all recorded in your histories?" asked Sisko.

"Yes." Then Tork winced, and gave a start. "That is what Hosir must have been referring to."

"Hosir?" Sisko recalled the intriguing elderly alien. "What do you mean?"

"Before I left," Tork explained, "he asked me how I knew that the Two Hundred and Third Hive's rebellion had failed. It is, of course, in the histories of our people. He must have been reminding me that we have a long and proud history. I am a student of it," he added. "I have spent years researching the texts."

"It must be fascinating," Dax commented.

"It is," agreed Tork. "I have discovered that the Two Hundred and Fourth and Fifth Hives quote the writings in a very slightly different way than they are known now. My theory is that over the millennia, our sacred writings have mutated slightly in use."

"Really?" Dax smiled brightly. "I'm a student of history, too. So, you've tracked changes over all two thousand seven hundred and sixteen generations then?"

"No," Tork admitted. "I have not had the time for that. Besides, the most substantial changes appear to have been in the very early Hives, which is logical."

"And intriguing," said Sisko thoughtfully. "How large were the changes?"

"Minor wordings for the most part," Tork replied. "Very little else. Most of my tutors thought I was wasting my time with such frivolous matters."

"No," Sisko said. "A people is the sum of its history and its present. If your history has been changed . . ."

"Not changed," Tork objected. "The revisions are really very minor. Our history is intact and accurate."

"Tork," Sahna interrupted suddenly. "Tell them about the notes that Hosir gave you."

Frowning, Tork answered, "But they are not relevant, surely?"

"They have a very advanced astronomy," Sahna explained. "Perhaps they could tell us what the information means."

"We could try, at least," Dax said. "May I be permitted to examine the notes?"

Tork hesitated, and then gave a shrug. "I do not see any harm in it." He pulled out his comp, and called up the data. "Here."

Taking the comp, Dax examined the screen carefully. Tork showed her how to scroll through the information. After a moment, she shook her head.

"It's very hard trying to work it out in your units." She reached under her seat and took out her tricorder. "If you have no objections, I'd like to patch it through my tricorder into the ship's computer. Then I can probably analyze it better. It will not harm your comp, or change the data in any way."

"Then I have no objections," Tork replied. "But I do not think that Hosir's message is relevant."

"Tork," Dax said gently, "I'm trying to save Bajor. I'm willing to try anything, even if it doesn't seem relevant."

He nodded. "I understand, and I wish you good fortune." He turned back to Sisko as she began to work. "Captain, I am greatly in sympathy with your aims. I, too, do not wish to destroy a planet. But my first loyalty is to the Hive. I will do whatever I feel is needed to insure its survival."

"And I understand that," Sisko replied. "I wouldn't ask you to betray your race, but I hope and pray that we can find some other way out of this quandary." He got to his feet. "I'd better go and check in with the major again."

Kira had the runabout well in hand, and he knew it. Sisko simply wanted some time to think about what he had just learned. If the Hive was working on a plan that had been determined by the designers of the Hive, it was being treated as a sacred legacy. He could see that it would be difficult, if not impossible, to convince the aliens to alter that Great Design. Matters were not getting clearer the more he knew; they were getting harder. How could he find a way to persuade a people to change their entire purpose in being?

"Looks like it might get a little bumpy, Captain," Kira reported. "There's a major storm brewing up right near the capital. Nothing the runabout can't handle, of course, but I'm a little concerned about the aliens."

"Not much we can do about the weather," sighed Sisko. "In fact, there's not much we seem to be able to do about anything right now, is there?"

"There had better be," Kira said forcefully. "We won't surrender Bajor without a fight."

"I know that," admitted Sisko. "And that's what I'm trying to avoid."

As they drew closer to the planet, Sahna came up front. "I hope I am not in the way," she apologized. "But this is the first planet I have ever seen. May I watch?"

"Of course," Kira answered. "I'm sure I don't have to tell you to touch nothing, though." She returned her attention to the controls. "You can see where we're heading, in fact. That area with the circular cloud formation."

"Clouds," Sahna concentrated. "Ah. Suspended water droplets in the atmosphere. It is something I know of only theoretically."

"Well, it's going to become practical knowledge real soon," Kira assured her. "We're going through the edge of it."

Worried, Sahna asked, "Is that dangerous?"

"Nah," Kira assured her. She grinned. "It might even be fun."

Sahna watched, enthralled, as the runabout entered Bajor's atmosphere. The craft shook slightly as the air buffeted it. The shields glowed under the heat of entry, kicking off trails of light beside the ship. Tork gave a strangled cry, but when Sisko looked back, he saw that the Hivemaster was still with them. He really was getting better at this.

After a few moments, they entered the leading edge of the clouds, and nothing but whiteness was visible about them. Sahna gave a sigh of disappointment.

"We'll be able to see again soon," Sisko assured her. "In fact, we'll be landing in just a couple of minutes. It might be a good time to get back to your seat."

"If you insist, Captain," she said, disappointed. She made her way aft to rejoin Tork and Dax.

"We've got landing clearance," Kira reported. "And a reception committee awaiting us, I gather." She grimaced. "I hope it's not going to be too formal."

As they left the lower layers of the clouds, the Bajoran capital was spread below them. Both Tork and Sahna gasped, though for very different reasons. For a second, it looked as if Tork was about to go catatonic again, but then he managed to relax slightly.

"That was . . . disturbing," he admitted.

"I wish we could do it again," Sahna breathed in delight.

And then they angled down, descending toward the Council buildings. The view was certainly spectacular, as they flew low over the rebuilt city. It was very different from Sisko's first sighting of it three years earlier. Then the buildings had been left half-wrecked and despoiled by the Cardassians as they retreated. Now a great deal of civic restoration had taken place. The temples—generally the largest and most ornate edifices—were back to their former glories. The bridges had been repaired, and the gardens the Bajorans so loved were in full bloom.

All of which might end very soon.

"The Bajorans are very proud of their architecture," Dax commented to Sahna. "They consider the raising of buildings to be a work of art."

"I can believe it," Sahna replied. "It is a lovely view."

The roof of the Council chambers appeared below them, and Kira brought the runabout down expertly to a gentle landing. After depowering the engines, she sprang the airlock.

"Well, here we are," Sisko murmured. He rose and walked back to the others. "Are you both prepared for this?"

Tork took a deep breath. "As prepared as I can be, Captain," he replied. "Shall we get this over with?"

Nodding, Sisko led the way out of the runabout.

Tork followed him nervously, clutching the edge of the hatch as he left. He gasped, and shuddered as he looked upward, at the open sky. "It is . . . unnatural," he wheezed, obviously distressed. "There is no roof."

"It's perfectly natural," Sisko answered. That, of course, was the problem: Tork was completely unused to uncontrolled nature.

"It is . . . distressing," Tork commented. "But I will endure." He walked beside Sisko toward the entrance ahead. Beside it waited five figures. "Are these the representatives of the Bajoran people?"

Sisko nodded. "They wished to greet you as you arrived." His eyes narrowed as he surveyed the group. He recognized Shakaar, of course, and, beside him, Kai Winn. Trust her not to be left out of this! Two of the figures were guard escorts, but the fifth . . .

"Jaro!" exclaimed Sisko. "I hadn't expected to see you again."

"At least," added Kira angrily, as she caught up with him, "not this side of a jail cell."

"It's nice to see you, too," murmured Jaro, with mock politeness. "At this hour of crisis for our world, we are all patriots first."

Kira glared at him. "You're scum first," she snarled.

Shakaar laid a hand on her arm, but she shook it free. "How could you even *think* about working with him?" she yelled at her old friend.

"Because he's right, Nerys," Shakaar answered calmly. "At a time like this, we have to work together."

Kira gave him a withering look. "Then check your back periodically," she snapped. "Because one of these days, there's going to be a knife in it."

"I can see these are going to be very fruitful negotiations," Jaro observed.

"Please, my children," said Kai Winn, raising her hands. "Can we not present a unified face of peace toward our alien visitors?" She smiled gently. "We are, after all, here to welcome them and engage in discussion of the situation, and not to fight amongst ourselves."

"The Kai is right," Sisko said. He hated having anything to do with Jaro, but there was clearly no alternative. "Shall we go inside?" He glanced up at the darkening sky. "It looks like it may get a trifle moist out here soon."

"Of course," Shakaar agreed. "Please, follow me." He nodded to Tork and Sahna, and then led the way indoors. In a matter of moments, they reached the Council chambers. The two guards took up position at the doors, and Shakaar led the others inside.

The room was dominated by a large conference table. The entire far wall was made of glass or some transparent substitute, giving a view out onto the city below. Tork didn't even flinch at the expanse this time.

There were only about a dozen other Bajorans present, all looking grim-faced and anxious. Sisko recognized none of them, which was hardly surprising. Politicians tended to come and go very quickly here. Even though the government had stabilized a great deal under Shakaar and Kai Winn's firm control, the Bajoran people were not happy with the direction their world was taking. Few incumbents were ever returned for a second term.

As Sisko had requested, two of the leaning boards had been fabricated for Tork and Sahna. They accepted their comfort gratefully, while the rest of them took their seats.

Shakaar was at the head of the table, with Winn to his left and Jaro to his right. Sisko, Dax, and Kira were seated by the Hive dwellers, and away from the table. This signified that they were not expected to speak unless invited directly to do so.

"First of all," Shakaar said formally, "I would like to thank Hivemaster Tork for attending this meeting. I understand that it involved no small inconvenience and distress to him, and we are grateful."

"I am pleased to be here," Tork replied. "I hope that our discussions will bear fruit."

"So do we," Shakaar agreed, his tone grimmer. "For the sake of both of our people, let us pray that we can come to some accord. First, I must ask: Is it true what we have heard from Captain Sisko, that your people aim to bring your Hive to Bajor and absorb it as you did our colony on Darane Four?"

Inclining his head, Tork said, "Unfortunately, it is. The Hive needs replenishing after the creation of two daughter Hives. Only a world with life-forms meets our needs, and Bajor is the closest."

"It's what we feared," growled one of the ministers. "They come to steal our *pagh*. We *must* fight these demons!"

"Please," said Winn, in her irritatingly condescending tones. "We are here to talk, not to accuse." She turned to face Tork. "And how may we persuade you not to come to Bajor?"

"I do not know," he replied. "The Hivemasters in concert are pledged to this course of action. I can see no way to sway their decision. If it were up to me, I would speak on your behalf. Your world is advanced, and you do not seem to be too insane. But I am only one voice, and unlikely to be heard."

"Then what is the point of this meeting?" exclaimed Jaro. "If nothing we can do or say will persuade you, why are you here?"

"To offer you help," Tork answered, surprised. "We will

lend you ships and help you to build a space colony. Or we will even help you to relocate to another world, if that is your desire."

"Relocate?" Shakaar appeared stunned. "You have no understanding of what you are asking. We could never leave Bajor."

Tork began to tremble. "But you *must*," he insisted. "If you do not leave, you will be annihilated when the Hive absorbs your world. You cannot remain."

Shakaar leaped to his feet. "We cannot leave!" he roared. "It is you who do not understand. For a hundred years, the Cardassians ruled our world, grinding our people under their boots. We fought back for every inch of this world. It is *our* world, and not one of us will simply walk away and hand it over to you. If your Hive comes here, we will fight while there is a single Bajoran alive. If we die, we die with our world."

"This is insanity!" Tork exclaimed, very agitated. "It is not logical to die for a handful of dirt!"

"It may not be logical," spat Jaro. "But we are *Bajorans*. This is our home. We will defend it, or perish in the attempt. You cannot have even a handful of our dirt unless you trample across all our murdered bodies first."

Tork shook his head from side to side. "No," he protested. "This cannot be. I beg you, do not do this. Let us help you to leave, to find a new home."

"There can be no other home for us," Kai Winn said. She stood also. "This is our only home. The Prophets have assured us of this. We could not leave, even if we wished. It is our destiny. Planet and people are linked through faith. The Prophets will protect us." She looked directly at Sisko. "The *Emissary* will protect us. Your plans will fail, because they are born of unbelief and evil."

"There's nothing like waving the flag," muttered Kira.

Utterly bewildered, Tork stared about the room at the hostile, implacable faces. "You must speak reason," he protested. "We wish to help you to live. We do not wish to kill you."

"If you insist on following through with your plan," Shakaar informed him coldly, "then you will *have* to kill us. Each and every living Bajoran. If you can." His face was filled with anger. "And we will all die cursing you and your entire race."

"You seem to have a conscience," Winn added. "Can you live with yourself knowing that you have caused the death of an entire race?"

"But this is not necessary!" protested Tork.

"You have made it necessary," Shakaar replied.

"It is only a planet!" Tork exclaimed. "A ball of water, mud, and rock. It is not worth dying for."

"It is our home," Jaro said. "It is not worth living without."

At that instant, the sky outside seemed to bubble with blackness, and a forked arc of lightning slashed across their view. Tork gave a strangled cry of panic even before the loud clap of thunder shook the room. Then he shrieked and dived to the floor.

"You see!" he howled. "It is madness to live on a planet! It is filled with violence and unpredictability. You are all insane to live like this!"

A second bolt shattered the sky outside, and Tork shriveled into a ball, only his shell now visible.

Sisko stared at the catatonic alien and sighed. This conference could hardly have gone any worse. Tork's overly wound-up nerves had finally snapped, and he had retreated from the reality he couldn't handle. Sisko glanced across at Sahna, who looked nervous, but not yet panicking.

"He will recover soon," she promised. "But this . . . weather . . . is too much for him."

"There is clearly little purpose to further talk in any event," Shakaar said. "Your minds are made up, and so are ours. It seems that we have no recourse left to us but war."

"I wish it could be otherwise," Sahna said sorrowfully. "I do not believe that it is right to destroy this planet. You have a fine civilization, and I would regret its destruction."

"It may not come to that," Jaro said smoothly. "There is another option."

"And what is that?" asked Shakaar.

"This." Jaro withdrew a blaster from his robe and pointed it at Sahna. "We have two of the aliens now. Unless the Hive promises to call off their attack, we shall kill them."

CHAPTER
22

"WHAT DO YOU think you're doing?" exclaimed Sisko, jumping to his feet. He stared at the small blaster that Jaro held. It should have been detected before he entered the Council chambers; obviously Jaro had supporters even on Shakaar's staff.

"It should be obvious what I'm doing," Jaro replied, irritated. "I'm trying to save Bajor." He gestured with the gun. "Now we have two hostages."

"They are under Starfleet protection," protested Sisko. "I promised them safe passage, and I intend to keep my word."

"They're murderers and thieves," Jaro said. "You owe them nothing."

"I gave my word," Sisko growled, taking a step forward.

Jaro moved the blaster slightly to point it between Sahna and Sisko. "Captain, don't be foolish," he begged. "I have no desire to harm you."

"That's odd," Sisko answered. "Because I have a strong urge to beat you to a pulp."

"I'm only doing this to save my world," Jaro insisted, his eyes wavering between Sisko and Sahna. As a result, he didn't see when Shakaar moved in from behind.

The ex-rebel's fingers closed about Jaro's wrist and jerked the blaster upward. At the same time, Shakaar delivered a sharp blow to the base of Jaro's neck. With a grunt of shock and pain, Jaro released his blaster and fell forward across the conference table. Shakaar picked up the blaster, and then threw it into the nearest trash receptacle.

"The aliens are here as diplomatic envoys," he growled as Jaro attempted to stand. "Your behavior is disgusting, and I will not tolerate it."

Jaro finally managed to straighten up, massaging his neck. "You'll pay for that," he hissed.

"Oh, come now," Shakaar retorted. "Can't you manage anything better than hollow threats? I've had enough of you for now. I think you'd better leave." He stared pointedly at the door.

Limping, Jaro glared at the first minister. "You'll regret this," he said. "If we had held them hostage, we might have saved Bajor."

"Do you really think that the Hive would have called off their plans because of two small hostages?" asked Shakaar. "Don't be absurd. And even if they would, we would not dishonor ourselves in such a fashion."

Dax stepped up to Sahna. "Tork asked if we wouldn't do anything to save our worlds. Well, now you can tell him that there's one thing we won't do: We won't break our word."

Sahna nodded. "You have acted honorably," she admitted. "I do not care what the Hivemasters say, the Bajorans are not insane. I may not be able to understand their love for this dirt they insist on calling home, but I can see it does not affect their integrity or their courage."

"This meeting is now closed," Shakaar announced. "I am saddened that we did not reach a compromise, Sahna, but this situation has obviously gone too far for that. You must forgive me, but I am forced to prepare for war with your people."

Sahna inclined her head. "For what it is worth," she said

gravely, "my sympathies are with you." She turned to Sisko. "I release you from your oath, Captain. I shall not be returning to the Hive."

Sisko frowned. "What do you mean?"

"I mean that I will stay here, on Bajor, of my own free will." Sahna gave him a level look. "I may not understand these people, but I truly sympathize with them. Bajor deserves to survive, and if the Hive is going to destroy it, then they will have to kill me to do so." She turned to Shakaar. "I regret I can do nothing positive to aid your people, but I will not harm you, either. I shall be here, with you, when the Hive arrives."

Kira shook her head. "That's very noble and brave of you, Sahna," she said. "And very stupid. You can do no good by throwing away your life like this."

"On the contrary," Sahna answered. "I can set an example to my fellows on the Hive. I believe the decision to absorb Bajor is abhorrent, and I protest that decision with my life. There is no point in arguing with me; my mind is made up."

"And what about Tork?" asked Sisko gently. "How do you think he's going to take your decision?"

Sahna shrugged. "He will hate it, Captain," she admitted. "But he will not change my mind." She smiled. "It may give him added incentive to discover a solution to this problem."

"Or it might just drive him crazy," Dax added.

"I do what I must," Sahna replied. "I can do no other."

Shakaar moved to join them. "I thank you for your gesture of support," he told her. "I would be honored to have you be my guest for as long as is necessary."

"Thank you." Sahna gazed down at the curled-up Tork. "I must wait here until Tork recovers to tell him of my decision. Then I will be happy to join you."

Sisko collapsed into his chair. "This *is* crazy," he muttered. Sahna was willing to die for her beliefs, as were the entire Bajoran people. And Tork seemed convinced that there was no way to resolve this peacefully. What other options were left to them now?

And how much longer did they have to explore those options?

Boran strode into the Masters' chambers, a delighted smile on his face. "Good news," he announced. "The servitors will be finished with their tasks in less than one day now. We are ready to begin shifting the population."

"Excellent." Dron rose to his feet. "You and your crew have worked wonders, Boran. You are all to be highly commended." He looked at the remaining Hivemasters in the room. Raldar was missing; Dron judged it best that he stay out of sight for a while. And Tork was with the aliens still. Otherwise, everyone was now present. "Makarn, your report?"

The Science Master rose to his feet. "The—ah—special Determination has been made, and the results are awaiting your command to be fed to everyone's comps, Grand Master. The population has been divided into half, and assigned their new spaces."

"Excellent." Dron nodded. "Then immediately following this meeting, you will transmit the information. Splitting will commence immediately. Everyone will move quickly and efficiently to their new posts in preparation for the schism. Now, for the matter that will most concern us." He moved his own comp to the table before him. "I have made a separate Determination to sort out our assignments to each Hive. I will remain Grand Master of this Hive, of course. Pakat, you will become the new Grand Master of the second Hive."

Pakat looked astonished and startled, as well as pleased. "Thank you, Grand Master!" he exclaimed. "It is an honor I did not expect."

"But one that you well deserve," Dron informed him. There was a murmur of assent from around the table—one that Hosir rather obviously did not join. "With you on the new Hive will be Premon and Makarn. All three of your subordinates will become your replacement Masters for this Hive. Boran and Raldar will remain with me on this Hive, and their understudies will become the new Masters of Industry and Security for your hive."

"I had thought," Hosir commented, "that Hivemasters were Determined, not appointed. Yet you are promoting underlings who have not been Determined to positions of power. Others might see this as a despotic move, you know."

"It is nothing of the kind," snapped Dron, irritated. "These are extraordinary times in which we live. The Great Design is being implemented. We do not have time to go through the Determination to see who is best qualified for the posts. We may find ourselves at war with these crazed aliens shortly, and we must be prepared. This is a one-time-only measure to insure we are not caught unprepared."

"And what of me?" asked Hosir dryly. "Am I to be split down the middle, perhaps, and assigned to both Hives?"

"I wish that we *could* split you down the middle," Dron said with utter sincerity. "We could both use your wisdom," he added, lying. "You will, however, become advisor to Pakat on the new Hive. I suspect he will have great need of your keen mind there."

"And you will be most pleased not to have it here, I warrant," Hosir answered. He tapped on the table with his fingers and then smiled. "I note that you have not commented on where Tork is to be assigned. Have you given him up for lost?"

"No," Dron lied. "I merely saw no need to speak of him since he was not present. However, since you wish to know, he will remain here on this Hive."

Hosir nodded. "I hope you find work for him," he gibed. "Otherwise, he might get bored. And bored hands seek out trouble, as the writings say." He pretended to frown. "Or do they? Tork seems to think that the writings have a few glitches in them."

"If he does," Boran said firmly, "he should be soundly disciplined. The writings are without error."

"Quite," agreed Dron. "We all know that."

"Yes," said Hosir, in his dry way. "It appears that we do." He smiled blandly about the table.

"Now," said Dron, "the hour of our destiny has come. Makarn, send the signal to begin. We will prepare to become two Hives. The Great Design advances! We are all privileged to live in these exciting times!"

It was quiet now in the Council chambers. All of the Bajorans had left, including Kira, who was getting updated on the status of the defensive forces. Only Dax, Sahna, and the still-comatose Tork were left with Sisko, and none of them felt much like talking. Sahna was watching and waiting beside the curled-up Tork. Sisko stared out of the large window as the storm raged above the city.

It seemed an appropriate omen for the struggle inside him. He couldn't see a way out of this problem, yet he knew that it was up to him to do something. *Why me?* he wondered. *Why am I always seen as the one who fits all their prophecies and has to save the day?* How could he be expected to pull a solution to this mess from thin air? And yet . . . and yet, this was what he was trained to do. By joining Starfleet in the first place, he'd put his life and abilities on the line. It was his responsibility to do the impossible—or, at the very least, to attempt it.

There *had* to be a way out, something he could do. He couldn't simply wait for Bajor to be annihilated. The only other option was to attack the Hive and attempt to destroy it. Either way, he was talking genocide. That was not an option he considered viable—either as a part of his personal philosophy, or as a Starfleet directive. That meant he simply had to find another option.

Options . . . "Dax," he called, quietly. "We need to talk."

"Of course, Benjamin." She crossed to join him. "What is it?"

"The Hive needs resources to live," he said slowly. "Primarily, it appears, they need food plants and other botanical goods that can only be obtained from a living planet. Is there any way we could bring them the living materials that they need? They could then simply take apart barren planets for their mineral requirements."

"Perhaps," Dax answered dubiously. "But we'd need a huge amount of such supplies to stock two Hives. It would take months, and perhaps even a year to assemble sufficient resources. From everything that's been said so far, I gather the Hive's needs are a lot more urgent than that. I don't think they'd agree to hold off that long."

Sisko sighed. "You're probably right. But work up a proposal, will you, and see just how feasible it is? And any other options that you can come up with that might give us some time to come up with a better suggestion."

"Of course, Benjamin." Dax returned to her work with the tricorder.

A jagged, searing flash of lightning lit the sky. Sisko started counting without thinking, and on "three," the roll of thunder came, rattling the glass in front of him. Some storm. At least it provided a little distraction.

There was a gentle rap on the door. Sisko was half annoyed at the interruption, and half pleased to be dragged out of his morbid thoughts. "Come," he called.

The tall figure of Yarka entered the room. He looked tired and haggard, which was hardly surprising. "Emissary," he said by way of greeting. "I hope that you've had better ideas from meditating on the words of the Prophets than I have."

Sisko laughed sourly. "Hardly. I don't have an idea in my head, Vedek. I wish that I did, but I keep coming up empty."

Yarka moved closer. "You will know the way," he said. "You are the one who protects us." He sounded absolutely convinced of this. "Emissary, surely there is no coincidence here in the fact that there are two aliens with you."

"Two shall convert," Sisko murmured, quoting the words of Andaki that he had heard earlier. A vague hope started to enter his mind. "Sahna has declared her stand for your people. But Tork hasn't—and can't."

"Perhaps he will, when he recovers?" suggested Yarka.

"Even if he does," Sisko pointed out, "it means very little. What can the two of them do to help us? I don't think that the Hive will stop because they ask it to."

"The Prophets have spoken," Yarka said, with simple

faith. "As to what they mean—I cannot say. I am only a Vedek. You are the Emissary, so perhaps their truth will become clear to you soon."

"Clear?" Sisko laughed ironically, and gestured at the storm outside. "Everything's as hazy to me as those clouds."

"But beyond the haze there is light," Yarka pointed out. "It is a matter of seeing past the obvious, that is all."

"I wish that I had your faith, Yarka," Sisko said.

"Peace," said Sahna, suddenly. She looked around. "Tork is recovering."

Peering down, Sisko saw that there was indeed a crack in Tork's armor, as he started to unroll himself. A moment later, the shaken Hivemaster staggered to his feet. He glanced outside the window at the continuing storm and shuddered.

"I am sorry for my behavior," he said. "But it became too much for me."

"You've been very brave," Sisko told him. "I'm amazed at what you've been able to do. It simply isn't enough, though."

Tork nodded. "I know. It seems that I have sorely misjudged matters. The Bajorans will not give up their world, will they?"

"Never," said Yarka, fervently. "It is our home, the home that the Prophets have given us. Their light will surely illumine your soul, and you will change as your companion has changed."

"Change?" Tork was confused. "What do you mean?"

Sahna stroked his shell tenderly. "Beloved, I have made a decision. I will remain here on Bajor, and not return to the Hive with you."

Blinking, Tork struggled to understand. "Why?" he asked. "You cannot be serious. Bajor is to be absorbed."

"I know." Sahna bowed her head. "It is an immoral act, one that I cannot be a part of and be true to my conscience. I will therefore stay and die with the Bajorans."

"No," Tork whispered. "Sahna, we are to be One. You cannot abandon me now."

"I must do what I feel is right," she replied. "Tork, look to your hearts. Do you not feel as I do? That it is more important to be true to your beliefs than to live?"

"Of course," Tork admitted. "But that is different."

"It is no different," Sahna replied. "I will not be a part of the death of any Bajoran. I will die first." She relented slightly. "Beloved, I am not trying to force you to make the same decision, but I can do nothing else."

Tork was clearly in pain. "How can I abandon you?" he asked. "Especially when it would mean your death?" He clutched at his head with his hands. "I do not know what to think, what to believe."

"That is because you have no faith," Yarka said urgently. "When you rely only upon yourself, you have nothing to fall back upon when your strength fails. We have our faith in the words of the Prophets to uphold us when we would fall. They have promised us a savior at this time of crisis, and I begin to believe that savior might be you."

"Me?" Tork stared at him in bewilderment. "I do not see how I can help anyone. My One-to-be has told me she wishes to remain here and die. I do not approve of what the Hive is to do, but I cannot stop it. And I am filled with fear of your world. Friend, there is no one who could help you less than I."

"That is because you are thinking only of your own strength," Yarka answered. "Again, I tell you: You need a better strength to rely on."

"I do not know these Prophets of whom you speak. How can I then accept them or believe in them?"

And then the answer came to Sisko. It was suddenly formed within his mind—almost as if the Prophets had placed it there. "Then you must meet the Prophets," he said firmly. "That is the answer."

"What?" Tork stared at him as if he were crazy. "This man speaks of a religious experience. You cannot simply order one when you wish it."

"Sometimes you can," Sisko replied, feeling more and more certain that he was right. "When I first came to Bajor, I didn't believe in the Prophets, either. Then I had an experience. I'm not sure it was exactly religious, but it cleared away a lot of my own doubts and fears. It enabled me to come to terms with my own soul, and to move forward. Perhaps the same will happen to you. Yarka," he turned eagerly to the Vedek. "Do you think you can borrow an Orb for me?"

"An Orb?" Yarka raised an eyebrow. "It will be difficult, especially at this time of crisis—but who would deny the Emissary what he needs?" He gave a wide smile. "I believe the Prophets have revealed their plans to you." He bowed and hurried from the room.

Dax had unraveled herself from the computer screen she had been accessing. "What are you planning to do, Benjamin?" she asked.

"I aim to take the runabout," Sisko explained. "And the Orb. And Tork. And then enter the wormhole and see if we can't contact the Celestial Temple. Since I don't have a clue how to resolve this problem, let's see if the Prophets will tell Tork how to do it."

"Do you think it'll work?" Dax asked anxiously.

"It had better," Sisko said. "It's the only idea I've had. And I have a good feeling about it."

"I'm glad to hear that," said Kira from where she stood in the doorway. "It might be the last one you'll ever have. I've just received word from DS9. The Hive has split into two, and both of them are under power. Armageddon's heading our way."

CHAPTER
23

ON THE BRIDGE of the heavy cruiser *Charak,* Gul Gavron watched the main viewscreen intently. They were finally closing on the Darane system, and should soon be close enough to pick out their target. "All vessels to alert," he ordered. "Begin powering weapons. Raise shields and prepare for contact."

His staff scurried to obey his orders. On his tactical display, he could see the wedge-shaped display that showed all of the other ships under his command. His ultimate hour of glory was about to arrive. He was known for his tremendous victory at Mintos Alpha, but that had been almost twenty years ago. A soldier's reputation was only as good as his latest victory, and he hadn't fought in a campaign in over a decade. His enemies had conspired to keep him out of the lines of action, afraid that he'd become too popular.

And now they needed him. All of Cardassia needed him. This alien Hive had targeted their world for destruction, and only he and his fleet stood between them.

Perfect.

This would be his ultimate hour of glory, and his first step toward becoming Gul-Tar. Keve was getting senile; everyone knew that. With a major victory such as this, Gavron would be able to challenge Keve's standing and assume the mantle. What would make such a triumph even better would be to see the expression on the face of Dukat. It was common knowledge that Dukat believed himself the favorite of Keve, and destined to become the next Gul-Tar. Well, that was about to change.

"Confirm readiness," he barked.

"All systems operating at peak efficiency," his aide, Tarvok, reported. "Weapons are ready, and shields are holding at maximum." He consulted the screen at his elbow. "All ships report the same status."

"Excellent." Gavron's attention went back to the screen. "How long until visual?"

"Any moment now," Tarvok said. "We're closing on Darane Four. Sensors report two large objects almost dead ahead."

There! There was a flash of light toward the upper edge of the screen, and Gavron's eyes focused on it. Seconds later, he could see a vague shape, and a second beyond it. Then the Hive began to take a definite form on the screen.

"Send a warning," he ordered his communications officer. "Tell the aliens that they have ten time units to surrender, or we shall attack." He knew that this offer would naturally be rejected, but it was a formality he had to follow. A surge of excitement infused his blood. There was no greater joy than that of facing an impending battle.

He stared about his bridge, proud of every officer seated at his post. This was the cream of the elite, the best of all the warriors in the three fleets. He had handpicked every one. Each of them would willingly die for either Cardassia or Gavron. Each would fight like a demon to avoid such a death. And there were thousands more like them on the other ships of his armada. One hundred and twenty warships in all, each of them a lethal hunter.

These aliens would never stand a chance.

The Hives were now quite distinct. According to his instruments, they were in motion, and already several planetary distances apart. The Cardassian fleet was heading toward the closest, the one that had set its sights on absorbing Cardassia. That aim would soon be dashed.

"Keep watching for their ships," Gavron growled at Tarvok. "They're bound to launch soon if they mean to intercept us."

"Acknowledged."

Gavron hunched forward, trying to suppress his excitement. It would not do to be too eager for the carnage that was about to occur. He simply hoped that this would not be too easy a victory. . . .

"The aliens have rejected the offer of surrender," the communications officer reported.

"Good," Gavron replied. "That means they wish to fight. And we shall show them what it means to fight Cardassians!"

There was a shout of agreement from everyone on the bridge to that sentiment. Gavron smiled proudly. Soldiers, every one of them, and as eager for the battle as he was himself.

"The Hive is launching ships," Tarvok reported. "Six hatches have opened. Targets are emerging."

"Excellent." Gavron's eyes burned. "Prepare to engage. The battle is joined!"

"Do you really think this will work, Benjamin?" asked Dax, as she helped him prep the runabout for launching. "The entities in the wormhole don't always communicate, you know."

Sisko took the Orb case from Yarka and gently placed it in restraints behind the pilot's seat. "They don't usually refuse when an Orb is involved, remember? Besides, I have a strong suspicion that the entities want this to happen."

"A religious experience?" asked Dax with a slight smile.

"A hunch," Sisko answered, with a wider one. "This just feels to me to be the right thing to do. If the entities are so concerned with the Bajorans, for whatever their obscure reasons, then they will not allow the Hive to destroy this world."

"For what it's worth," Dax said, laying a friendly hand on his arm, "I think you're doing the right thing."

Yarka nodded. "It is the will of the Prophets," he agreed. "For this Tork to convert, he needs a sign, and the Prophets will grant him that sign." He smiled. "Emissary, you will be the instrument of our salvation yet again."

"I hope," Sisko added. "Right, that's about it. All I need now is Tork. Where is he?"

"Saying goodbye to Sahna," Dax replied. "If this doesn't work, the two of them may never meet again."

"Well, I hate to break up a lovers' parting," Sisko told her, "but we'd better be on our way. We don't have very much time. Would you mind asking him to get in here?"

Dax nodded. "Good luck, Benjamin."

He grinned widely. "Thanks, old man. I'll see you soon." He sat down at the controls, and began powering up the systems. He heard Dax leave, and realized that Yarka was still there. "Was there something else?"

Yarka shook his head. "I merely wished to thank you in advance for your efforts. May the Prophets go with you and keep you safe—and may they inspire you both." Then he bowed and left the ship.

A moment later, Tork stumbled inside the vessel. "I am sorry if I delayed you, Captain," he said.

"I understand." Sisko glanced around. "And I'm sorry to have had to rush you. But the Hives are on the move, and we have very little time left to us now. Make yourself comfortable. I'm going to take the runabout back to the wormhole at maximum thrust. It may get a little rough on you, so be prepared."

"Of course, Captain." Tork flopped onto his leaning board. "I am ready."

"Good." Sisko turned back to the controls. "Then here we go."

The runabout lifted from the roof of the Council building, and rose slowly into the air. As soon as they were a safe distance up, Sisko kicked in the thrusters, and the vessel shot upward into the billowing storm clouds. Lightning crackled about the craft as if in omen for what was to come.

The shields protected them from strikes, of course, and moments later they were above the clouds and on their way.

Sahna watched the runabout vanish into the clouds with a heavy shell. She had tried to prepare herself for the thought that she might never again see her beloved Tork, but she knew that no amount of preparation was sufficient. Her hearts burned inside her. It was easier to wait for death than to contemplate never seeing Tork again.

"They'll be fine," Dax said, encouragingly. She seemed to sense what Sahna felt.

"I know," lied Sahna. "But it is . . . difficult for me." She took a deep breath and tried to force her attention away from thoughts of Tork. "Is there anything that we can do to keep busy?" she asked. "It will make the passage of time somewhat simpler if we can."

"Of course there is," Dax answered. "In fact, I've got something I wanted to show you. Come with me back to the Council chambers."

Intrigued, Sahna followed her new friend. When they were there, Dax called up one of the computer programs she had been working on. "This is the data that we downloaded from Tork's comp," she explained. "The logic is very different from the Federation computer codes, but since it *is* logic, our computers have been able to crack some of it."

"And?" asked Sahna, feeling excitement mount within her. "Does it have any significance?"

"Yes," Dax replied. "Given your assertion that it contained astronomical data, I had the computer run a match with local star charts." On the screen, Sahna saw a display that was obviously that of the Bajoran area of space. "It matches almost perfectly. The astronomers of the First Hive must have been geniuses, because they scanned this data from your home system. There's only a bare indication of planets, because they're very difficult to detect over such immense distances. But if I read the data correctly, this information is partly a map to be followed, aiming it at the Darane system."

Frowning, Sahna objected, "But that is not information.

The Hive arrived there anyway. Of what use is it to know they aimed us to arrive where we did in fact arrive?"

"Well, at least it shows that their original planning was sound," Dax replied. "I think you were correct in revering these members of the First Hive. Their achievements were astonishing. But it's not the aim that intrigues me. It's this." She gestured at the screen. "The target world in this data isn't given, of course. There was no way that the First Hive astronomers could have picked out an individual world from the distance of the Magellanic Clouds. But there is a blueprint for a target world. The plan was to match it when the Hive drew close enough to Darane to start scanning for likely worlds."

"But we know what was sought out," Sahna protested. "Darane Four."

"No," Dax informed her. "That is the world that was selected, true. But it isn't the world that this data calls for."

"What do you mean?" Sahna was completely puzzled now.

"The First Hive data in this record indicates that the target world was not to be Darane Four at all. The criteria listed here call for an uninhabited world—a world without any life on it whatsoever."

Sahna stared at the screen and then at Dax in utter confusion. "I do not understand. What does this mean?"

"There's more," Dax told her. "Beyond that data, there are a long string of command codes that make very little sense to me at all. Perhaps together we can discover what they mean."

Newly appointed Science Master Tovin stared around the command center in awe. He had worked here for years as Makarn's assistant. He knew its every function, and what must be done at all times. But this was his first time in here as Hivemaster, since Makarn was now on the second Hive. Even now, it was moving farther away from the first Hive.

The room was amazingly quiet, considering the work that was being done here. At their panels, the Hive's pilots were moving the immense vessel slowly through the Darane system, as they began to orient on the Bajoran system in preparation for their journey. The computers hummed quietly to themselves, processing the intricate calculations that such delicate maneuvers required. There were almost a hundred workers here, all busily absorbed in their tasks.

And each and every one of them was under his command. Tovin felt a surge of deep satisfaction as he surveyed his subjects. It was a great responsibility he had been handed, and he was determined that nothing at all should go wrong.

"Master," called one of the technicians. "There is a problem."

Mentally cursing his misfortune, Tovin moved to the female's side. "What is it?" he asked, crossly. His first moments as Science Master, and already a problem! It did not auger well for the future.

"The data from the astronomy section is . . . confused," she replied, gesturing to her computer screens. "It is as if they are transmitting gibberish. We cannot set a course with such figures."

Tovin sighed. What was going on up there? "I will settle it," he informed the technician. "Ignore the data for the moment, and continue with the other calculations." He strode back down the length of the room to his raised observer's seat. Resting against it, he keyed on the communications unit. "Astronomy," he ordered the computer. A moment later, Bree's elderly face filled the small screen. "Bree," he snapped, "there seems to be a problem with your data."

"There is no problem," she contradicted him. "You are receiving what we are transmitting."

Tovin scowled. "You are *transmitting* nonsense?" he asked, astounded.

"Yes. It seemed to be appropriate." Bree's snout twitched in amusement. "I hope it is causing you headaches."

This made no sense at all. "It is not funny," Torvin snapped. "You are delaying the progress of the Hive."

"Good," Bree replied. "That is our intention."

It took a few seconds for the meaning of this to sink into Torvin's consciousness. Then he stared at the screen, appalled. "You are doing this *deliberately?*" he gasped. "You are betraying the Great Design?"

Bree's face set in a hard glare. "The Great Design has betrayed us," she said. "We know that the world that was absorbed had living beings on it. And we know that there are more intelligent beings on the world that you Hivemasters have targeted next. We will not allow this."

"*You* will not allow?" Torvin repeated, stunned and furious. "You have no right to—"

"We have *every* right!" exclaimed Bree. "You have made us all murderers! The blood of an innocent race is on our hands. And it will *not* happen again. The entire astronomy section is with me in this, and we are spreading word of what has happened. We of the Hive will not tolerate what you wish us to become." She cut the communications, and the screen went blank.

Torvin shook as he stared aghast at the screen. His first day on the job, and *this* had to happen! Moaning, he clutched his head between his hands. What was he to do? Nothing could have prepared him for such a catastrophe. Without their data, the Hive would not be able to continue. And *he* would have to answer for it.

His fingers hovered over the screen's controls for several moments while he struggled within. He did not want to have to report failure to Grand Master Dron—but he dared not delay telling him, either. Finally, he stabbed down, and screwed up all of his courage. "Get me Grand Master Dron," he ordered the computer.

A moment later, the screen lit up, and Dron scowled out at him. "Torvin, this had better be very important," he said. "I have many concerns at this time."

"It is, Grand Master," he gushed. "I am sorry to disturb you, but there is a serious problem with the astronomy department. They are transmitting nothing but gibberish to us, and deliberately so."

"What do you mean?" demanded Dron.

"They have decided that they do not approve of the Great Design, and are attempting to sabotage it. Without their data, we cannot move the Hive. They are disrupting every-thing!"

"It is not as bad as that," Dron said sternly. "Security will handle their attempt at revolt. We may have to do without their aid for a while, that is all."

"But the data we need to move the Hive?" pleaded Torvin. "How can we proceed without it?"

"You do not have to," Dron said, sighing. "If you check your computer records, you will find that Makarn entered most of the necessary figures before he joined the new Hive. Simply call it up, and follow that. It may be slightly off, but it will suffice for the journey to Bajor. Meanwhile, I will put a stop to this foolish revolt. Return to your work, and get us back on progress."

"Of course, Grand Master!" Torvin snapped off the screen and scuttled back to the technician. "Ignore all input from the astronomy sector," he ordered in a confident voice. He did not wish his underlings to know how frazzled he had been. "The required data for moving the Hive has been stored in the computer files. Call it up, and use that instead." There, that should settle that! Torvin was worried that he had left Dron with a bad impression, but there was no helping that. All he could do now was to overcome the bad start by insuring that everything else ran smoothly.

The objective would be reached. Bajor would be absorbed.

CHAPTER
24

THE CARDASSIAN FLEET closed the gap between them and the second Hive. Gavron watched the progress, alternating between his tactical display and the view on the main screen. He could feel his heart beating strongly, and the blood pumping through his veins. Battle would soon be joined.

"Closing," reported Tarvok. "Estimating three units to first impact. Hammer section preparing to strike."

"Order them to fire when targets present themselves," Gavron instructed. "The alien ships are in their double formation as before?"

"Affirmative," Tarvok answered. "Commanders report they are ready to engage. Two units."

It all came down to this in the end. The survival of the fittest. And the Cardassians had always been the fittest in any battle. They would win, as they always did. "Now," breathed Gavron, hunched forward eagerly, waiting to see the first strike.

The leader of Hammer formation whipped toward the first two ships of the Hive fleet. Gavron knew what was coming, but he still tensed, waiting to see it. Fire streaked from the tips of the warship, streaking toward one of the alien ships. There it impacted on the target's shields, causing a brief surge in light.

"Their screens are holding," Tarvok announced.

The attacker started to come around to fire again, and moved to avoid being trapped between the two ships and decimated, as the Bajoran vessels had been in the earlier battle. But the two Hive ships were surprisingly agile. They spun, accelerated, and started to close in on the Cardassian ship.

A second Cardassian vessel cut across their bow, opening fire. This, too, splashed harmlessly off their shields.

And then the battle was joined, and there was too much confusion to be able to concentrate on the larger picture. Gavron allowed the reports to wash over him as he focused on one small section after another. It was important to see how their tactics worked. In the earlier battle that the *Karitan* had witnessed, the Hive ships had worked in pairs, using monofilament netting as their weapon. The Cardassian captains all had orders not to be trapped by the alien ships in that fashion.

Despite the order, some craft were too slow in response to evade being trapped. Gavron saw one of his ships dodge one attack, only to run into a second as they accelerated away. The Cardassian ship fragmented into a cloud of components.

The Cardassian attack, though, was doing more than holding its own. Taking a page from the enemy's tactics, two ships combined to attack a single enemy craft. Their combined firepower took time, but they could overload their target's shields, and eventually destroy it. Of course, they had to watch out for further attacks as they did so.

"Five ships lost," Tarvok reported. "Four of the enemy annihilated."

Explosion followed explosion on the screen. His tactical display showed the maneuvering, and from time to time, lights would wink out. Green for the Cardassian forces, orange for the aliens. At the moment, everything looked fairly even. The number of ships deployed was almost identical, and they were trading losses. Of course, Gavron didn't expect this to last. His men were battle-trained veterans, while the forces of the Hive had only fought one battle before in their lives. They could not possibly hold against his superior soldiers, especially not using the tactics that they had before.

Three more of the enemy were taken out, sending the unmatched ships scurrying for . . .

Wait a moment! Gavron stared at the tactical display. Despite the fact that they were now without their partners, the Hive ships were not retreating. On the contrary, the three single ships were now maneuvering to reenter the fray. What did this mean? Had they evolved a new plan?

That they had indeed became clear seconds later. Gavron had ordered his men to ignore solo ships after one of the pair had been destroyed, assuming that they would be out of the battle.

What was going on?

The three single craft, unbothered by the Cardassian attackers, swooped back into the battle. As they passed close to the Cardassian ships they had targeted, something was fired from each craft. It looked a little like a photon torpedo.

"Evasive action!" Gavron roared. "Tell those captains to—" But his orders were too late to help.

The "torpedoes" exploded *before* they hit their targets, which made very little sense.

Until three Cardassian warships simply fragmented in space.

"What is happening?" yelled Gavron. "What did they do to my ships?"

Tarvok merely shook his head and scanned the displays in front of him. "Unknown for the moment," he replied. "It's impossible to get sensor readings through all that weaponry. It'll take a few moments."

Frustrated as he was, Gavron realized that Tarvok was doing his best. "Rescind my previous orders," he commanded. "Tell the captains to *not* ignore solo ships any longer. Every enemy vessel is to be treated as a hostile and engaged."

As he watched, three further green lights blinked off on his display.

The unthinkable was happening. The enemy was starting to win this engagement. And he had no idea how they were doing it.

"What will happen to me?" asked Tork. There was no mistaking the fear and concern in his voice.

Without looking up from the controls, Sisko replied, "That is in the hands of the Prophets, as the Bajorans would say. I can't tell you what will happen because I don't exactly know."

Tork considered this for a moment. He didn't seem to mind the view of space through the runabout's window at all now, apparently having other things to worry about instead. "Then how do I know it will be real?" he asked.

"It *won't* be real," Sisko answered. "The aliens are completely different from us. They may not even possess bodies as we know them. Instead, they adopt the guise of people from your mind. It will appear to you that you are standing in familiar places and conversing with people you know. But you will in fact be meeting with the entities who constructed the wormhole we'll be entering very shortly. They do not see time in quite the same way we do. To them, it is one continual present. The concept of linear time— which seems natural to us—took them some getting used to . . . if they understand it even now. Everything you see and hear will be fragmented."

"Then I do not see the point of this. If it is not real, why must I experience it?"

"Think of it as a different perspective," Sisko suggested. "A *very* different perspective. The entities may not comprehend a lot about us, but they are highly intelligent and motivated. Sometimes they can see flaws in us that we never knew existed. Sometimes they reveal things about us that we can't see. At other times, they help to clarify our thinking. They should be able to clarify some of the confusion you're experiencing."

Tork sighed. "I would very much like to have my confusion removed," he confessed. "It seems as if these past few days have been an assault on everything I have ever believed in. I do not know which way to turn."

"Then let's hope that the entities can offer you some direction," Sisko said. "Now this next part may be very disconcerting. We're about to enter the wormhole. It manifests itself quite spectacularly, so be ready for this."

Tork nodded, and stared out of the window in evident fascination. So much for his agoraphobia! He had apparently overcome it without too great a struggle.

And then the runabout reached the critical threshold of the wormhole. In an explosion of light, it unfolded before them. No matter how often Sisko traversed it, the sight was never less than impressive. A huge whirlpool of colors seemed to draw the tiny ship into its funnel. Golds, silvers, reds, blues, yellows, and hues of colors he could barely begin to imagine swirled about them as they plunged into the mouth of the effect. Flashing past them were bands and streaks of magentas, ochers, and umbers; sparkles of light and color danced about them in a kaleidoscope of brilliance.

Tork gasped, more from awe than from fear, and stared out at this tremendous display. "It is . . . beautiful," he finally said.

"It is that," agreed Sisko. He tapped in the commands to halt their forward vector. The ship's computer began station-keeping, otherwise they would be sucked in and through the vortex. "Now, if you can tear your eyes away from the view, it's time for you to meet the entities."

Reluctantly, Tork turned to follow Sisko to the casing that held the Orb. Sisko bent and lifted the shell, placing it on the closest seat. Then he moved to stand behind it. This was not to be his experience.

"Everything will be fine," he assured the alien. "Simply look at the Orb, and then concentrate. Nothing else. Then let whatever happens happen." He gave the Hivemaster a reassuring smile. "Don't worry, you may even enjoy the experience."

"I hope that I will learn from it, at the least," Tork answered. "I am ready."

Sisko nodded, and then gripped the edges of the two small doors on the front of the Orb. "Here we go," he whispered, and then pulled.

As the doors opened, the light from the Orb streamed out, bathing Tork in its warm, comforting glow. Tork's eyes sparkled, and then he seemed to lapse into a trance. Sisko smiled ruefully, recalling his own experience with the Orb and his meeting with the entities when he first arrived on *Deep Space Nine* three years earlier. Nothing had prepared him for what he had experienced, and he suspected that Tork was discovering just how unique this experience was.

It seemed to Tork as if reality shifted. As he stared into the glow of the Orb, the runabout dissolved around him. He found himself standing in nothingness. There was only whiteness about him. He felt neither heat nor cold. There seemed to be no directions, and nothing else in this universe with him. Yet he was not scared. He felt perfectly at ease.

"Strange . . ." a voice seemed to whisper about him. There was no visible source for the sound, but it sounded friendly. "Different."

And then he stood in the Hive. He was in his favorite spot in park nineteen, where the river meandered past a small island. Here grew the beautiful blue *sami* flowers that Sahna loved so much. He was tempted to reach down and pick a handful, but stopped, thinking that this might not be allowed. He tried to remember what Sisko had said about this not being real, but it was hard to believe. It *felt* so much as it always did. There was the faint breeze from the air units stirring the air, and he could smell the light scent of the *sami* in front of him. He could hear the rippling motion of the water beyond.

"Logic," said a familiar, beloved voice. He turned to see Sahna watching him, an oddly intent expression on her face. "It is a linear concept."

"Sahna," he said, amazed. "How did you get here?" And then he realized that it couldn't be her; it had to be one of those entities of which Sisko had spoken. "I am sorry. You startled me."

"Logic," the alien-Sahna repeated. "A linear concept. Cause and effect. Clue and resolution. Beginning and end."

"Yes," he agreed, confused. "It is a linear concept."

"That which is," said a second voice. "And that which is to be, inferred from that which is." Tork saw an alien-Hosir approach.

"Yes," Tork agreed again. "That which follows comes from that which precedes."

"Interesting," the alien-Sahna said.

"Odd," added alien-Hosir. "Cause and effect . . ." He seemed to be savoring the sound of the words. Then, sharply: "How do you know what you know?"

If Tork had been confused before this experience, it was nothing compared to how he felt now. "I do not understand."

"That we can see," alien-Sahna agreed. "But think, and tell us: How do you know what you know?"

Tork struggled to make sense of the question. "Partly by discovery," he said. "What I find out for myself, I know. Partly from facts that are given to me by others."

"How do you know they know what they know?" asked alien-Hosir.

"They know it by the same process that I know things," Tork answered, hoping he was understanding the question correctly. "Some things they have discovered; others have been passed down to them."

The scene abruptly changed. Instead of standing in the park, Tork was in his own room. Facing him now was Harl. "And others pass along what others have told them?" the alien-Harl asked.

"Yes. It is a line of knowledge that goes back millennia."

"Linear knowledge," said the alien-Hosir, who had simply materialized. "Linear progression."

"Yes," agreed Tork.

"But how," asked the alien-Sahna, "do you know that it is linear without interruption?"

"I am sorry," Tork replied, confused. "I do not understand what you are asking me."

"Linear," alien-Sahna repeated. It seemed to be their favorite word. "One, two, three . . . How do you know it is one, two, three?"

"And not simply two, three?" asked the Harl-being. "If it is linear, is it completely linear?"

This was not making things simpler for Tork. "You want to know about authority?" he asked. "When things are passed along, their worth depends on their authority. Those who are accurate pass along accurate information. Our history, for example, comes from the people who made it. It has been passed along from generation to generation."

He was suddenly back in the Council chambers of Bajor. "History," said an alien-Sisko. "Passed along, one two three? Those who experience the event pass it along."

"Exactly," agreed Tork. "That way, we know it is accurate."

"Only if the one, two, three are unbroken," said an alien-Dax. "The problem with linear: One must follow another. If one is missing, then the linear is shattered."

"Shattered?" asked Tork. Why couldn't these aliens simply tell him what they meant? This was too unsettling, conversing in this fashion. "I do not comprehend."

The alien-Hosir snorted. "History," he said. "One event follows another. One event causes another. One event influences another. It is linear. It is . . . *logical.*"

"Yes," agreed Tork.

"Behavior," said the alien-Sahna. "That is not always logical."

"No," admitted Tork. "Emotions can sway logic where behavior is concerned."

"Emotions can sway the linear, then?" asked the Harl-being. "It can make the linear nonlinear. It can introduce . . . error? Lies? Deceit?"

"Yes." Tork was finally starting to see the point of this

discussion. It was a very roundabout way to reach the point, but he suddenly saw what the aliens were asking. "You mean that information that is passed along in a linear fashion is capable of being corrupted and changed. Sometimes by error, and sometimes deliberately."

"Yes," agreed Sahna's look-alike. "The linear is subject to interruption. One, two, four. Or to start at four and not one."

"Or three and not one," added the Hosir entity.

Three and not one . . .

Tork almost fainted as he realized what the aliens were suggesting. "No," he whispered. "You *can't* mean that?"

He was standing back in the Hive again, this time in the Masters' chambers. He stared at the conference table as the holographic image of Darane IV was destroyed again and again as he watched.

"Destruction," said the alien-Harl. "It is the final linear event. There is no further linear beyond destruction."

"For us," the alien-Sahna added, "there is no destruction, because we are not linear. For you, the linear is all that you are."

Darane was sucked dry again and again as he watched in horror.

"Is this one or is this three?" asked Hosir's image. "One is a builder, a keeper of linearity. Three is destruction, a beginner-again."

"No," gasped Tork, trying not to accept what they were showing him. "You are wrong. You must be."

He was in the runabout with Sisko and Dax. It couldn't be the real runabout, because there, Dax was not present. Otherwise, he wouldn't have been able to tell the difference.

"We show you only what is in your mind," the alien-Sisko said. "This is not our mistake, if it is a mistake."

"This is what you have been keeping from yourself," added alien-Dax. "This is the logic, the linear, that you have striven to suppress."

Tork felt giddy and sick to his hearts. "It cannot be," he insisted blindly. "This is delusion, not logic."

"The logic is within," Sahna's image told him. "You must be true to yourself. You must be linear. You must follow one, two, three."

"You must face reality," said an alien-Dron. "There *is* image and reality. But you must distinguish them both."

"Reality," added the alien-Sisko, "can hide behind an image. It can disguise itself. But it is linear. The image can be removed."

"The image *must* be removed," the alien-Sahna insisted. "And you must do it. It is important. If you do not do this, then the linear Bajor will be destroyed. It will become no more."

He was back beside the stream in the park. Only the alien-Sahna was with him now. "I am image," she told him. "You know the real. But there are places where you have confused the image with the real. Be linear. Seek the truth. Understand, and then follow what you believe. Is that not the essence of being linear?"

"Yes," he admitted. "It is. If I know the truth and do not follow it, I am denying it. I am hiding it. I am becoming corrupt, as others have before me." He took a deep breath. "It will not be easy."

"We have learned that many things are not easy," the image of Sahna replied. "When we first experienced Sisko, we discovered that there is linearity. Now we can speak of *first* meeting Sisko. Before, we could not. That is linear. It is not easy for us to be linear, but it is possible." She reached out a hand to touch his shell, and it was the touch of his Sahna, his One-to-be. "It is not easy for you to follow the truth," she added.

"It is not easy," he agreed. "But it is possible."

She smiled at him. "You have grasped the truth," she said. "May it illumine you. Now—"

He was back in the runabout. Tork knew this for a certainty. It didn't seem more real than his vision had, but the knowledge was sufficient. He blinked and then looked up from the Orb to Sisko. "I have seen," he said softly.

Sisko closed the doors and the light from the Orb was

extinguished. Tork felt as if a part of him had been dimmed also. "That was quick," he said. "Just a few seconds. Did you get the clarification you desired?"

"No," Tork answered honestly. "But I did receive the clarification that I needed. I now know what I have been hiding from myself. I know the truth."

"And that is . . . ?"

"That my people have been lied to, Captain." It was hard for him to admit this, but he knew that he had no option. He had to hold on to the truth. He had to be linear. "That what we have believed for millennia has been an illusion. That our history is a sham. That we have become murderers through deceit."

CHAPTER
25

"IT'S A BEAUTIFUL sight, isn't it, Nerys?"

Kira turned from the view of the city she had been studying and smiled sadly at Shakaar. "Yes, it is." She bit at her lip uncertainly. "I was just thinking how well we'd done to rebuild so much, considering how little the Cardassians left us."

Shakaar moved to join her at the window. "I was thinking the same thing just a short while ago," he confessed. "We really have done pretty well, haven't we, for all the petty political fighting?"

After a few silent moments, Kira asked, "Do you think it was worth it?"

"Don't you?" Shakaar gave her his old grin. "Nerys, you never doubted that fighting the Cardassians was the right thing. And when Kai Winn and Vedek Bareil made that peace with the Cardassians, you supported it wholeheartedly. Why this disenchantment now?"

"Because in a day or so it might all be gone." Kira gestured at the view. "All that work, and maybe for nothing."

"It wasn't for nothing," Shakaar said firmly. "It was for *us*. For our souls. Rebuilding our world gave us meaning and hope. Even if it is all destroyed by the Hive, it will have been more than worth it. Bajor has been reborn, Nerys." He smiled, sadly. "You know, I actually got out of my office the other day and went to a concert."

"You?" Kira was astonished. "Listening to *music?*"

He laughed. "It does sound odd, doesn't it? But the government's been sponsoring art, and I thought I'd better see where some of that money was being spent. It was a concert by Theron—have you heard of him?"

Kira shook her head.

"Well, he's an up-and-coming composer, I gather. Anyway, I sat through the whole evening, and surprised myself by really enjoying it. If you ask my uneducated opinion, he's every bit as good a composer as Varani is." Shakaar paused, and then added: "If we still have such seeds of greatness, nothing we do is wasted. Even if the world *does* end tomorrow."

After another pause, Kira asked him, "What are our chances?"

"Not good." Shakaar sighed. "We've got ground-based phaser cannons set up, for example. But planet-based fire against something like the Hive will do barely more than a little damage. Thanks to Jaro, we have a couple of small squadrons of fighters, but, again, they'll be little more than irritants. I try to sound confident with the others, but I can't lie to you, Nerys. If the Hive comes, Bajor is doomed."

"There's a cheery thought," muttered Kira. "And it's just the weather for gloom." The storm still raged outside.

"We can only pray that Captain Sisko can avert the disaster," Shakaar said. "It's our only hope."

"If anyone can, he will," Kira said with conviction. Then she snorted. "Listen to me. Who'd have ever thought I'd say something like that? Remember how I used to curse the Federation for refusing to help us out in our war with the Cardassians?"

"I remember a great number of things," Shakaar answered. "You've changed a great deal, Nerys, since we fought together. It's an improvement, too. You're a stronger, better person for it."

Kira smiled. "Thanks. And—" She broke off as her communicator sounded. "Duty calls." She tapped it. "Kira here."

"Dax," came the response. "Can you come to the Council chambers? I think we have something that you'll want to see. Bring Shakaar . . . if he's with you." Did she detect a note of humor there?

"On our way," Kira replied, trading glances with the first minister. They left his office on the run.

"What is happening?" repeated Gavron, as he studied the tactical display. Two more of his ships had collapsed following near-misses by the enemy's torpedo-like weapons. "I'm losing men, and I want to know why!"

Tarvok glanced up from his sensor panel, nervously. "It's still difficult to get any readings," he explained. "But at a guess I'd say that the aliens are using a variation of their earlier weapon."

"Monofilaments?" growled Gavron. "But how?"

"I'd say that the torpedoes are releasing a net of some kind, anchored to the launch device. When our ship moves, it cuts directly through the net, and is destroyed."

Gavron glared at the screens. That did make sense, and it also complicated the fight. "Then we cannot ignore the solo fighters." But if they started trying to shoot down everything, the Hive would be able to escape. "Order Hammer and Anvil wings to target any enemy craft. The rest of the fleet is to follow me. Prepare for an attack run on the Hive. I want all photon torpedoes primed and ready for launch."

"Acknowledged," Tarvok replied, and he began to relay the orders to the rest of the fleet.

Studying his tactical, Gavron saw that he had ninety-three ships left. Hammer and Anvil would be . . . twenty-seven of those. That left him sixty-six attackers. There would undoubtedly be further defenses that the Hive would throw at him, but some of those sixty-six ships should get through to inflict serious damage.

"Science officer," he called.

"Reporting," answered Ladra from her station.

"I assume you have been scanning the target?"

"Of course," she acknowledged.

"I need to know the best possible targets on the Hive to strike," he informed her. "Any weak areas. All the airlocks. The engine nacelles. Anywhere they might be vulnerable to strikes."

She nodded. A schematic came up on a small auxiliary screen in his chair arm. Several points were highlighted in flashing green. "Launch bays," she informed him. "The skin of the Hive is impervious to scanning, but those spots are where the attack ships were launched." Further indicators at the rear of the target lit up. "These appear to be engine emplacements," she explained. "I cannot determine how vulnerable they are, but logic dictates that they are a weak spot." Finally, several areas on the leading edges of the craft's two huge, outspread wings. "Collection points," she said. "The vessel utilizes dust, debris, and gases it collects as fuel. If these are destroyed, then it will not be able to ingest materials."

"Excellent." He turned to Tarvok. "Prepare to relay this information to the cruisers," he ordered. "I will assign targets. On my command, the attack will commence." He worked through the list of strategic points swiftly, assigning his attack ships in teams of five to each sensitive area. Even given defensive fire, some of the ships should get through to strike their targets. He reserved one of the hangar bays for his own craft and escorts. "Targeting details being transmitted," he said, with gruff satisfaction.

The alien ships were still engaging Hammer and Anvil wings. Both sides were taking a severe mauling. Two more enemy ships were swallowed in flares of explosions, and one of his craft disintegrated as it was struck by another monofilament torpedo. There were still thirty-eight of the enemy out there, to twenty of his forces. His men were being decimated, but they would buy him time for this attack.

"Now," he growled. "Signal the advance. Lock on to targets and prime weapons. The attack commences!"

"What are you talking about?" asked Sisko. Tork's diatribe against his own race wasn't making much sense.

"It has all come together in my mind," replied Tork. "It is time that we exited the wormhole. I must return to the Hive with the information that I now understand. I will explain as we travel."

Nodding, Sisko set the controls to reverse their course. The thrusters kicked in, spinning the runabout, and then he engaged the drive. Once again, they sped past the mad whirlpool of color that raged about them. "The entities clarified matters for you?"

"Yes," explained Tork. "They made me face what I suppose I had subconsciously already come to realize. I was blocking myself from accepting the truth, but I can no longer deny it.

— "In my studies of the sacred writings, I had noted that the texts quoted by the Two Hundred and Fourth and Fifth Hive were slightly different from those attributed to the First Hive. I had always assumed that this was due to faulty transmission of the writings because of the revolt of the Two Hundred and Third Hive. In fact, it could not have been, because later Hives referred back correctly to the First Hive writings. I had made an error of assumption that has now become clear.

"The First Hive writings were altered by the Two Hundred and Third Hive. What we believe to be the pure writings are, in fact, corrupted. Hosir must have at least suspected this, because he asked me just before I left how I knew that the Two Hundred and Third Hive's rebellion had failed. I knew it because the records said so.

"But the records have been altered!" He shook his head. "I had simply accepted the histories on faith, without using my intelligence to study them."

"We all do that," Sisko told him. "We accept things without question because we believe them to be correct."

"Perhaps," agreed Tork. "But in this case, the deceit was deadly."

The runabout exited the wormhole in a final blaze of light. The passage constricted behind them, and then vanished. Sisko glanced at Tork.

"Where to?" he asked.

"*Deep Space Nine*," Tork replied. "I must contact the Hive. Captain, could you also recall Sahna and Dax from Bajor? I know we are going to need their aid for what we must now do."

"Of course." Sisko patched into the Bajoran net. A moment later, he was looking at Kira's face. "Major, return to DS9 with Dax and Sahna. I don't care if you have to kidnap her to get her to come along, just do it."

Kira managed a smile. "There's no need to be that extreme," she answered. "Sahna is dying to get back anyway. She and Dax have discovered something very significant, Captain."

"Save it for later," Sisko replied. "I want you moving *now*."

"Understood." The screen went blank.

"What could they have found out?" Sisko mused.

"I have a suspicion that they have discovered much the same information that I have," Tork replied. "Sahna had the data that Hosir gave me before I departed the Hive. It is in a strange code, but I suspect it is the real information that the First Hive wished to pass on to future generations."

"Let's save this until everyone is together," suggested Sisko. "Am I right in thinking that this might be a way to stop the Hive and save Bajor?"

Tork nodded. "Yes, Captain. We may be able to restore the original programming to the Hive. But I do not think that it will be accomplished peacefully. There are too many powerful forces on the enemy side."

"The *enemy* side?" Sisko echoed.

"Yes, Captain." Tork smiled. "For what it is worth, we are definitely allies in your quest to stop the Hive. I pledge to do my utmost to see that Bajor survives."

"Well," Sisko muttered to himself, "it looks like the Prophets came through again."

Bree sighed and then straightened up from her workstation. "That is it," she announced to her colleagues. "I have completed the text of our message, and it is ready to be transmitted to the Hive at large."

"Then do so," a voice called.

"It is not that simple," Bree replied. "Access to the comps has been denied by a security override. Our act of rebellion has alerted Dron and his fellows to our knowledge. He is working to insure that we are isolated, and that we do not cause dissent before Bajor is absorbed."

"Then we must stop him," another said.

"Again, it is not that simple." Bree shook her head. These were intelligent people, but they simply didn't understand the nature of the political beast. "Dron, through Master Raldar, controls the security forces. They, in turn, control what messages reach the Hive. We cannot take on the security forces; we would be in open rebellion. And likely to lose," she added, realistically. "We are not fighters."

"Then you are saying we can do nothing? That Dron will succeed?"

"No," Bree answered. "I am saying that we need a different approach to the problem. We are scientists. There must be a way for us to see around this problem and to overcome it."

One of the younger members of her staff approached. "I have some comp skills," she said, hesitantly. "If access to the comps is coded, I may be able to deduce the coding. If I may try?"

"Of course." Bree moved aside to let the other work. "That is an indication of what I mean. If Dron is being sneaky, then we had better learn how to be sneakier." She looked at them all with affection. "After all, we *are* a lot smarter than they are, are we not?"

Before anyone could respond, there came a heavy blow on the door. "Security!" a voice called. "Open up!"

"No!" one of the astronomers exclaimed, panicking. "We cannot allow them in."

"We cannot keep them out," Bree contradicted him. "They could burn down the door, which will only delay them."

"What do you propose?" he demanded. "That we surrender?"

"No one is suggesting surrender." Bree hobbled across to the door and hit the entry plate. It irised open to reveal a half-dozen males beyond. Each carried a tingler weapon. "Ah, come to harass us, have you?"

The leader moved inside and glared at her. "Master Raldar has asked us to keep you confined and isolated," he replied. "You are acting in a treasonous fashion, and that cannot be allowed to continue."

"Really?" Bree peered at him intently. "I know you. Are you not . . . Dimas?"

"Yes," the officer replied, scowling at her.

"I thought so. I was one of your tutors." She snorted. "I always believed that you were an intelligent pupil. A shame that I was so wrong."

"I am not the one who is wrong," Dimas replied with dignity. "I listen to the voices of the Hivemasters, which you do not."

"Well, then," Bree told him, "did they tell you *why* we object to their voices?"

"We do not need to know that," Dimas replied. "Only that you do not listen."

Bree snorted again. "Oh, well spoken!" she mocked. "I can see that you are using your brains only to keep your ears apart. Next thing, you will be telling me that you are only obeying orders, and it does not matter what those orders are."

"I—" began Dimas, and then he caught himself. "You are attempting to bait me to prevent me from doing my job."

"Yes," Bree agreed, surprising him. "But I ask you also to hear what I have to say. You know me: am I a dangerous or vicious person?"

"No," Dimas said, reluctantly.

"And if you were ordered to kill us all, would you obey without thinking?"

"The Hivemasters would never order that!" protested Dimas. "It is unthinkable."

"They have already killed," Bree informed him. "The blood of thousands of innocents is upon our hands. And if we do nothing, the blood of more will join it."

She could see the struggle that was going on within Dimas. He had been trained by Raldar to obey orders without question. But she had instilled in all of her pupils the need to question everything. Which would win out here?

"What do you mean?" Dimas asked, finally.

"The planet that was absorbed had intelligent beings upon it," Bree explained. "Even now, the Hive is in progress toward another inhabited world. These people will not leave it, so Dron aims to kill them and absorb their world anyway."

"Kill?" echoed Dimas. He looked stunned. "Do you have proof for what you say?"

"Plenty of proof," Bree informed him. She gestured to where the young female worked on the computer. "We are attempting to make it known to the Hive at large. Everyone must know that Dron is making all of us guilty of murder. But we cannot override the security codes."

Dimas strode to the computer and gestured for the woman there to step aside. "I must review this data," he told her. "If what you say is true . . . then I can override the lockout and disseminate the information for you."

Smiling, Bree turned to her scared companion. "You see?" she asked. "I knew that there had to be a way. Dron has seriously underestimated the Hive if he believes he can force us to become killers."

Dron slammed his fist down on the conference table with fury. "Raldar!" he growled. "You idiot! Can nothing you do be trusted?"

Nervously, the Security Master wrung his hands together. "I do not understand," he protested. "What have I done now?"

"The security force that you sent to arrest Bree and the other astronomers," Dron snapped. "It has not done so. Worse, it appears that they have gone over to her side. Someone is systematically removing the security blocks from her computer and allowing her access to the comp networks."

Raldar shook as he studied the information screen. "I do not understand," he moaned.

"That has become abundantly clear," Dron informed him. "This is your last chance. Go to the astronomy section. Take with you only security men you trust implicitly. Stop these traitors *now*. Kill them if you must, but stop them!"

CHAPTER
26

GAVRON WATCHED HIS screens with deep satisfaction. Hammer and Anvil wings were continuing to engage the enemy craft. Both were suffering heavy losses, but inflicting the same. On the main screen, he caught the tail end of a fight, with one Cardassian cruiser raking a Hive ship with concentrated phaser fire. The alien ship attempted to pull free, but the Cardassian pilot was—of course!—superb. He locked on to the other craft no matter how it twisted and turned. Despite its shields, the alien vessel couldn't sustain such damaging fire. A moment later, it was a silent fireball, and the Cardassian ship slipped past it and on to another assault.

"All craft in attack formation," Tarvok reported. There was excitement in his voice. "Preparing to engage . . . now!"

Gavron's pilot moved the flagship into the correct alignment, and then boosted for the Hive. The gunnery officer sat hunched over his controls, eager for the right second to launch his cargo of photon torpedoes. On the tactical screen, Gavron could see his other ships starting their bombing run. He smiled, anticipating the devastation to come.

Laser fire erupted about them as they drew closer to the Hive.

"Automatic fire," Ladra reported from her science station. "Computer controlled, most likely. Shields holding."

"Is it enough to damage any of our ships?" asked Gavron.

"Yes," confirmed Ladra. "But it would take several direct hits. The faster we make this run, the better."

"Understood." Gavron ignored the threat. Computer-controlled fire was notoriously unreliable in combat situations. He could afford a few losses.

One went down even as he thought this. There was a brief explosion on the screen, and then further raking fire from the waiting Hive.

"Steady," he growled, but the pilot didn't really need encouragement. He seemed more eager for the attack than worried about being hit. Morale was high, that was certain.

The forerunners of the attack formation were now drawing close to the Hive. Laser fire burned through space at the ships, missing more often than it scored. But another Cardassian ship erupted into a flower of flame, and then a third.

"First torpedoes away," Ladra announced.

Gavron saw the sparks of fire from his lead ships, which almost instantly began to peel away from the Hive to avoid being caught in the backlash. He grinned as he waited to see the impact.

Fire exploded in several places at once, scattering debris and smoke into the stars, to vanish almost instantly.

"Sixteen hits," Ladra reported. "Minor damage to two of the airlocks. Their shields are still holding for the most part."

Was that all? Gavron hunched down further, scowling at the image on the screen as his flagship came ready for its own run.

"Take us low," he ordered the pilot. And then, to the gunnery officer: "Fire all possible torpedoes as we pass."

The screen was now filled with the smooth metallic

surface of the Hive as they whipped across its surface. Tactical showed their target as drawing closer and closer. He gripped the arms of his seat, eager for the kill.

"Torpedoes away," the gunnery officer reported.

"Take us out of here," Gavron snapped. "Screen to reverse view."

As they pulled away from the Hive, the view switched to show the airlock they had aimed at. Further laser strikes splattered harmlessly off their shields. Gavron ignored them, concentrating on the target zone.

Vast explosions ripped through the area, twisting the smooth skin of the Hive into jagged teeth biting at empty space. Gases, smoke, and flames vented into the vacuum.

"Bring us around for another sweep. All vessels, commence second run," ordered Gavron.

Pakat felt the second Hive shudder. He looked at his screens. There hadn't been time to appoint a new Security Master, so he was commanding the defense squadrons. They had deployed their monofilament nets as ordered, and had now taken out almost half of the attacking force. But some of the enemy were getting through, and the Hive was suffering damage.

Warning lights flickered around airlock seven. A picture on the screen showed that it had been hit, and was venting gas and materials into space. The damage-control teams sealed the section, but there was now a gap in the skin of the Hive. The enemy was bound to make use of this weakness.

These Cardassians were definitely stronger than either he or Dron had anticipated, and they attacked with a ferociousness he had never imagined. Still, there were ways to turn that aggression against them. They were bound to target the damaged area, so Pakat smiled to himself.

They would not get the swift victory they were obviously anticipating.

He tapped the comp before him. Master Premon's face filled the screen. "It is time," he said. "Prepare."

"Understood." The screen went blank.

Pakat studied the images in the holographic display above

the table. It showed the alien vessels regrouping for a second assault. Their diversionary craft had been almost completely destroyed, and there were still sixteen of his forces left. These immediately began to single out targets among the remaining Cardassian vessels, and moved to intercept. The alien commander would most likely have some of his forces break off to engage the Hive ships, but the rest were bound to repeat their bombing run, with airlock seven being the main target.

He smiled. The Hive would be ready for them. . . .

"Prepare the *Defiant* for immediate launch," Sisko ordered as he reached Ops with Tork. He glanced around. "Chief," he snapped, spotting O'Brien. "How is she?"

"Everything's back to optimum," O'Brien reported with a grin.

"We may need everything she's got," Sisko informed him. "We launch as soon as Kira and Dax arrive." As O'Brien hurried off to the *Defiant*, Sisko turned to Lieutenant Soyka. "How long until they arrive?"

"Less than five minutes, Captain," Soyka reported. "They've just requested docking assignment."

"Good. Tell them to head for the *Defiant* as soon as they arrive. We'll launch as soon as they reach it, so get the clearances ready now."

"You've got it, Captain," Soyka replied. "And—good luck."

"Thanks." Sisko turned to Tork. "Right, let's go. Even if we do have a plan by the time we reach the Hive, we won't have long to implement it."

"I understand." Tork scuttled to keep up with him as they reached the turbolift. "I do have one or two thoughts as to how to proceed, but I feel that discussion should be put off until the others are with us."

"I quite agree." Sisko stepped out of the lift, and almost into Quark's face.

"Captain," the Ferengi began, "I really must protest—"

"Not now, Quark," growled Sisko, irritated. "There are more important things to worry about than your profits."

"Bite your tongue!" exclaimed Quark, horrified. "It's just that—"

"Save it," Sisko snarled, pushing past him.

Quark watched Sisko and the weird-looking alien leave. It looked as if Sisko had a plan. . . .

Hurrying back into his bar, he grinned at the few dozen patrons there. "I'm giving ten-to-one odds on Sisko being able to stop the Hive," he announced. "Any takers?"

There were indeed. . . .

"We can expect trouble now," Dimas announced, as he stepped back from the control panel. "Raldar is bound to know that I have overridden his orders. It is only a matter of time until they respond."

"I imagine so," agreed Bree. "But what form will it take, do you think?"

Dimas's snout wrinkled. "Knowing Dron, I would expect an assault on the rooms here. He will first of all wish to silence us."

"Pointless." Bree gestured to the computer. "The information is already being spread. Containment is no longer a viable option."

Dimas managed a smile. "You think logically; Dron is apt to be more emotional about this."

"I suppose he is." She shrugged. "So, you're the security expert. What is our best option?"

Dimas had obviously considered this. "If we wait here, they'll attack. On the other hand, I do not believe that most of your fellow astronomers would be capable of defense. I suggest that we leave here those who might be better off if they surrendered."

Bree nodded. "And the rest of us?"

He grinned again. "I think that attack is the best form of defense—don't you? While Raldar comes looking for us, we might be better off if we incapacitated them."

"What, all dozen of us?"

"The odds are irrelevant," Dimas replied. "We just have to know where to strike. At the moment, our best option is to take out the guidance controls. If we stall Dron's forces, by the time that they engage us, the information we've set loose will be disseminated to all levels of the Hive. And if we are the only ones who rebel against the Hivemasters, I shall be greatly surprised."

Bree gave him a delighted smile. "Dimas, you obviously learned a great deal as a youth."

"I had good tutors," he replied. "Now, shall we make our selection as to who will accompany us?"

The Cardassian fleet swooped toward the Hive again. Gavron detailed another fifteen of his cruisers to intercept the enemy's remaining defenders. Then he ignored the side fight, concentrating his attention on their looming target. He had thirty-nine ships remaining, including his flagship, and they were all still in full fighting mode.

"Target the two damaged areas," he ordered Ladra. "Concentrate main fire on the ruptured skin we struck last time. We will widen that gap and break the alien craft in two—they'll have no hope of regenerating it this time!" He turned to the gunnery officer. "Prepare maximum barrage. I want every torpedo you can manage rammed into that gap."

"Acknowledged!" exclaimed the officer happily. He was just as eager for this kill as Gavron was.

"Begin the next assault," Gavron ordered, and Tarvok relayed his command to the other ships of the battered fleet. Gavron smiled happily. The battle was hard-fought, but it was being won. This next bombing run would lay open the Hive. A third run would most likely be needed to finish it off, but that would be all.

It would be a glorious victory! One that would sweep him back to the fore in the military again, one that would bring him the power that he deserved. Those who had conspired against him in the past wouldn't dare to do so once he was the undisputed savior of Cardassia Prime!

All about him, his troops moved with calm efficiency. Every one of them could sense their impending victory and almost taste it. They were all proud to be a part of this glorious hour.

Then the run began. The remaining ships closed about

him as they spun down toward the Hive and back into the barrage of laser fire.

Which immediately stopped.

Gavron frowned, puzzled. What was going on? The enemy couldn't have run out of energy for their weapons yet, surely? Why the sudden shutoff, then? A nagging fear tapped at the rear of his mind. The aliens were up to something. . . .

"The Hive is changing configuration," Ladra reported. "I am reading strange movements."

"On screen!" Gavron barked.

As they drew closer to the Hive, the flattened shape of the wings was starting to alter. They were beginning to curve upward, as if the ship were trying to gather the attacking vessels to itself.

What was going on? The reason for the cessation of laser fire was now obvious—the cannons would have simply hit each other and the Hive in this formation. Did this mean that the Hive had some other weapon that they had not anticipated? If so, what could it be?

"I'm picking up an energy buildup," Ladra reported. They had already passed between the upspread wings, and were passing over the main body of the Hive now. Ahead of them, tantalizing, was the open maw of the airlock they had destroyed on their last run.

Disturbed and confused, Gavron snapped, "Pull out! Get us out of here as fast as possible! Order all vessels to take evasive maneuvers."

The pilot responded instantly, whipping the nose of the flagship up and outward, toward open space. Tarvok started to relay his orders to the rest of the fleet. It would be moments before they could follow Gavron's lead.

Moments they did not have.

The energy discharged across the space enclosed by the folded wings. It was that same, awesome force that had ripped apart Darane IV. The vast energies seethed as they burned, ripping apart the Cardassian attackers in blue fire, rending them into shards and then absorbing the metals and components.

The outer edge of the destructive wave scrawled across the wing of Gavron's vessel. The flagship groaned and shook as the wing was ripped apart and annihilated. Then they were free, spinning uncontrollably away from the Hive.

Behind them, rapidly vanishing clouds of metallic gas were all that was left of the Cardassian fleet.

CHAPTER
27

As soon as the *Defiant* was on course for the Darane system, Sisko convened a meeting in his ready room. Both Tork and Sahna were there, along with Dax and Kira. "I think it's time we compared notes," Sisko said. "Tork, why don't you explain what you've discovered?"

"It is frighteningly simple," Tork said sadly. "According to our official histories, the First Hive built the Hive and conceived the Great Design. That much is certainly true. Later, the Two Hundred and Third Hive rebelled, wanting to change the purpose of the Great Design. They were defeated, and the true way was restored. And that is certainly a lie, which has been deliberately promulgated down the millennia.

"In fact, the revolution succeeded. The rebels gained control of the Hive from the true Hivemasters. The problem was that they knew they could never win over the entire population of the Hive to their views. Instead, they made it appear that they had lost the fight, and their views had been suppressed. In truth, they changed the Great Design, but slowly, over the course of several generations. Their succes-

251

sors carried on their changes gently, so that it would not be noticed. Since the Great Design wasn't to be implemented for hundreds of generations, they had plenty of time to do this.

"The *real* Great Design stipulated that the Hive would cross intergalactic space and then seek out a world in the closest star system that they could. The important matter here was that it was to be an uninhabited planet. I am not certain what was to happen then, but it was to be a peaceful termination to the voyage. The Two Hundred and Third Hive changed that plan. They saw that the survival of the Hive was the highest priority, and they believed that the Great Design was wrong. They preferred the concept of continuing the Hive as it was, and duplicating it, to insure a greater chance of survival. They felt that re-creating the great journey was the best way to insure survival of our species. They altered records and programming of the computers to make it look as if their plan were still the original Great Design. I am now convinced of this, and I believe that we must confront the Grand Master and expose the truth. Once the Hive knows the facts, they will not allow him to proceed with the destruction of Bajor."

"I think you're being naive, Tork," Kira informed him. "Dron is in power, and things are going his way. He's not going to simply surrender because you have truth and logic on your side."

"We are not a violent people," Tork explained. "Once the truth is known, Dron will be powerless."

"There is more than you do not yet know," Sahna informed him. "Dax and I have been studying the data that Hosir gave you. We believe that it is the original coding for the Great Design."

"Really?" Tork was astonished, and then thrilled. "You have been able to translate it?"

"Some of it," Dax said. "The bulk of it consists of command codes that I can't fathom. Presumably they relate to the Hive operations. But the rest . . ." She looked at Sahna.

"What you have surmised is correct," Sahna agreed. "The

Great Design was indeed forcibly altered. The original plan called for the location of an uninhabited planet. When the Hive reached one that was capable of sustaining life but was barren, then this program was to be triggered."

"I see." Tork's snout wrinkled as he concentrated. "But what does the program *do?*"

"I cannot be sure." Sahna sighed. "Perhaps in the context of the Hive's computers I could tell you, but now I cannot. I only know that this was the original Great Design, and the one that we should try to restore."

Dax called up a schematic on the screen of the Darane system. "Here's Darane Four," she said, pointing. "The two Hives that were in orbit there have begun to move. One has headed into Cardassian space, and is currently being attacked by the Cardassian Third Fleet. The other started to move toward Bajor, but has for some reason paused. It is quite close in spatial terms to Darane Three. That is a decent-sized planet capable of sustaining life, but is barren. It's almost exactly what the First Hive notes specify for a target world."

Tork nodded. "Then if we move the Hive closer to it, we could still implement whatever the original Great Design was."

"I don't see why not," Dax replied. "Except, of course, for the small matter of the Hivemasters. I doubt Dron and his fellows will go for this."

"Then we shall convince them," Tork replied. He grasped Sahna's hand. "We have worked together to create a solution," he said happily. "The Great Design will be restored, and there will be no need to absorb Bajor or any other world."

"I am pleased, beloved," Sahna replied.

Sisko coughed. "I hate to rain on your parade, but there's still the minor matter of getting to the Hive's computers to run the program."

"Of course." Tork was all business again. "Is it possible to communicate with the Hive from this distance?"

"If they want to talk," Sisko informed him. "I'll try and patch through a call." He shook his head. "I hope that logic wins through, but I strongly doubt that Dron or whoever's in charge now is going to simply hand over power like that."

"What else can he do?" asked Tork simply.

Kira snorted. "Believe me, despots *always* have alternatives."

Gavron stared at his tactical display in shock and revulsion. It told him that he had exactly three craft remaining beside the *Charak*. Not even enough to wage a battle, much less win a war. His hopes and dreams had evaporated just as surely as his fleet had under the barrage from the Hive.

"Gone," he muttered, clearing the screen. The fact that all of the Hive's defenders were destroyed didn't matter much now. He glared at the terrible sight on his main screen. The Hive hung there, its destructive energy bolts invisible for the moment. But they would return if he attempted another assault on the Hive. There was no way to cross the surface of the vessel without being annihilated.

There was the other side of the Hive, true. That couldn't be guarded by the devastating bolts. It still had laser cannons, though, and probably more defending ships readying themselves for launch even now. And there was no weak spot such as the breached airlock that the Cardassians could pour their fire into.

"Orders, Gul?" asked Tarvok quietly.

Yes, orders. He couldn't sit here brooding, sighing over the loss. This Hive was still heading for Cardassia Prime. There was still the Home Fleet, of course, but there was no guarantee that it would fare any better then he had. He had to assume that he was the last line of defense for Cardassia Prime. There was no honor of a glorious victory left to him now, but at least there was a chance to stave off shame and dishonor.

He swung about to face Ladra. "Their engine nacelles," he said, slowly and carefully. "Did they suffer any damage?"

She studied her board. "One minor rupture," she announced. "There is a small breach of the hull in that area."

"Their engines are stable?"

"Yes."

Gavron considered this news for a moment. "Then we shall have to destabilize them," he decided. He turned back to Tarvok. "Signal the remaining ships. We attack again. The target for us all is the weakened area of the engines. We shall pass along the top surface of the Hive to avoid their energy weapon. Expect heavy fire, and ready all remaining photon torpedoes."

"Acknowledged." Tarvok turned to his panel to relay the orders.

"Gunnery officer," Gavron demanded. "How many torpedoes do we have left?"

"Twenty-four," the officer replied. "I can bring them all on-line for a single sweep if you desire."

"Do it," Gavron ordered. "Target them as soon as you are able. We may be hit on the way in, and I want to be certain that we fire."

"Understood."

Gavron studied his board. The damaged wing wouldn't really cause a problem. No vital areas had been destroyed, and propulsion was unaffected. One of the cannons was gone, but that mattered little at the moment. They could attack, at least—assuming these damned aliens didn't have any further surprises in store.

"Course laid in," the pilot called. "Ready on command."

"The command is given," Gavron snarled. "All ships to attack."

Once again, the *Charak* swung about and headed for the Hive. The final three cruisers with them fell in alongside, their own weapons primed and ready. This would probably be the final assault. If this failed, there was nothing much left.

The Hive drew closer again as they swooped toward the upper surface. As Gavron had expected, the laser cannons started firing.

"Shields holding," Tarvok called, as the ship shook from a direct hit. The ship was hit a second time, and he cried: "Down to ninety-five percent."

Laser fire streaked from the surface below at the four

ships as they made their run. The screen lit up, and they were down to three. Gavron stared intently at the screen, willing their target to appear, willing the *Charak* to greater speed. His fingers clutched the chair arm, and he could hear it creak under the pressure.

"Coming up on target," Ladra announced. "Range closing."

"Torpedoes ready," the gunnery officer called.

"Steady, steady," muttered Gavron. Another wash of laser energy crashed against their shields.

"Down to eighty-percent shields," Tarvok reported. "And falling."

There was no time to worry about that. All that mattered now was the target. Gavron ignored his own fear. They would succeed. They had to.

Another flare of light on the screen announced the destruction of one of his final two companions. He cursed the loss of firepower more than the loss of men.

"Target locked," Ladra called, and then the gunnery officer yelled, "Torpedoes away!"

Laser fire continued to rake them as they pulled away from the Hive, climbing and spinning to get a better view of what was to come.

"The other ship has launched its torpedoes," Ladra called. "Tracking them in." As she spoke, there was another burst of flame, and their final companion was gone.

But not before they had launched their attack!

Gavron stared intently at the main screen, which was focused in on the engine section of the Hive. There were a dozen huge nacelles, all active, as the Hive moved through space. He could barely make out the target area, a small rough spot on the smooth surface of the Hive.

"Impact in . . . three . . ." called Ladra, "two . . . one . . ."

Thirty-some torpedoes impacted in the same small area of the Hive. The screens overloaded as the blasts went off simultaneously. Ladra was still scanning, and called, "Direct hit!"

As the light died down and the blast dissipated into space,

Gavron could make out the Hive. It was still there, but there was now a gaping hole where there had only been a minor nick before. Fire and explosions raged in the hundred-mile-long gap, gouts of gas and materials spewed into space.

"Readings?" he called.

"The enemy is crippled," Ladra reported. "Two of the nacelles are completely destroyed. Three more are malfunctioning. Their main drive appears to be in serious trouble. I judge that they are attempting to shut it down."

"No!" Gavron snarled. "That cannot be allowed. If we can get their engine destabilized, it will wreck the Hive and save Cardassia. We *must* make another attack."

"Gul," the gunnery officer said quietly. "We have no torpedoes left. Phaser fire alone will be insufficient."

"I know." Gavron clambered to his feet. "We have only one weapon left." He didn't need to spell it out to them. Ladra and Tarvok merely nodded their understanding. "Bring us about," he ordered the pilot. "Lock on to the engine area and take us in at maximum speed." He turned to Ladra. "Prepare to flood the antimatter core."

"Acknowledged."

Gavron was pleased. There was no whining, no questioning. He had good troops. They would obey his commands, right to the last second of their existence.

Which wouldn't be very long now.

"Report!" yelled Pakat at the screen. Premon's shocked face stared back at him. "What damage has been done?"

Premon shook his head. "It is horrible," he replied. "People are dying down here. Two of the engines are gone. Three are going. We have to shut down the drive to prevent detonation. We are in dire trouble."

How could this have happened? Those damned Cardassians! "Agreed," Pakat said roughly. He tapped in further commands. "Pakat to launch bays. Is the next flight not yet ready for launch?"

"Momentarily," the leader answered. "We are almost prepared."

"Then *hurry!*" Pakat yelled. This was getting far too

dangerous now. He had never imagined that these Cardassians would be so relentless or so resourceful. He stared around his command center, furious and terrified. They had to stave off further trouble, though there was only one Cardassian ship left.

Several screens showed the devastated area. Huge gouges had been sliced from the Hive and vented into space. The number of dead and wounded was beyond calculation at the moment. The affected sections had been sealed off, but there was panic throughout the Hive. And now they would have to stop their flight to repair their engines.

The Great Design was severely compromised. Worse, the Hive was in serious danger. If they had to wait too long, then it would give the enemy time to prepare further forces.

"The final warship is returning," one of his technicians called.

Pakat stared at the display. He couldn't look directly out into space, of course, so he was forced to rely on the computer simulation. "Shoot them down!" he screamed. "Stop them!"

The laser cannons began their fire again.

Gavron stared in satisfaction at the Hive as they headed toward it. With their engines shut down, there was less danger of getting caught in its exhausts. They were coming at the Hive low, aiming to hug the vessel until they reached the gap they had created. And then . . .

Tarvok smiled at him. "It is a good day to die," he said, quoting the Klingon proverb.

"It is as long as we take them with us," Gavron answered. He smiled back. "You're a good officer, Tarvok."

"Does that mean I get a battlefield promotion?" he asked, grinning.

"Ask me when this is over." Gavron watched the Hive draw closer. "Ladra?"

"Ready on your command," she said simply.

"Mark," he told her. "Fifteen . . . fourteen . . ."

It *was* a good day to die.

* * *

The *Charak* hugged the shell of the Hive closely. Laser fire splashed across its shields, but the Cardassians paid it no mind. The shields were failing, but there was still time. Arrow-straight, it plunged toward the maw of the hole they had blown earlier.

Two seconds before impact, Ladra released the antimatter core.

One second before impact, the antimatter and matter cores flowed together.

Impact.

In the raging firestorm of the matter-antimatter mutual annihilation, the Hive was seized in the grip of forces it had never been designed to withstand. The engine room was vaporized, along with the rear third of the Hive. Those killed didn't even know they had been hit.

The shock wave tore into the remaining portions of the vessel. Stresses ripped the levels and decks apart. The shock tore everything that remained to pieces.

Twelve seconds after the *Charak* annihilated itself, the Hive blossomed briefly into a tremendous explosion that tore it completely apart.

CHAPTER
28

THE BRIDGE OF the *Defiant* was once again filled with people, all with a mixture of desperation and hope in their eyes. Sisko's glance took in the crew: Kira, preparing the weapons, which would most likely be needed; Odo, hunched over his panels, scanning and rescanning their path; Dax, concentrating on piloting the ship toward the ever-closer Hive; O'Brien, fiddling as ever with his equipment—nothing ever seemed to work *quite* up to the chief's expectations. Only Dr. Bashir was missing from the regular crew; Sisko had judged the doctor's treatment of refugees back on *Deep Space Nine* more important. One of his medics was filling in for him on the *Defiant*.

Standing beside his command chair were Tork and Sahna. Both looked just as tense as the *Defiant*'s crew. It couldn't be easy for them, Sisko knew, to have faced the reversal of so much that they had always believed in. But now they were totally committed to saving Bajor. It looked as if Yarka had been absolutely correct: two *had* converted.

He could only pray it would be sufficient.

"Anything?" he called to Odo.

The shapeshifter glanced up. "Plenty," he growled. "One Hive is now stationary in the Darane system for some reason. The other is—" He broke off and grunted. It was impossible for Odo to look paler than he did, but Sisko could almost swear he managed that miracle. "The other Hive is *gone.*"

"Gone?" Sisko echoed. Everyone turned to stare at Odo, who fidgeted uncomfortably under the group stare.

"I'm reading an immense amount of radiation," he reported. "And a growing cloud of debris and plasma. If I were to take a rough guess, I'd say that the Cardassians managed to destroy the Hive that was aimed for Cardassia Prime. They also seem to have been destroyed themselves. I'm reading nothing but radiation and a spreading cloud of plasma and dust."

Sisko turned to Tork and Sahna, who were both stunned. "I'm sorry," he said gently. "You must have had friends and relatives on that Hive."

"It is only fitting," Tork said, choking. "We destroyed Darane. It is only right that we suffer." He looked distraught, however. "So many, gone."

"We *must* prevent the same fate befalling the remaining Hive," Sahna said firmly. She was fighting back the pain she obviously felt. "If one can fall, then both can."

"Agreed," Sisko concurred. He glanced over at Kira. "Any luck in raising the Hive?"

"They're receiving us," Kira responded. "They're just not answering our hail, for whatever reason."

Sisko rubbed his chin. "They may have seen what happened to their sister Hive. Tell them they'll be next if they don't listen to us."

"Worth a try," muttered Kira, bending to her task. A moment later, she announced, "Grand Master Dron coming through." She patched it onto the main screen.

Dron's face scowled out at them. Sisko could see from the pain on it that he knew about the other Hive. "Sisko," the Grand Master growled. "What do you want?"

"It's not what I want," Sisko replied. He gestured at Tork

and Sahna. "It's what your own people want. Call off this attack on Bajor while there's still time."

Dron grimaced. "Bajor *must* be absorbed, now more than ever." He glanced away from the screen and then back. "You must have seen that the other Hive has been . . . destroyed by a suicide attack. Only we remain to implement the Great Design. Despite any setbacks, it will proceed."

"This is insanity, Dron," Tork said angrily. "It is not the Bajorans who are insane: it is you. Call off the plan, now. It is not the true Great Design."

Dron simply shrugged. "So, you have discovered the truth?" he asked. "It does not matter. I assume that the late Hosir betrayed the secret?"

"Partially," Tork admitted. "But there were many clues to give it away." Then he started, as the meaning of Dron's words sank in. "You *knew* the Great Design had been changed?"

"Of course I did, you idiot," Dron snapped. "All Grand Masters since the Two Hundred and Third Hive have known that. So have many of the Hivemasters. The original Great Design was changed because it was unrealistic and unworkable. The rebels saw that, due to our agoraphobia, the original Great Design was impossible. The new one is our only hope for survival."

"By theft and murder?" Tork was appalled. "How could you condone this, and support it? You were chosen because you were supposed to be the best. The sanctity of the Great Design was your responsibility. The welfare of the Hive was your first concern."

Dron's snout wrinkled in amusement. "Do not be so naive, Tork!" he sneered. "Surely, if you know so much, then you should know it all. The Determination is just as bogus as the Great Design. The comps merely fasten their decision on what they feel you want the most. It is no more infallible than any. I reached my position because I desired it, and worked for it, not because it was fated for me."

Tork was reeling under this additional betrayal. "All of it?" he gasped. "It has *all* been a lie?"

"Near enough," agreed Dron. "I am too weary to debate

with you on this matter now. Captain," he said, turning his attention back to Sisko, "I admit that I am surprised that you actually returned Tork and Sahna instead of holding them hostage, but I thank you. You may deposit them and then leave. You are no longer welcome here."

Sisko grinned. "I always keep my word, Dron," he replied. "I told you they'd be returned safe and sound, and they are. But I'm not leaving."

"If you do not, you will be destroyed," Dron informed him.

"They're launching attack ships," Odo called out. "I count ten of them."

"Red alert," Sisko said calmly. "Raise shields. Weapons to full strength."

"Dron!" Tork called. "This is insanity! There is no reason to attack this vessel. It means you no harm."

"Idiot," muttered Dron. He moved to cut off the communication.

"Wait!" cried Tork, frantically. "You must restore the original program and complete the real Great Design."

"Never," said Dron with finality, and the screen reverted to stars.

"Well," said Kira brightly, "that could have gone better."

Sisko turned to face Tork and Sahna. "Now what will you do?" he asked gently. "Dron knew the truth all along, and has no intention of allowing it."

Tork thought for a moment. Sahna rubbed his shell supportively. "I will follow where you lead," she said simply.

Tork nodded. "Captain, this transporter of yours. Could you use it to put us aboard the Hive?"

"Not with our shields up," Sisko answered. "And not through the Hive's shields, either. We need to get inside them."

"I understand."

"We can't drop our shields while we're being attacked," Kira pointed out. "We'd be sitting ducks if we did."

"Do not worry," Tork informed her. "There is an option." He crossed to her panel, and studied the screens. "The ten attack ships will close in shortly. We must deactivate them."

"Right!" agreed Kira, sarcastically. "And how do we do that?"

"I am a Hivemaster," Tork informed her simply. "I have all security clearances." He started to tap commands into the communication panel. "We shall simply transmit a signal that will shut down their weapons and propulsion."

A wide grin split Kira's face. "You're my kind of guy, Tork," she enthused. "Go to it."

Sahna turned to Sisko. "If we can get aboard the Hive," she said, "the propulsion unit is controlled from a command deck near the Council quarters. Would it be possible to transport into that?"

"I'd need coordinates," Sisko replied. "Chief, do you have the ones for the Council chambers?"

"Aye, Captain." O'Brien smiled. "And if Sahna knows how far away the control deck is, I can juggle the figures a bit and try to get them closer."

"Excellent." Sisko nodded to Sahna, who scuttled over to O'Brien's station.

The main screen showed the remaining Hive, growing as they approached it. Sisko couldn't see the ten interceptors, but the sensors were tracking them. He hoped that Tork could get the commands ready before it was necessary to fire on the enemy. It was getting harder and harder to think of the Hive dwellers as the enemy now. It was clear that only the Hivemasters had really been in control of what had happened at Darane. The bulk of the population of the Hive was oblivious to what had been done.

"Closing," Dax murmured.

"I'm reading the attack ships," Odo growled. "They're powering up their weapons."

Sisko glanced across to Kira and Tork. They were both crouched over her panel with intense expressions on their faces. They glanced at one another, and then Kira slapped her hand down on the controls.

"The vessels are losing power," Odo reported. "Their weapons systems are also standing down."

"Good work," Sisko said. That was one less problem to worry about.

"Incoming call from the Hive," Kira reported. "You want to acknowledge it or ignore it, Captain?"

"Put it on the main screen," Sisko decided. "Perhaps Dron wants to talk."

The Grand Master's face filled the screen again. "You have betrayed the Hive!" he screamed, focusing on Tork.

"No," Tork answered calmly. "*You* have. Restore the original programming now."

"No," Dron hissed. "You do not understand what it will mean. Whatever you do, you cannot succeed."

"We can and we will," insisted Tork. "You must cease this futile struggle now."

The screen went dead.

"I think we can take that as a no," observed Odo.

"What did he mean?" asked Sahna, worried. "He said that we do not know what we are doing."

"He's bluffing," guessed Kira. "He's just trying to get you to stop."

"Perhaps," agreed Tork. "In any event, it does not matter. We shall go through with our plan. It is the only way to save my people from the lies, and to save Bajor from destruction. We have no other options. We must trust that the First Hive knew better than Dron thinks they did."

"Approaching the Hive," Dax called. "Their shields are up."

"I'm reading an energy buildup," Odo added. "It looks as if there's some weaponry being trained at us."

"Laser defenses," Tork answered briefly. "My next command will override both them and the airlock controls. Once we are inside the Hive, the transporter should function." He tapped in a command.

"They're bound to be trying to change the codes," Sisko observed. "Let's hope they can't do it quickly enough to stop us."

"Shields dropping," Dax confirmed. On the screen, they could see a gap appearing as the airlock Tork had targeted began to open. "Taking us in." She flipped the *Defiant* through a roll, and into the capacious airlock. Thrusters brought them to a momentary rest, hovering, as the outer lock closed and the inner one cycled open. As soon as she had the room, Dax boosted the *Defiant* through the gap and into the Hive proper.

This was the first sight of the interior of the Hive from most of the crew. There were several gasps of surprise and delight and an admiring "Lovely technology!" from O'Brien. Dax concentrated on piloting the *Defiant* down the main axis of the Hive. Thankfully, most of the smaller air traffic had been cleared.

"The away team had better get down to the transporter room," Sisko said. "Tork: you, Sahna, Dax, Odo, and Kira. O'Brien, scan the target zone again. We don't want them materializing inside a wall." He took over the pilot's seat as Dax relinquished it. "I've always wanted to fly this thing," he told her with a grin.

"Don't damage it, Benjamin," Dax answered, winking. "It's our only ride home."

"I'll be careful."

As the away team left the bridge on a run, Sisko concentrated on taking them as close to the transport zone as he could.

O'Brien cursed, and glanced up from his panel. "Captain, I'm reading energy discharges close to the target zone. It looks like there's some kind of a fight going on down there."

"Well, that might explain why the Hive is stalled in space," Sisko replied. "You'd better put the away team down outside the region, and warn them to have their phasers ready. We may have come in on the start of a civil war."

As soon as she materialized, Kira had her phaser in hand, scanning the corridor in which she found herself with the rest of the team. Odo was beside her, his own weapon at the alert. Dax scanned with her tricorder. "Seven Hive dwellers ahead," she announced. "They seem to be assaulting the control deck."

"We should join them," Tork said, eagerly. "Perhaps they are trying to stop Dron themselves."

"Maybe," growled Odo. "Maybe not. Let us go first. You and Sahna follow behind. We're more used to this sort of thing than you are." He led the way down the corridor, as Kira kept up with him.

They emerged into a plaza that fronted on the control deck. Shutters were over the windows, and the seven aliens Dax had detected were staying behind barricades, firing at the shuttered area.

"An assault," muttered Odo. "But which side?"

Tork glanced over his shoulder. "That's Master Raldar," he exclaimed. "And six of his men. They're definitely on Dron's side."

"Then we take them out," Kira announced. "Whoever they're after must be on our side." She stood up and fired two sharp blasts from her phaser. Odo and Dax joined in. The six security men collapsed, without even knowing what had hit them.

"Did you kill them?" asked Sahna, anxiously.

"Stunned," Kira replied tersely. Raldar himself had escaped the first barrage, and, alerted by the phaser sound, dropped into cover. "Damn." She fired again, but succeeded in only hitting the barrier Raldar was behind.

"We'll not get past him easily," Dax commented. "He's in a good position, and he probably called for backup."

"But he's not prepared for me," Odo commented. He tossed his phaser to Kira. "I'll be back."

Then he melted into a puddle.

Sahna gasped, and jumped back. "What . . . ?"

"He's a shapeshifter," Kira explained. "Let's hope that Raldar has the same reaction." She grinned and watched from cover as Odo flowed across the metal floor toward the barricade. Raldar popped up briefly to fire his gun at them. It created some form of electrical discharge that singed the wall beside Kira. She ducked back, then fired again as Raldar vanished.

Peering out, she saw that the Odo puddle had vanished. Then, rising behind the barrier, she saw Odo re-form. There was a squeal from Raldar, and then silence.

"All clear," called Odo. "He won't be bothering us for a while."

Kira led the charge toward the barrier, as Odo pulled Raldar out of the way. "Now what?" she asked, flopping down beside him.

"We'd better contact whoever is inside," Dax suggested, as she, Tork, and Sahna reached them. "We have to get in there, and I don't really want to go in phasers blazing. We might damage the computers."

Kira nodded, and then called, "Hey in there! This is Major Kira. We're here to help. We have Tork and Sahna with us!"

After a moment, a voice called out, "Prove it!"

Standing, Tork replied, "I am here. We are safe and with friends. We must gain entry to the control deck."

There was another brief pause, and then the main door cracked open. "Come on," the voice called out. "Quickly. Security reinforcements are on their way."

Tork led the sprint for the half-open door. As soon as the small party was inside, the door was closed and barred and equipment was pushed back against it. Kira was astonished to see that the person who had let them in also wore the security badge affixed to his shell. "What's going on?" she demanded.

"Over here," called a slightly cracking female voice from the computer banks.

Sahna gave a delighted laugh. "Bree! What are you doing here?"

"Leading a revolt," Bree answered gleefully. "Dron is furious, of course, but the truth is getting out about the murders on Darane. It is causing tremendous unrest."

"If you think *that* caused trouble," Kira told her, "wait till you hear what else Tork and Sahna have discovered."

While Sahna and Tork filled their colleagues in on their discovery, Kira contacted the *Defiant*. "We're in the control room," she reported. "It's being held by friends of Sahna's, so it looks good for now. How are things up there?"

"Fine," came back Sisko's reply. "They're taking a few halfhearted potshots at us, but it's nothing we can't handle."

Kira returned her attention to Tork, who had finished his explanations. "Hosir left this data for us," he explained. "It will set in motion the real Great Design. It does not call for the destruction of any inhabited worlds. But we do not know what it will do instead."

"Then why are we standing around talking?" demanded Bree. "Feed it to the computers, and let's see what happens." She led the way to the main navigational panel. "Tirhe, start up the engines again," she ordered. "We must head for the closest desolate world."

As Tork started to download the information from his comp, the communicator chimed on the panel. Dimas checked the call, and looked up frowning. "It is Dron," he reported.

"Accept," said Tork, passing the comp to Sahna. "Continue," he told her. "I must try again to convince Dron." She nodded and went on with the data transfer. Tork stood before the screen. "What do you want?" he asked.

Kira saw that there was shrubbery behind Dron's face this time. He was out of his office, and moving. It wasn't hard to guess where he was heading. She nodded to Odo. "Another assault on the way."

"Then we'd better be ready," he answered. He glanced at Dimas. "Trouble."

"I expected it," Dimas admitted, hoisting his tingler. "We had better stand by the doors again."

Kira listened to the conversation as she sought out a good spot to defend. She settled beside one of the shuttered windows, phasering a small hole to see and shoot out of.

"You must give up this insanity!" Dron demanded. "You have no idea what you are doing."

"I am completing the Great Design," Tork informed him placidly. "Whatever happens now is what should happen."

Dron cursed. "Did it not occur to you to ask yourself *why* we changed the Great Design?" he questioned. "The original one was unworkable. It had to be modified."

"The First Hive built the Hive," Tork stated. "They knew what they were doing. I am willing to trust their judgment."

"Do not be such a fool!" pleaded Dron. "Their plan was to abandon the Hive and return to living on a planet. You *know* that this is unworkable. Our people cannot live in open spaces. You yourself are proof of this."

Tork shook his head. "I am proof that we *can* survive it if we must. If the Great Design is that we return to life on a planet, then so be it. We shall adapt, if we are worthy of survival." There was a gasp from one of the security guards in the room, but Tork ignored it.

"You are insane!" Dron exclaimed. "The aliens have warped your mind."

"No," said Tork coldly. *"You* wished to warp my mind. You and those like you lied to us systematically for generations. You tried to split Sahna and me. You had Harl framed for sabotage and murder. You have suppressed the Great Design, and even now you are willing to lie and murder to achieve your goals. You do not care about the welfare of the Hive. All that concerns you is your own power. And that is now finished."

"Not yet, it isn't," snarled Dron. "Surrender and stop your foolish plan now, or else suffer the consequences."

"We have nothing more to say to one another." Tork broke the contact. Then he glanced nervously at Kira. "I suspect he still has some plan in his twisted mind."

"You're right," Odo interrupted. He gestured out at the plaza. "Take a look at this."

Tork ran to join Kira, and they both peered out at the empty, barricade-strewn area. From one of the side streets, there came a grinding sound, and then the snout of a large machine. Running on large tires, it simply moved along, crushing whatever was in its path. The device was about twenty feet long and eight high. It had a large blade at the front, with a small nozzle protruding.

"A repair drone," Tork said, worried. "Used for demolition work."

"And I have a nasty suspicion that it's aiming to demolish us," Odo muttered.

There was a loud crack, and the muzzle spat flame in their direction. The three of them and the security guards threw themselves to the floor, just as the whole wall fell on them in the blast of a heavy explosion.

CHAPTER
29

KIRA YELPED AS portions of the shattered wall fell across her. Dust and smoke filled her lungs. Coughing and spluttering, she fought her way out of the debris, wiping at her tearing eyes and cursing every ache. She'd been very fortunate. The bloody mess that had been one of the security guards showed her that not everyone had been so lucky.

Gasping for breath, Tork surfaced among the wreckage beside her. Seeing he was alive, Kira glanced back at the control room.

The shock wave from the blast had sent the others reeling further back but they appeared unharmed for the most part. One of the technicians seemed to have a broken arm, and Bree had a large cut across her forehead. She was ignoring it and struggling back toward the navigation computer.

Odo formed from nowhere beside Kira. "We were fortunate," he told her. "The shutters absorbed some of that blast."

Glancing at her phaser, still clutched spasmodically in her hand, Kira grimaced. Might as well throw stones at that armored drone. She slapped her communicator. "Kira to Sisko. We need help, *now!*"

Sisko banked the *Defiant,* heading back toward the control deck. Laser fire splashed harmlessly against the shields. The Hive didn't dare deploy too much firepower inside itself for fear of structural damage. "We're on our way," he informed Kira.

"Powering up phasers," O'Brien reported from the weapons console. "According to the sensors, someone's opened fire on the control deck. They must be stark, raving mad. If they damage the instruments there, who knows *what* will happen?"

"I don't think Dron is thinking too clearly right now," Sisko informed him. "He's losing his grip on power, and is just trying to stop Tork at all costs. We don't dare take any chances on that drone opening fire again. Take it out on the first shot, Chief, and don't worry about casualties."

"Aye, Captain." O'Brien bent to the task. "Coming in range . . . now!"

Kira saw the *Defiant* hurtle into view, narrowly missing a collision with one of the towers. As it banked, the phasers lit up, and she looked away.

Twin beams lanced from the sky and onto the drone. For a second, she saw it silhouetted in a blinding light, and then it and three Hive dwellers who were tumbling from it vanished into nothingness.

She staggered to her feet, surveying the wreckage in the plaza through the gaping hole that had been the front wall of the control deck. It certainly looked as though a war had been fought here.

"Dron is dead," said Tork with some satisfaction. "He was one of those killed in the blast that saved us. Raldar was another. I did not recognize the third."

"Couldn't have happened to a nicer fellow," Kira muttered. She turned her attention back to Sahna, Bree, and the others. "How's it going there?"

"The transfer of data is complete," Sahna replied. "The program has been activated and is running. As soon as we reach Darane Three, the program should begin."

Bree looked nervous. "Are you sure that this is a good idea?" she asked. "I know it is the will of the First Hive, but . . . If Dron was telling the truth, then we are committing our race to life on a planet again. They will not be prepared for this. Perhaps we should wait? The urgency is past, after all."

"No," Tork answered, firmly. "If we wait, the remaining Hivemasters may begin a new assault. And if we ask the Hive whether to proceed with the *real* Great Design, I suspect that there will be a great deal of discussion. Many may favor returning to Dron's plan. We must act, and act now, however severe the consequences." Tork laid a gentle hand on Kira's arm. "Now might be a good moment for you all to leave," he suggested. "This is our destiny. We must face it alone."

"Understood." Kira holstered her phaser. "Good luck." She tapped her communicator as Odo and Dax joined her. "You're a sight," Kira informed her smoke-smudged friend.

"Speak for yourself," Dax said with dignity. "Unless you're planning on making blood your new uniform color."

Realizing she had been injured in the blast, Kira grimaced. "Another new uniform requisition," she sighed. "I *hate* filling out those forms." She tapped her communicator. "Kira to Sisko. Three to beam up. I think it's time we left."

Dax held the *Defiant* in synchronous orbit several planetary diameters out from the rocky surface of Darane III. She smiled back at Sisko. "Ringside seat," she announced.

Sisko smiled back. "Thanks, old man." He glanced around the bridge. Kira had just returned, a bandage across her left shoulder and a patch on her forehead. "How do you feel?"

"Lousy," Kira replied, grinning. "But I'm not going to miss this. Anything happen yet?"

"No." Sisko turned his attention back to the main screen. The Hive was slowly crawling toward the waiting planet.

The wings were bent again in the position that they had been when it had drained Darane IV. The huge mechanical construction hovered in space above the globe, now cradled in the space between the wings.

Nobody spoke. Sisko saw that O'Brien was feverishly activating every spare sensor and camera to record whatever was about to happen.

Then it began.

The strange blue fire began to play across the lower surface of the Hive, like lightning zipping back and forth. It started slowly, building in intensity, the light moving from blue into blinding white. It seethed and rolled in the gap, and then the first lance of fire leaped down to touch the surface of the planet. The first bolt was followed by several more, and then a barrage of fire rained from the Hive onto the dead surface of Darane III. In moments, the entire planet was glowing with the blue-white incandescence.

"Is something going wrong?" asked Odo.

"I don't know," Sisko admitted. "Just watch."

The globe was starting to writhe beneath the falling blasts of energy. It seemed to be seething, in preparation to explode. Just as it seemed to Sisko that the tortured world could endure no more, the light changed. A golden glow seeped down the blasts, crawling across the battered surface. The world was glowing still, but the light changed, shading into a deeper gold, and then umber.

The Hive *shifted*. A ripple spread across the gigantic wings, as if it were a cloaking device about to fade the vessel into invisibility. The stability returned briefly, and then the Hive started to fade slowly, becoming slightly transparent.

"My God," muttered O'Brien. "It's an inversion field . . . but the power of it . . ." His voice faded into a whisper of awe.

The Hive itself was fading. The glow about the planet increased, getting slowly brighter as a vast transfer of energy took place. The Hive was looking less and less real, the fires burning brighter and more gloriously. Then came a blinding explosion of light—

—and the Hive was gone.

Only the interplay of color from the glow remained. It whirled about the planet like a cloud of luminescence, touching everything. Fingers of splendid aura stroked the world, caressing it.

As the glow started to die down, Sisko could make out blurred images on the once-barren surface. There was water, he was sure of that! Vast oceans, smaller rivers, barely visible from space. The gray, dust-colored rocks that had once been the surface of Darane III were gone. In their place he could make out greenery.

"Close up," he ordered. "As close as you can manage."

Dax complied, and the screen shimmered and then refocused. They were looking down on vast expanses of trees—forests and jungles, growing on the once-dead world. Clouds were staring to form above them.

"O'Brien?" he called, not tearing his eyes from the screen for a second. "What do you read down there?"

"What *don't* I read!" exclaimed the chief, stunned and happy. "There's a viable atmosphere, plants, animals . . . and I'm getting the readings for several cities, all clustered on the southern continent," he added. "Millions of life signs. I'd say that the Hive dwellers made it safely."

Tork gasped as he straightened up. It had felt so strange to be in the grip of the forces that they had unleashed. For several moments, he was terrified that the powers he had set free would destroy them all, but a vast peace had settled upon him as the Hive had started to break apart.

Now he stood on the surface of their new world. Before him lay the city he knew so well from the Hive, transferred somehow intact to the surface of their new planet. Around him, other people were forming. He saw Sahna, and rushed to her in delight. Then Bree, and Dimas, and the rest of the Hive dwellers appeared on the surface of a planet.

A million Hive dwellers looked up and saw the open sky above their heads for the first time in their lives. They screamed, and whirled into catatonic balls of shell, retreating from the reality they couldn't face.

Tork stared around at his traumatized fellows, sadness in his hearts. "It is hard for them," he said.

"They will learn to adapt," Sahna assured him. "It is possible. You have proven that."

"Yes," he agreed. "Yes. I have."

Kira snorted good-naturedly. "It looks like it's all turned out okay after all," she commented.

Dax nodded. "They're certainly in for an adventure. I wonder how they'll do?"

"If they're all anything like Tork and Sahna," Sisko commented, "I wouldn't be too worried about them. Mind you, they're going to need a lot of help and advice, I suspect. Living on a planet is very different from living in space."

Kira gave a crooked grin. "Maybe there are a few thousand refugees from Darane Four who would appreciate a new home," she suggested. "If they can forgive the innocent Hive dwellers, maybe they could teach each other a few things."

Sisko smiled. "That sounds good to me. Do you think you could make it sound good to Shakaar?"

"You can bet on it," Kira replied. "In fact, Quark could bet on it." She snapped her good fingers. "Hadn't we better call Shakaar and tell him that Bajor's out of danger?"

"Yes," Sisko agreed. "I imagine he'll be most interested. And he's probably dying to tell Jaro just where to go about now." He gave the screen one last look. The new world looked beautiful as it started to cloud over. "They've got a fascinating adventure ahead of them," he said softly. "I almost envy them."

Dax smiled at him. "Only almost?" she teased.

"Yes." Sisko nodded at the screen. "I'll bet there's plenty of space for baseball diamonds down there, old man. Now, set course for *Deep Space Nine*. We've got a lot of work to catch up on."

As Dax started to follow his orders, Sisko sat back in his

chair. It had been a close call, but once again he had somehow come through. Maybe he was better than he'd once believed. Maybe he was simply luckier than he'd once believed.

Or, just maybe, Yarka was right: It was the will of the Prophets. . . .